George Yarak is a Lebanese noveli
He has worked as an editor and writ
pers, magazines, and publishers, and
lished in 2013. He lives in Beirut.

Raphael Cohen is a literary translator based in Cairo.

Guard of the Dead

George Yarak

Translated by
Raphael Cohen

hoopoe
AN IMPRINT OF AUC PRESS

First published in 2019 by
Hoopoe
113 Sharia Kasr el Aini, Cairo, Egypt
200 Park Ave., Suite 1700, New York, NY 10166
www.hoopoefiction.com

Hoopoe is an imprint of the American University in Cairo Press
www.aucpress.com

Dar el Kutub No. 13701/18
ISBN 978 977 416 910 6

Dar el Kutub Cataloging-in-Publication Data

Yarak, George
        Guard of the Dead / George Yarak.—Cairo: The American University
    in Cairo Press, 2019.
        p.   cm.
        ISBN: 978 977 416 910 6
        1. English fiction
        823

1 2 3 4 5   23 22 21 20 19

Designed by Adam el-Sehemy
Printed in the United States of America

1

CHANCE ALONE IS TO BLAME for what I suffer now.

I was hunting in the open country. It was sundown. Walking past the village garbage dump, I heard sporadic groaning. First, I thought I was imagining it, but with the repetition I was sure it was a person's voice.

Possibilities jostled. Had a shepherd's child scavenging for broken toys fallen and got hurt? Had a nomadic Bedouin from one of the tribes found a large tin can and been injured? Had a hunter shot his quarry, but still able to move, the animal had caused an accident? Had someone seen me coming and, to play a trick on me, hid and started groaning? I expected the guy to show himself at any moment, arms aloft and shouting, to give me a fright.

I backed the last possibility. Stunts were often pulled to scare people. Then, once the trick had been jazzed up to make it worth retelling, it was recounted to friends. Specialists in omission or addition made the version doing the rounds somewhat different than the facts.

I advanced toward the voice with the muzzle of the double-barrel shotgun pointing upward so it didn't bump into anything solid. The gun was still new, and I had gotten the money together for it lira by lira. Every time I took a step, the groaning faded away. I stood completely still and it started again, but not as loud as moments before. Approaching the source of the sound, I did not exclude any of the four possibilities.

I was primed for a surprise when I neared a pile of garbage, or an oil drum, or a mound that someone might hide behind. Smoke rising near the rust-eaten springs of a bed caught my eye. Some clothing and three pairs of shoes were smoldering. Right then the groaning grew louder. I strained to make out the spot it was coming from. Useless. The breeze made it impossible.

I wasn't frightened, just cautious and on the lookout for someone to stand up howling and laughing at the same time. Being prepared for the surprise would reduce its impact. I picked up a few stones and tossed them around the spot the groaning was coming from, thinking that might cause the concealed person to move. Then I would see him, and the game would be up, but after I threw the stones the groaning stopped.

I froze where I was for a minute. Two minutes. I looked around, listening closely, and heard the sound of rats scrabbling over sheets of metal. The groaning, however, was gone. I turned back in the hope that the trickster would think I was about to leave and reveal himself or start groaning again.

The instant I turned around, I heard movement. A man, his face covered in blood, flew at me with an iron bar. I ran. He chased me, raging: "It's you, you son of a bitch!"

The shotgun was over my shoulder, so it was impossible to wave it at him in self-defense or to threaten him. It looked like he had been watching me. I had only slung the shotgun over my shoulder when I pretended to turn back. It never occurred to me that a blood-covered man would jump out of the garbage and chase after me as if I intended to harm him. If I had foreseen that, I would have kept the gun ready for use and fired a shot in the air or between his legs to stop him in his tracks and make him realize that going any further might cost him his life. I would have done that as a threat, but I can't guarantee what I might have done if I felt in real danger. I had never experienced anything like it. I might have killed him with a single cartridge. I was quite capable of aiming between his eyes and hitting the target. Those who know me, know that I go out hunting with ten cartridges and come back with nine birds. The tenth I would have clipped, and the injured bird kept flying before dropping far off.

The man looked frightening. Blood covered most of his face, and I couldn't make out his features. No way could he catch me. After all, I was a champion sprinter, and a prize-winning shot-putter to boot. When I run, after a certain distance I feel I'm running on air. He was still behind me when he started swearing and threatening me. When the sound of his voice reassured me that there was sufficient distance between us for me to catch my breath, I looked behind me. I saw him totter and then collapse by the side of the road.

Had he died? Had he passed out as a result of blood loss? Had he faked his collapse to induce me to come to his aid and then grab me?

Who was this man, who apparently knew me personally? What else could his saying, "It's you . . ." have meant? His words accused me outright of having done something bad, but I didn't know what.

Perhaps the blood running down his face was the result of a shot to the head. There were lots of hunters at this time of year when the plovers passed through, and one of them might have hit him by mistake. An accident like that might happen. I remember one hunter from Beirut missed a low-flying quail and hit his companion in the neck and killed him. Another hunter shot at a quail and missed, but in a nearby vineyard a Syrian worker dropped dead. It turned out he'd been shot in the head.

The man groaning in the garbage dump might also have been a hunter, shot unintentionally. He thought that I had fired the shot and come back to check on him. Doesn't a criminal always return to the scene of the crime? But the garbage dump wasn't a good spot for hunting. Apart from the swarms of fleas and flies, its stench made being in the vicinity an ordeal. I had never seen a hunter bagging birds there.

Possibly, one of those who waylaid hunters from outside had thought the man rich pickings. He had disarmed him, then used the rifle butt, or something else to bang him on the head, and made off with the gun. He wouldn't have been happy with just the rifle but would have stolen his car too and scarpered. Nobody came here on foot unless they were from the village.

The blood-covered man was, most likely, a stranger, even if I hadn't seen a car parked around the dump. What puzzled me was him saying, "It's you . . ." He knew me.

Did he know me from my cousin's car repair shop where I worked in the summer holiday? Had he seen me in the pinball and pool place where I sometimes went to have fun? Did he see me reading the newspaper in the café, which became a gambling den in the evening?

I hadn't seen his face. Blood obscured most of it. Anyway, the shock and fright stopped me looking too close. The rays of the setting sun were dazzling too. When I turned around with him running behind me, I saw a man in his fifties or thereabouts, square built, with a small paunch, and a mustache and goatee. His legs worked fine since he was able to run quite a long distance. The same applied to his arms and the rest of his body. That made me think it likely he had a head injury. Even his voice I didn't hear properly. It came out of a mouth full of blood.

If the man was from the village, I would have recognized him even with his face cloaked. I knew everyone—from the way they walked, from their voices, or from their clothes—without having to see their faces. When you see a man several times a day over the course of years, seeing anything remotely connected with him is enough to know who it is. If you showed me a hand, for instance, and concealed the rest of the body, I would be able to tell you that it was so-and-so's hand.

Perhaps the man had relatives in the village that he visited every now and again, and he had seen me at one of the events held by our sports club in summer. Perhaps he'd seen some resemblance between me and someone else. Faces look alike. What made me lean toward that possibility was that he hadn't used my name when he spluttered his rude words. If he really knew me, he would have said my name to prove to me that he knew who I was and that he wasn't going to let me get away with it.

Probably he forgot my name during those excruciating moments. Excruciating for him because he thought that the person who had caused his injury had come back to see the result or to make certain that what he had done didn't need finishing off or some such reason. Excruciating for me because I was expecting a prank, not the appearance of a face covered in blood and an attack and threats from the person whose face it was.

When he failed to catch me and fell to the ground, I thought about going to help him before his condition worsened and he bled to death. If that happened, I would be overwhelmed with feelings of guilt that would stay with me until I met my Maker. I wasn't up to that. I would go up to him, offer assistance, and exonerate myself. I would tell him that I was just passing by, heard a groaning, and stopped, thinking that a friend was playing a trick on me.

He might be convinced and find me innocent. However, after some hesitation, I rejected the idea. I was afraid he would think I had come back to finish him off or that I was lying.

I was also afraid to tell someone who passed by. If I did tell someone passing that there was a bleeding man who might die, they would say, "Come and help me do something." Then it would be awkward. If I went it would be a problem, and it would be a problem if I didn't.

I was unwilling to dig my own grave or to live a nightmare awake, so I was afraid to make a report at the nearby police station. Such a report would require specific legal steps be taken. In my case, the matter might not turn out well. Assuming I did make a report, then a patrol would go and bring in the man for questioning. He would definitely accuse me of being the perpetrator, and I had no proof to rebut the accusation. I would be thrown in a cell as a result and subjected to interrogations punctuated with torture to make me confess. What would I confess? Until the truth came out, if it came out, who would get me back my good name and compensate me for time in prison as well as for all the abuse I suffered since being arrested?

I didn't leave. I walked along the road that overlooked the area where the man had fallen. The darkness that had slowly descended made it impossible to see. Passing cars did briefly illuminate the area, and for a few moments I could survey the place. I tried to focus, hoping to see whether the man had stood up, or at least crawled if he was unable to stand and walk. If he reached the road alongside the open area, it might save him from certain death.

I carried on watching. I would never relax unless I knew his fate. If, God forbid, he died, I would feel responsible for his death. That feeling disquieted me as it dug into my mind and soul. But there was nothing to be done. Nobody else knew what had happened to him. Apart, that is, from the perpetrator, who too might have been watching the scene from a distance. Perhaps he was driving around in his car to find out what had happened to his victim. If he went to the dump and did not find a body, his suspicions would push him to investigate.

The cars that had driven past, and continued to pass by, aroused no suspicions. I observed them all and did not see a driver, or someone sitting next to him, looking frantically around, as would have been the case if someone was on the lookout.

If it had been possible to make a phone call, I would have dialed a random number and informed the person who answered that there was an injured person in need of assistance. I would have given the location and hung up. I would have repeated the attempt with several people. Perhaps one of them would take the call seriously, feel a surge of humanity, put on his clothes, and go to help. The world is full of do-gooders. But the telephone at home was out of order. When it did work, you had to wait half an hour for a line. I ruled out the idea.

The village phone booths were a fifteen-minute walk away. Not being on the lookout for so long left a window, during which time the man might come round and reach the road. He would stop the first car and head for the nearest hospital. Then I would lose his scent and no longer know whether he remained where he had fallen after chasing me or had been able to stand up and escape. It was sensible not to leave as long as I was careful to keep pulling the strings.

It was now ten o'clock at night. At such an hour, carrying a shotgun would draw attention, even if the gun was pointed down and hanging over my shoulder. The sight would raise question marks for anyone who saw me, especially any outsider to the village who happened to be passing through. Yet the pouch hanging down on my thigh which contained around a dozen plovers indicated that I was a hunter, and not an armed militia man.

I don't know why I imagined that the man was still alive and had found a way out of his predicament. He had vanished without my noticing. I imagined what I hoped had happened, so as to relax and let my conscience relax and end the nightmare I had been enduring for six hours.

My presence on the road at midnight raised questions. I approached the space where the man should have been and had a last look around. I listened carefully, for at night even a quiet sound is audible. The place was calm; only the sound of cicadas, falling leaves, and passing cars disturbed the silence.

I went home. Mum and Dad were asleep. I had a late supper, brushed my teeth, put my pajamas on, and lay down in bed. I couldn't sleep. When I closed my eyes, I kept seeing the man's blood-covered face and hearing his voice. I tried to think about something else to allow me to sleep after an atypical day. But the expression, "It's you . . ." kept ringing in my head until first light.

That night I learned the value of a sense of security and peace of mind, which are the two best catalysts for refreshing sleep and sweet dreams.

2

YESTERDAY MORNING, WHILE I HAD been lying in wait for the rarely passing flocks of plover, three members of the Sovereignty Party were meeting at one of their houses in the village. On the agenda was kidnapping a certain teacher and teaching him a lesson to serve as an example for others like him.

He had been insulting the party out loud to his pupils in class and his colleagues in the staffroom, accusing it of backwardness, extremism, and narrow-mindedness. He even described its leader as an agent of foreign powers. The teacher belonged to a rival party. He had been transferred to the village school because it was not far from his village, following the intervention of a senior political figure.

The three at the meeting set zero hour for the end of the school day—4:00 p.m. The location was to be the square next to the school that had to be crossed going in or out. At that time of day, the square would be packed with people waiting to take their children home and with buses that took pupils to nearby towns.

The choice of that time and that place was deliberate. The three guys, and the mastermind directing them, wanted the furor about the kidnapping to reverberate around the village and its environs. If that hadn't been their objective, they would have chosen another time and place. It seemed they wanted the operation to send a two-pronged message.

The first prong was internal and connected to the party's response to the village big shots. They refused to let the party run things and tried to keep the village out of conflicts. It was, after all, surrounded by villages most of whose inhabitants were of another denomination and belonged to parties that looked at the Sovereignty Party with defiance and aversion. They wanted to say to the big shots—the head of the municipality in particular—that in the village, what we say goes. It's us who decides its fate, not you, and not those propping you up.

The second prong was external and directed at the vicinity, as if to say: There are red lines, and anyone who crosses them will meet the same fate as the teacher. This prong had an addendum: Although there might not be many of us, we aren't afraid and we aren't afraid of your veiled threats. We're ready to defend ourselves, and will never abandon our homes unless it's for the grave.

The three guys were Sailor, Grinder, and Rooster.

Sailor was a childhood friend of mine. My mother said that she nursed him as a baby and loved him just like she loved me. His mother said the same about me. The difference between us was his passion for lethal weapons and my dislike of that kind of weapon. He loved to be photographed about to pull the pin out of a hand grenade or posing with a machine gun or pointing a pistol at his head. His role in the operation was getaway driver.

Grinder, who was thirty, had been discharged from the army for his conduct. He was said to have killed his sister— she was rumored to have drowned—and thrown her body in the river after he found out that she was not, as she claimed, working as a nurse at a hospital in Beirut, but in a brothel. He had a black belt in kung fu and was proud of his athletic physique and bulging muscles. Even in the freezing cold he often wore a short-sleeved shirt to show off his pumped forearms. His role in the operation was to pounce on the teacher, drag him into the car, and put a black bag over his head to prevent him knowing where he was going and who was taking him.

Rooster earned his nickname because of his resemblance to Antoine Karbaj, who had the same moniker in the Lebanese television program *From Day to Day*. He was twenty-five years old and constantly at odds with his father, who owned half the village land and was close to the head of the municipality. He had joined the party out of spite to get one over on his dad. His role was to shield Grinder during the operation and ward off anyone who tried to defend the teacher or do anything else.

The identity of the mastermind was unknown, but suspicions revolved around two men. One was Bou Layla, who was normally held responsible for anything that breached the peace of the village, even if he was in fact innocent. The other was the Colonel, who was the first person to confront the head of the municipality and the members of its council when they decided to restore their authority, which had waned as the party's sway extended.

While I was catching up with a plover whose wing I had hit and which had dropped into the brambles, the three of them were in a car stolen two hours before from a hunter from Beirut. It was parked near the square in an isolated spot. When their lookouts, who were students, told them that the teacher was on his way to the square, they pulled masks over their heads and set off. They pulled up in the middle of the square. Rooster got out to ensure cover, flashed his machine gun, and needlessly fired a few shots. Grinder attacked the teacher. He punched him, then picked him up and forced him into the car. They made off to the astonishment of the people and the panic of the pupils. The scene of the kidnapping was straight out of the movies. So concurred the witnesses.

Inside the car, the kidnapped man asked, "Who are you? What do you want from me? Where are you taking me?" After each question, Grinder gave him a punch to shut him up. He had already tied his hands behind his back with thick cord to stop him moving.

The whole route from the square via the Zaarour neighborhood to Bayada, the three of them kept their masks on and did not take them off until they reached the open countryside. They were afraid someone might follow them, since they expected that word of the kidnapping would reach the army barracks or the police station. Speed was of the essence.

Sailor rebuked Grinder because there had been no need to fire shots over people's heads. That might have led a police patrol to pursue them. They might have to engage them if needed. Grinder had made a mistake, but things were still under control. Sailor said that his heart had been beating fast, not in fear but for an unknown reason. He said that he had felt things he had never experienced before, feelings only experienced by those who undertook such ventures.

They chose the garbage dump to settle scores with the teacher and send a message to those concerned that anyone who made a mistake with someone from the village would end up in the garbage dump. At the time I was resting under a willow tree reading a new chapter of Agatha Christie's *Dumb Witness*, the three of them were beating up the teacher, insulting him and his party and the party leader.

They did not intend to kill him. They wanted to discipline him to stay in line, to content himself with teaching and put a stop to giving political advice and insulting the party they belonged to. The blow that fractured his skull came from the butt of Rooster's pistol. As soon as he saw the blood spurting from the teacher's head, he suggested they throw him in the middle of the dump and leave. They untied his hands to give him a chance to escape. If they had left him tied up, it would have been impossible for him to stand up and he would have bled to death.

They changed out of the clothes and shoes used in the operation, which they set alight after having poured a can of gasoline over them. Those were the clothes and shoes I noticed smoke rising from. They had thought of everything and executed their plan. They even had a Plan B should Plan A fail.

The level of organization was noted by some people and made my father and others think it more likely that it wasn't Bou Layla behind the operation but the Colonel, who had studied math for four years at the University of Lebanon and taught it to the middle school classes at the village intermediate school. (His flunking topology four times prevented him graduating. He wrote an appeal to the faculty administration to allow him to re-sit the exam for a fifth and final time, but the appeal was rejected by the dean of the Faculty of Science.)

On their way back, they got rid of the masks. They stopped the stolen car on the edge of the village and split up, having agreed to meet that night in the party offices.

All of that was revealed to me by Sailor the following day after swearing me to secrecy. I tried to link each chapter of the kidnap operation with what I had been doing at approximately the same time out in the countryside.

When I saw the teacher, or more accurately when he saw me and tried to attack me, Sailor was drinking coffee at his aunt's house where everyone was talking about the kidnapping. Along with the aunt and her husband were a few neighbors and some young eyewitnesses, who, at the time of the kidnap, had been scoping passing schoolgirls with hungry eyes. Sailor did not participate much in the conversation. He preferred to listen. He felt proud inside when someone relayed something about the operation and added a touch of heroism to the account. He noted that those present had concluded that the perpetrators were from the village and not outsiders. Some of them tried to guess the names of the participants in the kidnapping, based on their physique and movements and the size of their heads. Sailor was happy that the list of names did not include his name or those of

13

his accomplices. That was proof of the effectiveness of their disguise and of the success of the operation.

While Sailor was at his aunt's house, Grinder was sitting in the kiosk that looked onto the square, a bottle of beer in his hand and a pack of pistachios between his thighs.

Rooster had gone home. He undressed, put on his pajamas, and slept. Luckily, the house was empty. His mother was at a neighbor's. His father was at the café, and his sister was doing yoga in the garden. He wanted to rest so he would be able to stay up till the morning. It was his turn to be up all night organizing the guard.

At the time of night when I had been watching the waste patch where the teacher had fallen, the three met up at the party HQ. While they were listening to each other's comments about the operation, the head of the municipality's house was full of people denouncing the operation and expressing their fears over its consequences, particularly after fingers had been pointed at certain extremist party elements. The name of Sailor was mentioned, but not the two others. However, there was no proof of his involvement in the operation. They penned a statement and distributed it the following morning. In it they held the village blameless for the attack on "the educator who teaches our children love, goodness, and beauty, and who deserves nothing less than gratitude and esteem," and slammed "the foolish action undertaken by the enemies of knowledge and peace." The statement concluded with an apology to the teacher and the school administration and with the hope that "the regrettable incident would not assume dimensions impacting on the harmony between the village and its neighbors and serve the aims of those who sow strife."

Meanwhile, the party issued a statement condemning the incident and blaming "hands from outside that aim to sow discord between the people of the village themselves and between the village and neighboring villages." It urged everyone to "reflect and act wisely in the delicate circumstances that the country is passing through."

Naturally, the party would issue a statement of that sort, particularly once it found itself in the dock. Equally, sensible heads in the party did not expect the matter to end well. The teacher who had been kidnapped was a well-known activist and from a big family. If his party did not respond to restore its prestige, then his family would not turn the other cheek but take revenge.

The morning was somber. People's faces looked anxious as if prepared for a day of uncertainty in the village. I was the most anxious of all. None of them, apart from Sailor, knew what had happened to me.

3

I WAS AT A LOSS.

At midday I headed to the road overlooking the waste ground hoping for a sign that the teacher had survived and gone back to his family safe and sound. The place was quiet. A tractor was parked at the side of the road parallel to the waste ground. The driver looked over his shoulder every now and again as if waiting for someone. Two hunters were heading out into the open countryside. Around them ran a dog that seemed not to have been out for a walk for a few days.

I imagined the dog smelling something strange and making for the waste ground. He stops, then walks around a particular spot and ignores the command of 'come' from the hunter, or gives a howl to signal that he has found something and that his master should come and look. The hunter and his companion obey the dog's summons and discover a body. The body of the teacher. I imagined them shocked then racing off to notify the police after having shouted out to passersby and the nearby houses.

Thoughts roared in my head. I did not calm down until the dog had crossed the waste ground, content to sniff the earth and run behind the two hunters. I inferred that there was no dead body there. If there had been, the smell of the corpse would have attracted the dog. After about twelve hours, it would have started to decompose. Plus, it had been under the rays of the autumn sun for around seven hours, which would accelerate decomposition and cause the body to putrefy and give off an intolerable smell.

This inference cheered me up. The news circulating that evening confirmed its accuracy and shook the village. Unknown assailants had kidnapped the head of the municipality's son from his home and Grinder's brother from the farm where he worked as a guard in retaliation. That the teacher was alive cheered me up as much as that news saddened me.

When had he left the waste ground? I had stayed up the previous evening until midnight, monitoring every movement in and around the area, but observed nothing. Perhaps he had crawled a long way until he reached a side road leading to the same main road I was wandering along now. The road curved away toward the open countryside though and prevented a view down it.

Assuming he had reached the road, no driver would have been brave enough to stop for an injured man in blood-soaked clothing. Possibly, the teacher had stood in the middle of the road and forced a passing car to stop, but that would have been very risky. The road was not lit and the darkness was intense. Headlights might not have picked him out from a distance and a car could have run him over.

Possibly, he had walked to his house in the neighboring village, just seven kilometers away. Or he had gone to the hospital about five kilometers away. His condition required medical attention and treatment. Most likely, he had not headed for home but for the hospital. If he had gone home, he would have had to be taken to hospital anyway, and he knew that.

So he made for the hospital on foot or by car. He went to emergency and received first aid. He asked to call his wife or one of his brothers. If that wasn't possible, he would beg the nurses to let his wife or brother know and give them the address.

Fear ran through me. The man, so it seemed, knew me personally. Even supposing he didn't know me, he had seen me. He had seen my face and the clothes I was wearing. He had seen the shotgun and the birds hanging on my thigh—evidence that might help track me down. I was positive that they were looking for me. He must have given them my name, if he really knew me, or my description, if he didn't know my name.

I walked along, turning my head in no particular direction. I felt like someone expecting to be jumped and beaten up, then thrown into the trunk of a car and driven off to an unknown destination. Just what happened to the teacher.

Goddamn hunting. If I hadn't gone out into the countryside, I wouldn't now be panicked and desperate. The kidnap of two men with no direct connection to what had happened suggested escalatory intent. I didn't know what end awaited them.

I wasn't going to sleep at home that night, or at my grandfather's or at one of my relatives'. Our house might be watched and, because it was located on the edge of the village, it wasn't safe. It would be easy to drag me off from there.

I had to let Dad know. When I came back last night, he was asleep and I didn't want to disturb him. When I woke up today, he had already gone out. I avoided telling Mum to stop her scolding me: "How many times have I told you, 'God protect us from hunting trips these days!'"

I made for the square. Young guys were stationed on the roofs and in the windows with unseen weapons. Whenever a car passed, I felt as if my heart would leap out of my chest. Its pounding sounded like it had detached and settled by my ears.

Evening and the café was half empty; that was unusual. I expected to find my dad there. The owner of the café, who was leaning against the door smoking a cigarette, told me as soon as he saw me that my father was looking for me. He had just left and probably gone home. I was reluctant to go to the house. I told one of the boys crowded in the pinball place to go and let my father know I was waiting for him at the café.

Dad came back in a hurry. I told him everything. He too thought that I shouldn't sleep at home. He said that the kidnapped teacher was a colleague of his, who had only been transferred to the village school about a month ago. Dad said that he had been introduced to him, and, as usual with his friends, he had shown him a photograph of me. One day he was standing chatting with him on one of the school balconies overlooking the schoolyard. By chance, I was passing by, and he pointed me out to him. I knew what he would say after pointing at me: "That's my son. See how much he looks like me." It's what he always said about me in my absence, and in my hearing when he wanted to introduce me to someone.

Now I was certain that the teacher knew me. He had, of course, given my name and description to those concerned. In his eyes, I was an accomplice in his kidnap and beating. If that wasn't the case—unlikely given his reaction at the dump—I might be the lead his faction needed to find the rest of the gang and reveal the mastermind. Even if I was innocent, I still might have seen the criminals or their car.

That's what they would think. They wouldn't believe me if I told them I hadn't seen either the kidnappers or their car. They would consider me complicit and a liar who didn't want to snitch on his fellow villagers. Then they might kidnap me and beat me up. They wouldn't let me go until I confessed everything.

If only Sailor hadn't told me. If he hadn't, I would have been at peace with myself. The information I had made me an accomplice. I might reveal it, at a moment of weakness, under torture.

They might be watching me, but they wouldn't dare kidnap me in a public place, as long as they could do it somewhere else, like on the way to my house, which was normally dark. There was no better spot to carry out such an operation. Who knows, perhaps they were already lying in wait for me there.

Dad suggested I spend the night at the school. The classrooms were left unlocked. It would be easy for me to slip through the small window of the garbage room into the playground and into one of the classrooms. I had often done just the same as a pupil, but in the reverse direction, skipping school to go hunting, or swimming in the muddy pond at one end of the village.

Dad said that the garbage room was emptied around sunset, meaning I could enter easily without getting my clothes dirty. He said he would find a safe way to give me some food and a blanket. With words cut through with suppressed anguish he whispered—even though no one could hear us— that staying in the village was dangerous for me. I had to leave until the danger subsided.

I sneaked into the school in the evening and spent the night awake in the classroom overlooking the courtyard and part of the road leading to the Zaarour neighborhood. Dad was unable to bring food and the blanket. Perhaps he noticed that he was being watched and, afraid to lead them to me, preferred not to risk it. I put four desks together until they resembled a bed, then lined them up against the wall. I could not fall asleep. Fear alone banished sleep, how then if it was in alliance with cold and hunger?

My exhausted eyes were on the point of closing when the engines of the buses started rumbling in preparation for their morning school run to the neighboring villages. As soon as they left, I found myself hanging from the classroom window, which was on the first floor, and jumping down onto the road. My knees let me down and I landed on my elbows. I did that because going out the way I had come in at night wasn't safe. To reach the garbage room I would have to cross part of the playground. One of the staff might spot me, or the principal, who arrived early to exercise by walking around the playground.

The village was yawning that cold morning. It too seemed not to have slept. The kidnap of two villagers was no ordinary event. The efforts made by the head of the municipality to secure the release of his son and Grinder's brother appeared to have been fruitless. Only tractors disturbed the calm.

I didn't believe I made it home. I barely reached the doorstep when Mum opened the door. It was as if she was expecting me, or as if her heart had intimated my return. She smothered me and cried. Dad was sitting by the stove. He told me that he had been unable to bring me food and a blanket because he sensed he was being watched. He was afraid to lead them to the place I was spending the night. My hunch had been right. They would never do anything suspect inside the village, because they knew that the guards were up all night.

While I ate a hearty breakfast after a night of nil by mouth apart from the water I drank from the school taps, and Dad toasted the bread and soaked it in the bowl of milk, and Mum looked at me with worry in her eyes, there was a knock at the door. I opened it. It was our only neighbor bearing news that darkened our morning. He said that they had killed the son of the head of the municipality and thrown his body on the country road. The fate of the other kidnapped man remained unknown.

Dad put his clothes on. "You have to leave. Today," he said.

Mum packed me a few clothes and things in a shopping bag. We didn't have a suitcase, since none of us had left the village before.

Dad accompanied me to the neighboring town and begged a friend of his from his days at teaching college to put me up for a few days after telling him why. The friend welcomed me and seemed sympathetic.

Dad drank his cup of coffee quickly. Then he hugged me, said goodbye, and left. I remained standing on the balcony watching him walk dejectedly away. Before he disappeared around the corner, he turned around, raised his hand, and closed his fingers into a fist that he shook before going out of sight.

4

THAT WAS THE FIRST TIME I slept in someone else's bed. I slept in the same room as my dad's friend's son. Black thoughts haunted me.

I was afraid they would hurt my dad if they didn't find me. I imagined they kidnapped him and threatened to kill him if I didn't surrender myself. His age interceded for him. He was also peaceable and on good terms with everyone. His friendships in the neighboring villages were well known. He often made visits to offer condolences or congratulations. True, he stuck to the party line and made his political views public, but he was against violence all the same. At the beginning of the war, he bought a machine gun from the mukhtar, the village leader, in installments after reports spread that our village was going to be attacked. Then he regretted it, saying he didn't like to have a gun at home, and that he, someone considered part of the supposedly intellectual class, believed in dialogue not bullets. He buried the machine gun behind the house after the mukhtar refused to take it back, even though my father would have let him keep the first payment. Later on, he found out that the report of the attack was a rumor put about by the head of the municipal council and the mukhtar so they could sell the guns they had bought from one of the local MPs.

I only fell asleep at dawn. I kept reliving the scene of the man with the blood-covered face attacking me, and I could not shake off his voice.

I was exhausted. Two nights passed, and I only managed to snatch a few minutes' sleep. At breakfast my host and his wife, their two daughters, and their son noticed how sleep-deprived I was, even though I tried to hide it.

When the husband went to work, and the two girls and the boy went to school, I also went out. Remaining in the house alone with the wife wasn't approved of.

I claimed I was going to visit a friend who lived in the town. I spent the day in the market and headed for the park when I got tired of walking. I rested for a while under a willow tree. I pulled a newspaper I had found by a trashcan out of my jacket pocket and leafed through it to divert myself. It wasn't that day's paper. I read about the clashes on the Green Line that divided the capital into east and west, the former majority Christian and the latter majority Muslim.

In the twenty years of my life I had never once been to Beirut, but I had heard the names of streets on the news. They were mentioned so much by people and on the radio and TV that I knew them by heart. They felt familiar even though I had never walked down them. Sometimes I wished I had been born there and not in the village. It was the sea that attracted me.

Photos of fighters in the paper drew my attention. I studied them. I looked at them through the eyes of the gun-obsessed Sailor. I could see him among them holding a Kalashnikov or an M16 and, like them, wearing a black headband and assuming a combat pose for the picture. Many times I imagined myself with them too, but I rapidly exited the scene, preferring to look at the gun and not carry it.

From the outset, I decided to be an onlooker. In the village, I did not take part in the weapons training that usually took place covertly in people's homes and at the abandoned chicken farm in the countryside. I also refused to do guard duty. I told them I would do it, but without a rifle. They made fun of me. If Dad had not taught most of them at school, they would have ostracized me. Plus, as an only child I had been exempted from military service. All my high school classmates had gone apart from me.

Around the same time, noon, the head of the municipality's son was being buried in an awe-inspiring funeral attended by the entire village.

Returning to the village was impossible. Carrying on as a guest at my father's friend's was also impossible. It was an unusual situation. I wanted to go to Beirut where nobody knew me and I knew nobody. Things would work out for the best there. Taking a chance? So be it. At least I would be responsible for myself and not have to ask my dad's permission, or his friend's, for every move I intended to make. What would I do here in this small town? Nothing, except wait for the situation in the village to improve. If the situation remained the same, or became tenser—and the second possibility was more likely—what would become of me?

In Beirut I would look for work. Any work. I knew it wasn't going be easy, but it was better than staying here. I slept. I ate. I walked the streets and rested in the park. Worst of all was my sense of being a guest, and guests, after three days, start to smell. That was what Dad said whenever Mum's brother's visits stretched on.

The little money I had with me would be enough for a few days if I was extremely sparing with it. Then I would be in God's hands. He does not forsake those in need.

I wrote a letter to Dad, explaining the reasons for my decision, and gave it to his friend who tried to dissuade me from leaving. When he saw that I was determined, he wished me good luck. On the doorstep, he tried to put some money in my shirt pocket. I refused, claiming that I didn't need it. I thanked him and his family for their hospitality, and I left.

5

AT THE RANK FOR TAXIS to Beirut, a white Mercedes was waiting for one more person to make up the passengers. When
the driver sensed that that passenger was me, he hurried over,
took my shopping bag, and put it on the roof of the car on top
of a foam mattress, some suitcases, and other stuff.

I clambered into the backseat and the vehicle set off.

We were five passengers, then the driver turned off the
main road into a side street. He said apologetically that two
more passengers were waiting for him.

"Where do you want to put them?" a passenger objected.

"You should have said before," I chimed in.

The driver didn't care. "It's not worth it for me to take five
passengers. Yesterday I waited two hours for a tank of gas and
it cost ten thousand."

Once they had helped the driver to put their things in the
back of the car, the first of the two sat in the backseat, and the
other in the front.

Around sunset and the highway was almost empty.

A convoy of Syrian trucks was trailing clouds of black
smoke behind it. The truck at the rear was towing a bus plas-
tered with pictures of Egyptian actresses, as well as a giant
picture of Hafez al-Assad on the back.

The driver did not dare overtake the convoy even though
the road ahead was open. I was scared that the bus would
come detached, crash into our vehicle, and force it off the road

and down the steep slope. None of us would survive to tell the tale. I had read in the paper that a Syrian bus had broken lose from the truck towing it on the Dahr al-Baydar–Mudeirej highway and crashed into a car coming the opposite way and really smashed it up. The accident caused the death of a man and his wife who were heading back to Beirut after attending a family funeral. The unfortunate pair had gone to offer condolences and the next day their families were accepting condolences for them.

It was hard to believe that the convoy was behind us.

The driver was smoking and ashing his cigarette out of the window. The wind blew some of the ash back inside. The passenger next to me pointed this out to him. He apologized but seemed annoyed by the remark. He said that he had heard on the news that clashes had broken out again in Beirut. Then he asked each of us where we wanted to be dropped off. He didn't shut up for the whole journey. He said he had been in the army, and after retiring had bought a red license plate and this vehicle to have a job while he was still able to work. When he got old, he would take it easy. He said it was better to put up with the stresses of working than for a man to stay at home.

It was an ill-fated moment when I asked him to turn up the radio for us to listen to the news bulletin. As soon as the newsreader reeled off the areas being flattened by artillery, the passenger in front of me accused the party behind the station of lying and being an agent of foreign powers and asked the driver to change it. The passenger sitting behind the driver weighed in, insisting that he stay tuned. They would have started insulting each other if I and others had not intervened to put a stop to the argument, which was about to turn into a fist fight inside the car. To satisfy both parties, the driver put on a zajal poetry tape, a competition between Zaghloul al-Damour and his troupe and Khalil Rukoz and his troupe that had taken place about seven years before in 1971 at the Beit Mery Fortress. The contest was engaging. It held the attention of all the passengers, as demonstrated by their silence. Even the driver only opened his mouth to preempt the singer with the last word of the verse. It seemed he was a good reciter. When the tape ended, he sang improvised lines. He commented on whatever he saw with a couplet. He told us that he had published quite a few poems in the army's *Soldier* magazine. He said he had been influenced by Khalil Rukoz, who had died young, and whom he viewed as the father and most important of the zajal singers. He had attended a show-down between him and Hanna Moussa in Mtein in 1959, at the end of which the legendary poet Saeed Aql had come on stage and kissed and congratulated Rukoz.

I listened to the driver, eager for his brilliant comments in verse. He seemed a rarity. People hid inside their clothes; inside the driver was a poet. Perhaps inside the person next to me was a killer, and next to him an oud player, and in the fourth a smuggler, and the fifth a Jehovah's Witness, and the sixth a poker player, and the seventh a pimp.

As we approached the Syrian checkpoint, we all kept quiet. A soldier who was standing inside a metal sentry box surrounded by sandbags motioned to the driver to pull up by the side of the road where three of his comrades were crouched in waiting.

The driver complied, muttering "God protect us." One of the soldiers asked him to open the trunk. He obeyed. Another ordered us to get out of the car and we did. He and his third comrade searched under the seats, lifting them up and putting them back in place. Then with the muzzle of his machine gun he inspected the things on the roof of the car. After this care-ful search, the fourth soldier asked to see our ID cards. Each of us proffered him our ID. He asked us the usual questions at checkpoints: What do you do? Where are you coming from? Where are you going?

"It's all over," I said to myself when the soldier took just my ID and went off to the base close to the checkpoint.

Perhaps someone had anticipated that I would run away and put an all-points alert on my name. Or perhaps an informant had fabricated a report to cause my downfall and take revenge against my father.

The passengers got back into the car, and I remained standing waiting for the soldier to come back. It would be a bad sign if he came back without the ID in his hand. He might make me stay behind and summon me to the base. But on what charge, I wondered. I wasn't interested in politics. It made no difference to me who was in power, this lot or that lot. In either case nothing would change for me. True, this was the first time I had left home, but I believed that the whole world was my country. I often repeated the saying of Imam Ali, which Dad always used to quote: "A poor man is a stranger in his own town, but strangers welcome the rich man."

The soldier was taking his time, and the passengers started muttering. They hoped the matter would end, well or badly, so that they could all continue their journey. It would soon be dark, and it was advisable to reach the city before nightfall. Those seated in the rear hoped I would be arrested so they could finish the journey in comfort. I read it in their eyes when I saw them looking at me reproachfully, but they wouldn't be happy if my wretched luck meant I was detained. The third passenger in the front would take my place to give the driver the space needed to steer well. My detention would benefit those on the front seat, not those in the rear.

I looked at the doorway the soldier had gone through. Whenever the light in the room cast a shadow, I started. I thought the soldier, having completed his task, was coming back and casting the shadow.

Now his delay reassured me. If he had found anything against me, he would have returned quickly. Perhaps he was talking to one of his colleagues, or going to the bathroom, or having a cup of tea. He had taken advantage of taking my

ID to do what he couldn't do when manning the checkpoint. Checking if someone was wanted didn't take such a long time.

My suspicion proved correct. When he emerged, his shadow preceding him, and I noticed the ID card in his hand, I relaxed. He gave it back and ordered the driver to go. I got into the car and apologized to the passengers.

As soon as we had moved off, the driver said, "If someone had given them a pack of cigarettes, we wouldn't have waited all that time." He quickly backtracked. Perhaps one of the passengers was a Baathist or belonged to a party allied with the Syrian army. Lighting a cigarette, he said, "It's the least we can do. Be good hosts. They are protecting us. Without them, God alone knows what would become of us." Nobody responded. The doubts that had struck the driver and made him change tack also seemed to muzzle the voices of the others.

I was thinking about where I was going to get out. All I knew about Beirut were the names of places you heard on the news: al-Shayah, Ein al-Rummaneh, Ashrafiyeh, the Damascus Road, the Museum, Sodico, Holiday Inn, Fouad Shihab Bridge, al-Sayfi. I thought about starting a conversation with the person sitting next to me, as a prelude to asking him where he was getting off. I might get off at the same stop. I was afraid of being asked questions I might not be able to answer. I preferred to remain silent and let things take their course. I was also afraid to be found out as a first-time visitor to Beirut who had no friends or family there, and no home. There was no need to tell him my life story to explain my reasons for coming to the capital. If I did, he might say just what my dad's friend said when I told him my decision: "People are fleeing Beirut, and you're heading there?"

Someone who knew I had left the village in fear for my life would appreciate my position. Someone who knew I refused to stay at people's houses because I felt I was a burden on them would also approve of the decision I took to leave the house of Dad's friend.

If I hadn't gone out hunting that luckless day, I wouldn't now be jammed in a car, being deafened by the drone of its tired-out engine.

I wasn't unaware of what awaited me. I had mentally prepared myself for everything. It was preferable to arrive in the daytime. A stranger arriving in a city whose ground his feet have never trod—that was a somewhat risky venture, particularly as the security situation was not reassuring. But regret was useless and turning back not an option.

The car stopped. The driver got out to allow the passenger sitting next to him to get out. I watched the passenger cross the road, carrying half his home's furniture on his back. He seemed to be a construction worker who slept on the site where he was working. I, who was not jealous of anything, even though I possessed nothing, envied him. I envied him because he knew where he was going, and because there existed a place to shelter him.

A poem by the Lebanese poet Mikhail Naimy, whose opening I still knew by heart from my elementary school days, came to mind: "The roof of my house is iron. / The pillar of my house is stone. / So storm, you wind / And mourn, you trees."

Now, on the outskirts of the city, I understood the meaning of the poem. In fact, I could almost hear the whistle of the wind shaking the branches and reminding them of their bareness. Without a house, there is no peace of mind. Someone without a roof over his head is hostage to sidewalks, building doorways, and vacant lots.

After a few minutes, the two passengers one over from me got out. The passenger sitting next to me smiled happily at the room after being squashed and moved over to the door. When he reached his destination, he got out. While collecting his things with the help of the driver, one of those seated in front got up and sat in the backseat. We were three passengers.

At a roundabout with an army tank stationed in the middle, the remaining two passengers got out and I was left on my own. I moved next to the driver out of politeness so as not to appear, seated alone in the backseat, as if I had hired the car as a limousine. My action had an effect on the driver. He offered his hand and introduced himself: "Bou Walid."

I shook hands with him: "Abir Litani."

Then he offered me a cigarette, and I took it with a thank you.

I don't know how he realized that I had either made a mistake in the route taking me where I wanted to go, or I didn't have a specific place in mind. People like him, because they meet so many different kinds of people, have insight and intuition.

I didn't hide anything. He might help me or show me somewhere to sleep. He looked at me then got lost in thought before saying, "Is there anything I can do to help?"

"Show me a place I can sleep tonight," I replied. "It'll be better in the morning."

He told me that he didn't have a house there either. He slept at his married daughter's house, and she lived in a district close to the Green Line. He said that he slept there whenever he brought passengers at night. In the morning he would go to the taxi station and wait his turn. Once he filled up with passengers, he would set off for the mountains. He might come back the same day if God helped him with passengers heading for Beirut.

He was clearly sympathetic once he saw I was a good guy. "It's written on the face," he said, and suggested that I sleep in the car. "It's the only solution. There's a blanket in the trunk. You can manage with that."

I welcomed the suggestion. What mattered was having a roof over my head. That night it made no difference whether it was a roof made of concrete or of metal.

Bou Walid stopped the car in the street parallel to the street where his daughter's house was. He pulled out the blanket and put it on the back seat. I got out of the car to reclaim my shopping bag from the roof. It was ripped open, and only my jeans, rubber shoes, a black leather belt, and Agatha Christie's *Hound of Death* were still in it.

He saw me looking confused as I peered at the bag and inspected its contents. But I soon pulled myself together and ignored the subject. I folded up the bag and threw it inside the car. I asked him to wait while I bought a bottle of water and something to eat for dinner. He said that we should go together to a shop about to close, and we went over. I bought a bottle of water, a pack of bread, a tub of Picon cheese, and a tub of labneh that the shopkeeper said was one hundred percent local. We went back. He headed off to his daughter's house. I returned to the car and had dinner.

I was sad about losing the clothes Mum had put in the bag. Perhaps the Syrian soldier who searched the bags had torn it with the muzzle of his machine gun, and the contents had spilled out onto the road without anyone noticing.

Despite the chill in the air, I walked around a little. I kept the car in view. For the first time I was walking the streets of a city that I had never imagined I would live in. I studied the buildings, most of whose apartments were dark, even though it was still shortly before midnight. Did people here go to bed early and wake up to go to work fully refreshed?

There was a burst of bullets not far off, followed by a burst of tracer fire. Then another few minutes and the boom of an RPG. I understood why the area was half-deserted. Those who remained in their homes were either determined to stay and preferred to die in their beds or had nowhere else safe to go. I prayed that the gunfire was not a prelude to clashes, and that I would not be deprived of the sleep that my heavy eyelids and groggy body were preparing for.

I stretched out on the backseat after bending my legs and lifting my knees toward my stomach. I covered myself with the blanket and fell asleep. I tossed and turned. Several times I was woken by rain falling on the roof of the car. The tapping of drizzle is perhaps the sweetest music you can hear, but not when you're tired and think sleep your only joy. Then it becomes more annoying than the buzzing of a mosquito as you drift off.

I woke up. I waited for the rain to stop before going back to sleep. During my brief slumber I saw Dad, not Bou Walid, driving the car along a mountain road with snow on both sides and me asleep in the back. Seeing the whiteness in the dream made me optimistic, as did seeing Dad happily crooning a sentimental song.

I wondered how he would react when he learned that I had left his friend's house and come to Beirut. He would read the letter and understand. He would respect my view. I wasn't a child. I could take care of my own business. Often when talking about me he even said: "However you knock him down, he picks himself up again."

I would not disappoint him even though standing on my feet in this unfamiliar city would not be easy. If this was a time of peace and security, the problems would have been easy. But in war, every move was a risk. Who could be sure that a sniper would not kill you crossing the road? Who could be sure that a shell would not fall next to you, during a lull, when you were reassured by the calm atmosphere, and blow your body to pieces? Who could be sure that a stray bullet would not penetrate the roof of the car and lodge in your head?

Lives were the property of their Owner, may He be exalted. No one dies before their time. Two sayings I repeated just like many people. Especially those who rejected the war and the killing but were forced to live in their shadow on the basis of: 'I'm no hero, I had to.'

I was dozing when I heard a tapping at the window and Bou Walid's voice: "Good morning. Hopefully you were able to sleep." He had not come empty handed. He had taken me into account with a manousheh with thyme and some tea in a plastic cup. We ate standing by the car. I thanked him again, wishing him good health and long life.

While he checked the engine, he reminded me of the location of the taxi station where he picked up passengers and invited me to visit him whenever I wanted. He wished me goodbye saying: "Look out for yourself."

6

NIGHTTIME IS THE ENEMY OF strangers. I learned that as soon as I walked the city streets.

Daytime, the streets were bursting with activity, especially when the security situation was calm. The fighters must have been in league. They would stop firing and shelling long enough to let people carry on with their normal lives, but the afternoon hours were sometimes a bit shaky. At night, the artillery opened fire and pounded inhabited areas. People living on upper floors headed down to shelters and safer floors below.

I fell in love with roaming the streets. The world of the sidewalks was exciting and fun. A world mixing blatant contradictions. The fake-watch seller jumps you, his fingers encircled by three watches, and cries out, "One watch for five, three for ten." Across the street, the owner of the genuine watch store huffs in annoyance at the window shoppers and the hagglers and insists on the price tagging the watches in the window.

The hawker of knock-off perfumes in their brand-name boxes insists that you hold out your hand for a squirt from the bottle, and hopes you will feel embarrassed and buy. Meanwhile, the owner of the perfume shop in the next street is busy gift-wrapping bottles for a waiting customer.

The guy who sets out his books on the pavement next to the barber's shop is willing to sell you a secondhand copy of Gibran, Naimy, or Rihani for half a lira. If you buy two, you're sure to get a book of his choice as a present. You have to accept it, or you lose your present. At the bookstore nearby, if the owner, or an employee, is feeling generous, he will say hello in response to your greeting.

The shoeshine man you see in passing is performing clownish tricks with his brush to dazzle you with his skill. You stretch out a foot to his box for him to shine and make good as new. Opposite is a shoe store, its windows blocked by passersby contemplating the new stock.

The old man missing a hand extends the good one for you to put in what your humanity sees fit. His mouth fills with prayers for the generous, and silent insults if you pass by and don't notice him. Alongside him, an old man is walking his dog; his sunglasses would feed a poor man for a month, three meals a day.

On the street corner a fella fleeces people with a three-card trick. Nearby a man is selling lupine seeds. Another is selling coffee from a copper pot as he clacks two saucers together in a monotonous rhythm. Then there's a seller of biscuits and cakes and another selling walnuts, one of which he shells and offers you. A fifth one can tell your fortune: he reads your palm by looking at your pocket, not your open hand.

Behind them are rows of stores and shops about to close their doors in the early evening, making do with what they have earned, while the street people remain behind as if their day has not yet begun.

I don't remember who said, or where I read, that the sidewalks reflect the city. From life on the sidewalks you can fathom the decency of the police or their degeneracy.

I don't remember who said, or where I read, that in New Delhi the streets are unlike any other place on the planet. Millions of people eat, drink, and sleep on them.

Don't belittle the inhabitants of the sidewalks. Like the taxi driver, they can spot the faces of strangers. They distinguish those who'll buy from those content to look. As a result, you see them pouncing on some and not approaching others. It's an intuition they acquire with the passage of time and faces.

I had read in novels (and seen in films) that streets like those I roamed every day housed buskers who played for passersby or themselves in the hope of making a little money to buy food for them and their families, but I did not see a single musician on the streets of Beirut. It was as if this city was content with the playing of bullets, the blast of artillery, and the shouts of children fleeing to the shelters.

Once the street people got to know my face, affection grew between me and most of them. The secondhand bookseller, most of all. He let me borrow books for free, on the condition that I returned the loaned book before I could take another. His memory was awesome. He knew all the books I borrowed. He was a cultured salesman. They said he bought books in sacks from fighters who had obtained them from villages and areas whose inhabitants had left. He bought them by the kilo and sold them for a pittance.

Without the street people, Beirut would have been tedious. During the day, time flew past. But as soon as the sun set and the streets emptied, my mood changed. I became depressed, as though the night was falling on me alone.

I kept walking wherever my feet took me. When I got tired, I sat down on the curb. I did not stay sitting for long, in case a militia patrol went by. I could be thrown in prison on some charge. They might accuse me of spying on their positions, working for a rival militia, or planning to rob a store. Then I would disappear without trace.

The night before last I slept on the backseat of a car parked next to a shoe factory. I liked sleeping in cars, after having tried it in Bou Walid's taxi. I extended a stiff wire through one of windows that was slightly open and lifted the button that locked the door. I was scared about oversleeping and being caught dozing by the owner of the car. If that happened, people would come running at his shouts of, "Thief! Thief!" If he was armed, he would kill me. The law would not touch him or even tread on his shoes. It was the law of the jungle. The strong ate the weak. It was enough to claim that he had caught me red-handed stealing his car or something in it to get himself off.

Yesterday evening, though, God answered my prayers—and that doesn't happen often. The area was under heavy shelling. I went into a building for protection until the situation calmed down. Then, a resident insisted I go with him to the shelter.

Luckily for me, the bombing continued sporadically. Whenever there was a lull, I let those still awake know that I wanted to leave, and they implored me to stay. "Are you crazy?" said one. "It's chaos out there. Where will you go? Stay here." Another took my hand and said, "Sit down so we can play cards." Dinner was a mouthful of labneh, a few olives, and a tomato. I slept deeply on a foam mattress. I didn't know whether the shelling resumed or not. I slept heavily normally, so imagine how I slept during those days when sleep was in short supply.

Where to sleep tonight? I walked and walked, my small bag under my arm or in my hand. I often used it as a pillow. I made it seem as though I was carrying food home so that the armed men did not stop me and pepper me with questions. True, I had no home, but no one else knew that. Sometimes I thought the opposite. I felt that everyone knew I was homeless, as though it were written on a placard on my back. More than that, I felt they were reading the details of my life.

At night, streets and building look very much alike. I walked down countless streets more than once, thinking it was the first time. During the day, things were different. Some neighborhoods required you to wear out your shoe leather to work out how to leave their maze of streets once you had entered. To memorize the streets, you have to walk them. Walking was an exceptional geography teacher.

I walked.

I stopped.

I sat down.

Power cuts made the nights darker. Car headlights perforated the dark with beams of dazzling light. The sky was piled with black clouds. Little by little the gentle breeze turned into a strong wind. I lowered my head and plowed my way against its gusts. I saw a tornado start to spin, spitting thick dust from its periphery. Shortly after the wind died down, it started to drizzle. I felt it soft and gentle on my face. The old lottery ticket seller whom I heard in the afternoon telling his companion as he looked at the sky, "In winter, clouds coming from the sea always bring rain," had been right.

It rained. God sent His bounty in buckets.

By the light of a passing car the pouring rain looked like a jungle of crystal filaments. Under the awning of a store, I watched another car pass to enjoy the same sight again. I fixed it in my memory to relive whenever I wanted. It did rain in the village, but never so hard. Even the rain was more merciful in the village than in the city.

I could no longer feel my feet because of the cold. They had got wet and I walked unsteadily. I thanked God for His having stopped me throwing away the bag. I sat on the doorstep of the store. I dried my feet and changed my wet socks for a clean pair. I made use of the rubber shoes. Because of the water, my worn-out shoes looked nothing like shoes. I got rid of them. I threw one next to a trashcan and the other into the middle of the road. It floated on the current of water and went down a drain. I imagined it venting its anger:

He hasn't taken me off his foot in five days, apart from a few hours. He's tired me out walking day and night. His five toes have left marks on my uppers, and his socks have stuck to me. If I was still of any use, he wouldn't have chucked me away. Wearing out has saved me from the unbearable smell of his feet. I often felt abject when he gazed at those like me in store windows. I envied them. They were new and shiny, while I was old and dirty. They were comfortable and respectable; I was exhausted and an outcast. I don't know what's happened to my partner. I remember I saw our owner throw us away together. Perhaps my friendship had grown dull, and he decided to continue life alone. Perhaps when he got rid of him and me, he regretted it and picked him up in the hope of finding me too. But living in sewage seems preferable to the smell of his feet. Once I got used to life under the ground, I regretted the days I had spent upon it.

The rain stopped pouring, but the torrent of water kept sweeping away everything it encountered. The roadway had turned into a river. There was nothing I could do. I took off my socks and put them back in the bag. I rolled my trousers up above my knees and made my way through the ankle-deep water. The shoes protected my feet from stones and anything harmful. Moving warmed me up.

Walking against the flow made me happy.

I went into an elegant building. The flame of my lighter guided me to the shelter. Its door was locked with a sizeable padlock. The cold was gnawing at my bones. The pain of hunger or from having stopped smoking since my cigarettes ran out was beating in my head. I looked for a cigarette butt on the stairs. I went up to the top floor without finding a single one. There were paper plates to feed the cats by the front doors. If they hadn't been there, I would have thought the building abandoned. I could not conceive of an inhabited place without cigarette butts.

I sat down on the steps to the shelter. I leaned against its door and curled up. Exhausted and sleep deprived, I dozed off.

I opened my eyes and saw a black shoe gently prodding me. I raised my head and saw an open mouth beneath black spectacles ordering me out and threatening me. I picked up my bag and left. Once I had gone a little way, I stopped opposite the man with the open mouth and gave him a rude hand gesture. He got angry and started picking up stones and throwing them at me as he ran after me.

Today is my fourth day homeless and on my own. No one has been willing to give me a job in exchange for food and a place to stay. At midday, I took two pieces of falafel without the owner of the restaurant noticing. As soon as I ate them I grew hungrier. I decided to try the same again. The suspicious glances of the vendor persuaded me to desist. I wished that a bomb would explode near the restaurant making the people evacuate the place. Then I would steal all the food I desired and keep eating until I burst.

On top of a garbage bin near the restaurant, I saw half a falafel sandwich wrapped in white paper and surrounded by a swarm of flies. I went up to the bin as if I intended to throw something away. I took the sandwich and gave it a quick once over. I devoured it and thought that ten like it would not satisfy me.

I felt that my stomach had had enough. The thought of a cigarette preyed on my mind. There is no greater pleasure than a cigarette after eating. The old gum seller gave me a cigarette. He almost burned my face as he lit it with a lighter whose regulator was broken. I smoked the cigarette and felt a pleasant light-headedness, something I always felt with the first cigarette after a break of a day or two.

I was not going to be able to carry on like this. Going back to the village was not an option. The only option was to join one of the militias. At least they would provide board and lodging. In exchange, I would perform my duties: guard duty, fighting in battle, and other missions.

7

I PREPARED CONVINCING ANSWERS TO every question I might be asked at the barracks.

A sentry seated on a small wicker chair in a corner of the entrance responded to my greeting with annoyance. He looked me up and down several times in a way that made me understand I had better explain what I wanted as quickly as possible.

I told him I wanted to meet the barracks commander about something important.

He tried to find out what this important thing was. I told him I could only disclose it to the commander. Of course I didn't have any secret. I said so to make the sentry take me seriously. Asking to meet his commander might make him hesitate before doing anything inappropriate.

I improvised that approach—it wasn't one of my preprepared answers—when the guard started looking at me as if I had landed from another planet. I wanted to warn him indirectly not to squint at me with disdain. He had the power to wreck my plan and stop me going in if he didn't like the way I looked, or if he just wanted to exercise his authority over me. So it was essential to succeed from the start, which meant gaining his confidence. I won it the moment after a sonic boom when he pointed to two thin streaks in the sky caused by two Israeli jets flying at high altitude. Somewhat sarcastically he said, "Without the Israeli jets, we would have forgotten the color of the sky."

I didn't reply. I just smiled sympathetically at his funny comment, but I was afraid it concealed a trap. He wanted to gauge my reaction and figure out my political stance. One group saw Israel as an enemy that had to be fought, along with its backer America. Another group thought that the Jewish state was an ally.

The guard got nothing at all out of me. He smiled then resumed scowling, so maintaining the boundaries usually erected by an armed man like him in the face of a defenseless person like me. He didn't need to search me. The shirt tucked into my trousers and hugging my body showed I wasn't carrying a pistol. Even so, he asked, "Do you have a gun?"

He asked me to wait while he informed a comrade that someone wanted to see the chief. 'Chief' was one of the words that heightened my aversion to the party in the village. That and the sessions for latent sectarian incitement, which people left in a mood to kill anyone from the other denomination or from rival parties, if they met them in the street.

As I stood waiting by the guard, who had started yawning in a way that made me do the same, a covered military jeep pulled up carrying two fighters in uniform. A 500mm machine gun was securely mounted on the back of the jeep with no one manning it. The guard asked them to take me to the Chief. They welcomed the idea.

I climbed into the jeep and said hello to the two guys, who said hello back very warmly. Perhaps they thought I was a relative of the Chief or linked to him in some way.

The barracks was vast, although it did not appear as such from the road by the entrance. I saw disused half-tracks, troop carriers, and 120mm mortars. Perhaps they were spoils of war.

A girl in green shorts and a black blouse looking out from a balcony caught my attention. What was a beautiful girl doing in the barracks with all these men? The question flashed through my mind, but I didn't stop to think about it. I had other more important things on my mind. I kept quiet.

The two guys didn't ask questions. They kept quiet too. They dropped me off by a two-story building, and one of them pointed out the Chief's office.

I got out and went over what I had decided to say to the Chief. I would tell him that my father was a veteran party member, that the party newspaper arrived periodically, and that although I wasn't a member, I was a friend of the party, and all my friends belonged to it. I would tell him the reason why I had had to leave the village and come to Beirut. There was no need to conceal or distort the facts or lie. The party had eyes and ears all over the place.

Why risk it and leave question marks hanging over me? In the situation, honesty was the best policy while lying would be playing with fire. I would openly admit that I didn't have relatives in Beirut, or friends, that I had come to him in the hope he would ensure me a place to sleep, plus food, and that I was willing to do guard duty and other tasks, even unpleasant jobs like collecting the garbage and taking it to the dump and cleaning the toilets.

Those ideas vanished when I saw him. He was wearing a combat jacket, with his sleeves rolled up above his elbows to show off a tattoo on his right forearm whose design I couldn't make out.

He didn't stand up when I came in but remained seated in a swivel chair. He talked while moving the chair with his body. His hands were resting on the table fiddling with a cigar in a transparent wrapper, an action that left a negative impression, but I didn't lose hope. He seemed arrogant when he eyed me as though I was a beggar. I regretted having chosen this barracks and cursed my luck for having met an officer like this one.

He wasn't alone. There was another person in the room who was looking for something in a metal cabinet right behind me. That was a little awkward. I would have preferred the room to be empty apart from the two of us.

As soon as I said my family name, he knew the name of my village, and, by chance, he knew some of the guys a bit older than me. He said he had gotten to know them at one of the training sessions and liked them because of their courage and commitment to the party. He described them as 'men' fighting for the cause and not for personal gain. Then he asked me about some of them and about the situation in the village and its environs. He said, "You are heroes because you remain steadfast in a region the majority of whose inhabitants are from the other denomination."

When I told him why I had come, he wasn't surprised. It seemed I wasn't the only person who had been forced to leave his family and seek refuge at the barracks. He said, "Go and ask for Azizi. He'll take care of you."

I asked for Azizi. They told me where to find him. He got his name because he didn't use a comrade's name, but called them 'azizi'—my dear. I noticed that when he repeated the word 'azizi' between every sentence. He led me to a room among a group of similar-looking rooms. He pushed open the unlocked door, and I saw four bunk beds, each with three tiers. There was also a table covered with leftover food and cans of tuna and sardines, and a plastic wardrobe. On the wall was a picture of the party chairman addressing the masses. When I saw the picture, I remembered Dad who often said that the extraordinary charisma of the party chairman had made him the leader.

Azizi pointed to a bed with two bunks above it, complete with a pillow and two unused blankets. I am unable to describe my feelings when he said, "This is your bunk." I felt like I owned half the world. I soon found myself sitting on the bed and inspecting the bedclothes. It was a throne, not a bed. I was too embarrassed to ask whether the two upper bunks were occupied or not. What mattered was I had found somewhere to spend the night. And not just the night, but the day too if I wanted. Then we went out onto the balcony and he pointed out the armory.

I did not disclose my aversion to guns. I told him I was only good at handling a hunting rifle. He said that everyone in the barracks was armed, and it would be strange for only me not to have a gun. Then he took his machine gun off his shoulder and showed me how to use it. In ten minutes he had taught me how to strip it and load the magazine. He informed me that there were ongoing training sessions, and I had to choose the specialization I wanted according to my qualifications. He pointed out that first I had to go through basic training in things like stripping down and reassembling personal weapons, shooting, and various military matters essential to know before moving onto a specialist area. He advised me to opt for artillery if I had a certificate in math or science.

Azizi was friendly. I didn't feel that I had just met him half an hour before but had known him for ages. I told him my story in brief. He was moved and insisted on hearing the details. He invited me for lunch when I was ready. "I'll wait for you at the entrance to the barracks in half an hour," he said looking at his watch.

We went to a small restaurant across the street from the barracks and sat at a table piled with two plates of fava beans, a plate of mashed chickpeas, another of boiled chickpeas, and a third with a few olives, some sprigs of mint, and two onions.

I told him my story from the moment the blood-soaked man appeared at the rubbish dump until the moment I reached the barracks. From that lunch onward, we became friends or friends-in-the-making.

When we parted, I recalled what he had said. Choosing the artillery was a nice idea. Taking part in combat from a distance was safer than attacking or defending, but I had a certificate in philosophy, not math or physics, and that wouldn't qualify me for the artillery unit. If it was up to me, I would choose to be a sniper, and I would be outstanding. Someone who could shoot partridge, quail, or sandpiper, the mark of a skilled hunter, would find it easy to pick off people.

I would train as a sniper but avoid killing.

I would train because I had to, to avoid becoming homeless again.

Such thoughts ran through my mind as I lay on my bed trying to relax after a night where I had only managed to sleep a little.

A comrade woke me up around sundown and asked me to help him and two others carry boxes of ammunition from the armory to a truck.

Once we were done, I presented myself to the officer in charge of the armory. He gave me a Kalashnikov automatic rifle and accessories in the form of a pouch big enough for three magazines and seven boxes of bullets, plus two combat outfits and a pair of boots. Then he entered my full name, the serial number of the gun, and other information in a thick ledger.

I went up to the room and stashed the automatic rifle under the blankets and the pouch and the boxes of bullets under the bed next to the boots.

In the evening I didn't know what to do with myself. I knew nobody. The novel I was finishing I had left in the bag. If it had been with me, I would have killed a couple of hours reading and then slept.

The only option was to go out of the barracks for a stroll. On my walk, I noticed that the barracks was set among residential buildings, most of whose upper stories had been damaged by shelling.

My stroll didn't last long. After half an hour I was back. I had somewhere to go back to. A lovely feeling of security.

The barracks at night was totally quiet. The calm was punctuated by a jeep heading out or a civilian car coming in from a special mission.

There was a television on in one of the rooms, and a few guys were watching a local football match. I discovered this from the commentary, not from the shouts of encouragement that accompany that kind of sport. In another room, two guys were reading. I subsequently learned that they were university students. One was in his third year in law school, and the other was in his second year in the media department. It occurred to me to resume my studies when I would be able to concentrate on learning. At the present time I was still messed up. I had no money and no desire to go back into education.

Tomorrow I would go to the taxi station for the line between Beirut and the town close to the village. I would send Dad a message with Bou Walid telling him that I wanted money to buy underwear and other essentials, and a kitbag in preparation for the training.

I didn't know whether fighters got paid if they were full-time at the barracks or whether everyone was a volunteer. I thanked God for giving me more than I deserved. He had given me a bed to sleep on, two blankets to keep me warm, and a roof to live under.

My mother's prayers were not far from His heart. They had had their effect on Him, the One who Hears and Responds.

8

ALL THE GUYS AT THE barracks had a codename. Their real names never went further than their ID cards except for administrative purposes. It was forbidden to mention them, especially during missions and in combat. Only nicknames were acknowledged. Because they were used so much, they took the place of real names and erased them over time.

I didn't find this strange. In my village, there was no shame in being nameless; shame lay in not having a nickname. Your name was given to you by your family, in honor of a saint, or in memory of a dear friend who had emigrated, or out of respect for a dead grandparent.

Nicknames were a different story altogether. You didn't get one for just anything. Your friends, or those older than you, gave it to you inspired by something remarkable you had done or something bad, or inspired by an occasion testimony to a talent of yours, or a weakness.

You might go for a long time without a nickname, but no one would call you by the name on your ID. They would append you to your father's nickname if he was still alive. If he was dead, the rule did not apply.

They nicknamed me Son-of-the-Teacher because my father's nickname had been Teacher since it became known that he had passed the exam for teacher training college, where he studied for three years and graduated as a teacher. After graduation, he taught at the far-off Ein al-Asfour intermediate school, then in the village intermediate school after the helpful intervention of an MP.

I was stuck with my father's nickname, preceded by son-of, until I shot a bird called the ittriss, after it had been missed by hunters known for their good aim. The ittriss is a male plover, slightly smaller than the female, but smarter. He's also known for his spiraling flight path, which makes him extremely difficult to hit.

The next day, I was surprised by the neighbor's son calling me Ittriss. I thought he was calling someone else, then he pointed to show that he meant me. "Don't forget," he said, "I was the first one in the village to call you Ittriss."

You might know who first called you by your name, but it was very unusual to know who gave you the name. If someone knew who it was, he didn't have the right to say. Keeping secrets was ingrained because of the drug smuggling and hashish growing practiced by many local people, as well as their trying their luck gambling on winter nights.

I liked the nickname, not because I thought it was great, but because it saved me from my father's nickname. I wanted it to spread around the village as fast as possible. That would never happen unless the regulars at the square, the café especially, acknowledged it. The café would give a new nickname the stamp of permanence, for if it was circulating in the village but not in use at the café, it faced oblivion. The café recognized the nickname, then the village adopted it. The café owner had a major role in the whole process. His repeating the name in a loud voice as he called out to its bearer was a step on the road to recognition.

It wasn't just the name that spread. The event that gave birth to it went with it. The name was impossible to separate from its origin. Foundling nicknames, as we termed them, were those born without some event. People used them for themselves and changed them when they wanted, and several people might be known by the same nickname at the same time. Such nicknames were borne by shepherds, orchard keepers, and the workers who harvested grapes and figs, most of whom were nomadic Arabs. They would visit our village and pass through the square. If they sat in the café, they did not stay long. Their hearts told them that their presence was not wanted, because they were outsiders. For my village, outsiders were those who knew people's nicknames but not their real names. They also did not have a unique nickname. The significance of our nicknames lay in their uniqueness.

To preserve this tradition, the café owner would record nicknames in his ledger for debts and the dates of deaths and important events experienced by the village (a visit by the metropolitan or his deputy, or a famous zajal poet invited to lament at a funeral).

I remember that my grandfather on my father's side was not happy about my nickname. He insulted those who used it. Of all his grandchildren I was the only one to be named after him. He was inordinately proud of his name because it sounded good and was not much used. It was enough to say it, without the family name, to know who was intended. For a long time, and for the same reason, I was also proud of my given name. I didn't know anyone else called Abir. I don't know how my great-grandfather came up with that name, which wasn't among the names common in the village. Even my grandfather himself didn't know the source of the name and what had motivated his father to name him so. From my birth and having been named after him, he did not call my father by his name, Habib, or his nickname, Teacher. He called him Abu Abir. My grandmother did the same. When he heard that I was being called Ittriss, he threatened out loud to teach a lesson to the lice on the hair of the head of anyone who did not call me by my real name. In the past, my grandfather's threats had frightened people. His record from the French Mandate period was full of heroic deeds. The village elderly knew them well and still talked about them. But old age had slowed him down. His threats would not have gone beyond the walls of his house if my grandmother hadn't confided them to those sitting next to her at Mass on Sunday.

My grandmother's view was no different to my grandfather's. I remember she hit the seller of lupine seeds and cotton candy with a broom because he didn't call me by my real name. On the outside Dad seemed indifferent. He didn't argue with anyone because of my name. He often deliberately called out to me in a loud voice as he passed through the square at sundown. It was as though he wanted to remind the men lounging on chairs by the entrance to the café and in front of the shops of my real name. I deliberately kept walking, pretending not to hear him so that he would call again in a slightly louder voice. Complicity over this developed unintentionally between us. He didn't have anything important to tell me when we stood under the chinaberry tree in the middle of the square. He would ask me a few normal questions, and not let me answer any of them fully before interrupting and hitting me with another. We stood talking for a while to convince anyone who saw us that there was something urgent that demanded it.

Mum didn't care, but, like my grandparents, she carried on calling Dad Abu Abir, rather than Habib, in front of the neighbors and at gatherings. At home, however, she used his name as was her custom.

Giving nicknames was not limited to people. Neighborhoods also changed their names. The residents had their own name for their street, different to the name used by the residents of the other streets. A neighborhood might have as many names as the number of neighborhoods that bore it animosity.

Even the name of the village, Bayadir, was only used in real estate circles and on the map. Its inhabitants called it Beit al-Qamar, in reference to a plant that looked like the moon that only grew on our land. Visitors thought that some poet or author was behind the name. Older people supported that idea. They said that Shahrour al-Wadi had given it that name in a poem when he had passed through. Nobody, however, retained anything of the poem. Others ascribed the name to a beautiful woman who lived a time in the village. She drove the men soft in the head and they likened her to the moon. When disease took her, they called the village Beit al-Qamar in her memory.

At the barracks, when I was asked my name, I understood that my codename was intended, not my real name.

I did not think long. "Ittriss," I said.

That was the name I wrote on a piece of paper that I stuck on the bag of clothes before throwing it inside the truck that would precede us to the training camp.

9

MY HEAD BETWEEN CHUNKY BOOT and muddy gravel. The trainer's boot was mountainous. He pressed it down hard when I made any move indicative of complaint or pain. He was almost crushing my skull. Something hot flowed slowly down toward my mouth. My ear was bleeding. The pressing of the trainer got harder. Swearwords flew out of his mouth along with spittle. His voice sounded distant as if coming from the ends of the earth. My head started to spin. My eyes went blurry.

Whenever I moved my head and looked upward I saw the front of the boot superimposed on the top of the trainer's head. Whenever I looked forward, I saw my comrades standing in two ranks, some tall, some short.

The bastard wanted me to be an example for them so that they would think twice before messing around. I had done nothing to warrant such punishment. He spotted Starling looking behind him and assumed I was talking to him when we were supposed to be keeping silent. It wasn't really like that. I was standing directly behind Starling and I don't know what made him turn right around toward me.

The trainer called me over and ordered me to lie down and crawl, and not stop until he told me. I tried to make him understand what had happened. He grew furious, as if I had insulted his mother. He kicked me so hard in the stomach I shot a meter in the air then hit the ground again. He started pressing his boot on my head. When he relented, my face had gone numb. I brushed the mud off the left side and could feel the grooves the boot had left on the right side.

I did not protest, based on the military precept of 'carry out orders, then protest.' That was the first lesson we had learned and committed to memory, even before the party anthem. I often made fun of it and who said it, seeing as there was no point in protesting once the punishment had been implemented. Assuming I was in the right, would a blunt apology or "no offense," be enough? I would not swallow being demeaned. The day might come when I would get justice in my own way. I hobbled back to the ranks.

We were in combat jackets, under the sun, by a large pit full of filthy water. One by one we had to crawl through it with our faces in the water, otherwise the trainer fired a shot over the head of the miscreant. When my turn came, I got slowly into the water. My face was in the water. The thickness of the mud hindered my motion. I planted my elbows in the bottom and moved forward. I raised my head slightly. The trainer warned me not to do it again if I valued my life. I continued crawling to the end of the pool, wondering how they could push our faces into the mud and then expect us, when saluting the party flag, to stand with our heads held high.

The question dropped away with the water that a comrade, who was lame and exempt from training, sprayed over our bodies as soon as we came out of the pit. I stood opposite him as he rinsed off the mud. I moved closer to the nozzle of the hose and scrubbed my head thoroughly. I felt cold when he stopped training the water on me.

When Sultan came out of the pit, we saw a worm coming out of his ear. Bonnet Head grabbed it, rinsed it, and ate it. The trainer applauded him, and we joined in. The clapping continued until Bonnet Head placed his hand on his stomach as a sign that the worm had gone down.

After the crawl through the pit, we stretched our exhausted bodies out on the ground. There was a gap of about half a meter between each one. The trainer walked over us, stomping deliberately on our chests. He went forward and backward. Backward and forward. They said that was how they turned us into hardened men and fierce fighters. I had never felt as humiliated as I did in those seemingly endless moments. Their plan to humiliate us seemed premeditated. The spiritless make authority relax. The self-confident disturb it.

I only regained my dignity at the firing range. At the end of the practice, I was in first place. The trainer, in everyone's hearing, said that in all his military service he had never seen a better shot than me. That acknowledgment was a source of pride for me, although I had expected it. Most of the trainees had never fired a cartridge before, not even at a tin can or an empty bottle. Some had only ever seen a rifle on TV or at the cinema, and at the army parade on Independence Day.

From the age of twelve I had been hunting. I started with a catapult, made out of poplar wood and a length of car or bicycle inner tube. One day I felled a bird with it that we called the "air fucker" because of how it fluttered in the same spot thrusting the air for about two minutes. After the catapult came the pellet gun; I was such a good shot with it, I could hit a matchstick at ten meters. After I passed my exams, Dad bought me the shotgun, and I became a full-fledged hunter. The villagers and my friends made my marksmanship proverbial. Beirutis, who came to the region during hunting season, watched me bring down birds however fast or high they were flying. Leaning on their shotguns, they watched in amazement. They often bought birds off me at prices that were astronomical for a lad like me.

At the camp, I found shooting easy. Wooden targets shaped like men with a concrete wall behind them, and tree trunks about a meter high. To begin with, you shot at a fixed target at forty meters. I was only happy if my ten bullets, the number allotted to each of us, lodged in the head. Many comrades failed to hit the target, their bullets missing by miles.

We trained with live ammunition at the firing range. When it came to a dummy offensive against a fortified position, we carried our weapons unloaded. I was on the attacking side once and among the defenders once. That kind of training was fun and amusing. It reminded me of the war games we played as kids with sticks for guns, and our voices making the sound of bullets.

Training was not limited to the fighting arts. It included a section on 'military culture.' I didn't think war required that kind of knowledge. Wasn't it enough for fighters to learn how to fire their guns and practice some maneuvers to go to the front?

The instructor who taught us that subject was pleasant and always going off on a tangent. I listened to the digressions more than the explanations of the theories, because, according to the instructor, they were examples taken from the battles that had been waged or were waging in Beirut and the provinces.

The instructor was around fifty years old. He stood there with a long thin ruler in his hand, which he used to point at the three maps stuck up on a long wooden board as he explained the theory. Then he gave examples from the field. The attack on such-and-such area had succeeded because it concentrated on this and that. The attack on that strategic location had failed for a number of reasons. He would enumerate one reason after another, and those listening to him would think him a hero who would never lose a battle if he was allowed to command.

During the early classes, I felt a bit bored. Dropping the class was not possible. Fooling around or being flippant was forbidden. The homeland and our existence were in danger, and we the youth had to defend them, otherwise we were cowards who did not deserve our country or to remain in it in dignity.

Subsequently, however, I started to look forward to the military culture classes. I even found the instructor pleasant and took notes of what he was saying in his Akkar accent. I tried not to miss anything important. Military thinkers who impressed me included Sun Tzu, even though his ideas went back to 500 BC. Our teacher himself seemed bewitched by them and their author. Ideas still valid for today. Tzu said that the short war is an effective war, that speed is the essence of warfare, and that dissimulation and deception are its basis. I learned by heart his saying: "When you surround an army, leave an outlet free. Do not press a desperate foe too hard." I was struck by the teacher's comment that the hope of survival offered by retreat helps a quick defeat.

From Bonaparte's principles, I learned the importance of organization and administrative and logistical support, and to maneuver with separate forces and strike with combined forces.

One rule emphasized by Mao Zedong stuck in my mind: the need for cohesion between the people and the army. A slogan of Lenin and Stalin caught my attention: "Use up forces in preparation for battle rather than battle for using up forces."

I also understood the role of the slogans that encapsulated the principles and political views of the party. Likewise, I understood the role of anthems, slogans, and chants, which had a dual purpose: first to inspire enthusiasm, second to sharpen resolve.

I learned that resorting to martial songs on long marches diverted the fighters and helped them endure and cope with the slow passage of time. We often went on runs at night and sang patriotic songs even though we were exhausted. We ran long distances to get warm, and when we grew tired, we went into our tents and slept.

On the final night, the weather was freezing. The camp commander summoned me and asked me, Shakespeare, and Starling to go to nearby fields to fetch firewood.

I carried out the order.

On the way, Starling imitated the howling of a dog. Anyone who heard the howls without seeing their source would have no doubt that they came from a dog, not a person. Starling was a big guy with a beard. He said he wasn't going to get rid of his beard until the war ended. He had a strange sense of humor. He would lie down on the ground and look up at the stars. We often thought he was dozing, and would go over to wake him up, only to find him with his eyes wide open, lost in thought. He claimed he had the power to move the clouds into the shapes he imagined as he lay thinking. He loved women. He stole his mother's jewelry and spent the money on hookers, drink, and hash. I was impressed by his idea that war was like a hooker. Neither of them was ever satisfied: the first with blood; the second with men. He was in the same situation as me. He had no relatives in Beirut. He ate and slept at the barracks. He was a member of several parties. The importance of a party for him lay in the food and bed it provided. The slogan of one party was tattooed on his forearm. When he was pissed with that party, he tattooed another party's slogan on his other arm and removed the first tattoo. He had taken part in the training to have a break from the barricades. He rarely went out without a revolver. The 14mm was his pistol of choice. You could start a counter-offensive with it. He said that as he took aim at a bat passing overhead.

Shakespeare was short and skinny. He earned his nickname because he could barely read and write. He had never been to school. Initially, he thought Shakespeare was a film star. He swelled with pride when he learned that the name belonged to the most famous English poet. Sometimes he talked in his sleep, but it was impossible to make out a word he was saying. If you didn't find him at the barracks or at the frontline, he would definitely be at the pinball place by the barracks. The right side of his face had been disfigured by acid. A girl from his village had thrown it at him. He had taken her cherry and denied it. He still loved her. I caught him once in the tent playing with himself. There was a photograph of Egyptian actress Souad Hosni cut out of a magazine in front of him. When he saw me, he said, "For her intent, not her beauty." *Her* here referred to the girl.

The three of us walked in the dark, pleased at the distinction granted us by the trainer. We piled up dry branches and tied them into half-a-dozen bundles. Each of us picked up two bundles and we headed back.

A white Honda was parked down a path off to the side. It was not difficult to work out why. The Kleenex tissues strewn around suggested that it was a good spot for making out.

We approached the car, drawn by its rhythmic swaying and steamed-up windows. Shakespeare put his two bundles down on the ground and went over to the driver's door. He tapped his fingertips on the window and pointed his flashlight inside the car. A man covered his eyes with his hand to shield them from the sudden light, and, pulling up his underpants and trousers which were around his ankles, got off a woman. The shock made the woman freeze where she was: lying on her back, hair disheveled, one breast bare, and half her midriff exposed.

Starling went over to the other door, the side of the girl.

I tried to persuade them not to do what they had in mind. They didn't listen. Starling even pushed me and told me to keep out of it. I dropped my bundles of wood and sat on them to observe what was happening. The terrified man got out of the car. He started begging us not to hurt him or his companion. "Take everything," he said, "but let her go." Starling started slapping him. The man tried to deflect the blows by hiding his face behind his hands. Then they started fighting, but Shakespeare resolved the situation. With the butt of his pistol he hit the man on the head and he passed out.

The woman got scared and started to cover herself up. Her pleading sobs did not deter Shakespeare from pulling her out of the car by the hair. Then he grabbed her from behind and covered her mouth with his hand. Starling could not believe his luck. He knelt down, putting his knees on her shoes to stop her legs moving. Taking the hem of her dress in his teeth, he lifted it up until her panties were visible. He slowly pulled them off, then threw them toward me. He gripped her legs and buried his head between her thighs.

When her companion came round, Shakespeare let go of the girl and started on him. He took the man's head in his hands and banged it against the ground until he knocked him out again.

While this was going on, the woman gave Starling the slip and managed to run off. Shakespeare caught up with her and pounced on her. She resisted. He slapped her and dragged her back to the car. He forced her to bend over with her hands on the hood. He eased open her thighs with his legs and took her from behind. Starling went after. With her in the same position, he lifted her ankles onto his shoulders and entered her.

The poor girl was crying silently as she looked at her friend lying a few meters away. As soon as they had finished with her, she rushed over to him.

Shakespeare looked for her panties. When he found them, he studied them and gave them a sniff. Then he kneaded them in his hands like a baker kneads a lump of dough, stretching it out before putting it in the oven.

Back to the camp with the bundles of wood. Starling went first. He dropped his bundles on the ground and started dancing around waving a bra that he pulled out of his pocket.

We agreed to keep things secret. We went to sleep unable to believe that tonight was the last night.

The twentieth day was exceptional. At noon, a senior official accompanied by a number of aides arrived. We formed ranks in front of a platform that had taken half the day to construct. The trainer gave a short speech. He was followed by the official who talked about the importance of training and discipline, and the need to guard the homeland from the enemies lying in wait.

I was surprised when he mentioned my outstanding performance on the firing range. To everyone's amazement, he broke off his speech and asked me to raise my hand to let him know who I was. I left the ranks and raised my hand. I lowered my head in gratitude for his having generously singled me out.

He said, "We congratulate you," and resumed his speech.

Then we were awarded medals for completing training that bore the name of the martyr Usama al-Bahri. The medals inscribed with the party slogan hung on our chests, which still bore the imprint of the trainer's boot.

10

FROM THE CAMP I WENT straight back to the barracks. I was free to spend the two days' post-training leave anywhere, but I spent them there. My reputation as a marksman preceded me, as did the commendation of the senior official. The next morning, the commander summoned me to his office and congratulated me. He told me he was proud of me and those like me who brought honor to the party. He said that he had given the order for me to join the unit commanded by Napoleon since it needed a good marksman. As I was leaving, he said that his door was always open if I needed anything.

I told Azizi that I was joining Napoleon's unit. He made no comment. I understood his silence to mean that I had been unlucky and was going somewhere he wouldn't have wished for me. I avoided asking questions so as not to embarrass him. Perhaps he didn't want to disclose what he knew, because he didn't know me very well. Or perhaps he wanted me in the unit he was attached to.

I met Napoleon and found him pleasant enough. He welcomed me and said that he had heard good things about me and was happy that I would be one of his men. I almost objected when he counted me as one of his men, but I didn't. Perhaps the expression was usual for unit commanders, but I refused to be anyone's subordinate, even the party's itself. As if he sensed my unspoken objection, he was effusive on the fraternal spirit that imbued his unit. He said that we, all of us, were one hand, and that what afflicted one of us, afflicted all of us. He stressed that everything we saw and heard, nobody else must know. When he saw me nodding my head as he spoke, he stretched out his hand and I shook it as a sign of agreement.

In the first two weeks I took part in many missions: setting up mobile checkpoints, raiding a drug dealer's house, arresting a gang specializing in car theft, guarding the barracks, night duty on the demarcation lines. During all of these tasks, Napoleon behaved as befitted a conscientious officer. My admiration for him grew when we stopped a guy from another confession at one of our checkpoints who was concealing a pistol at the bottom of his leg. He treated him decently and ordered the two soldiers charged with taking him to the security center not to cause him any harm.

The admiration did not last long. One night, he summoned me and said that we had a top-secret military matter to deal with. He had chosen me and another comrade called Ninny to take part in the mission.

At zero hour, we set off in a military jeep. Ninny was driving, Napoleon sat next to him, and I was in the backseat. Some twenty minutes after leaving, we parked the jeep in an unlit street and transferred to a car parked on the same street. Napoleon opened its door with a single key and we got in. He drove and Ninny sat next to him; I sat in the back. I had never seen the car before, but since Napoleon had the key, I assumed he must have been its owner.

After less than a quarter of an hour, we stopped in a bustling street whose stores were closing for the day. It was time for the owners and employees to go home, content with the income the Lord had provided. While Napoleon kept his eyes trained on a particular part of the street, he explained the mission to Ninny and me. His gaze was fixed on one spot, as if he was afraid that if he looked away, he would miss something that might jeopardize the mission.

After the explanation, we understood the reason why we had come to that street in particular. We learned that the target was the owner of a jewelry store. We had to teach him a lesson because he was harboring agents in his home and then facilitating their crossing the Green Line in his car.

The man came out of his store carrying a black briefcase like any businessman and was followed by the lad who worked for him. The jeweler watched the lad as he shut the two padlocks on the shutters, then leaned over to the side of the doorway and secured a third lock. After inspecting the first two padlocks and making sure they were secure, he patted the lad's shoulder and they walked off together for a short distance and then parted ways.

The man headed toward his car, which was parked in a bay. A white metal sign affixed to the wall showed the car license number. He placed the briefcase on the front passenger seat, took off his jacket and threw it lightly onto the same seat. He sat down behind the wheel, adjusted the rearview mirror, started the engine, waited a short while, then drove off.

We followed him.

Napoleon ordered us not to open fire unless it was in self-defense. He said he would give us the necessary instructions at the appropriate time, and that there was no need for our automatic rifles. Pistols would be enough. I was like someone on a daytrip. I looked out of the windows on both sides and watched the cars pass alongside. From time to time, I looked at the jeweler's car, which was about fifteen meters ahead. When he turned off onto a mountain road, we turned too and remained behind him. For cover, so that he did not realize he was being followed, Napoleon let a car overtake and slide between our car and his.

We were surprised when his left side indicator showed that he was going to pull over. We overtook him and slowed down, then waited next to a nearby building. The man got out of the car, went into a pharmacy and came out holding a small white plastic bag. He passed by us in his car and I tried to make out his face but could not see it clearly. He was wearing glasses and driving with his left hand. His right hand might have been tuning the radio or doing something else.

We followed him again.

We reached a crossroads. A truck was causing a holdup as it maneuvered backward and forward toward the narrow entrance of a warehouse. Napoleon avoided stopping behind or alongside the man. Two cars stood between us. As soon as the road cleared and the cars sped off, we returned to the previous formation with him in front and us behind.

When the cars thinned out, we sped past him.

After quite some distance, Napoleon stopped the car and got out. He stood in the middle of the road waving his hands for the man to stop. He stopped. Napoleon ran toward him, opened the car door, brandished his pistol, pointed it at his head, and ordered him to park the car at the side of the road. He complied.

Ninny and I watched in astonishment. We had no idea what we were supposed to do. We remained seated but were ready for every eventuality. Then we saw Napoleon bludgeon the man with the butt of his pistol and come back with the black briefcase that the jeweler had brought from his shop.

Before Napoleon handed the briefcase to Ninny and got in the car, the jeweler fired two shots, one of which hit Napoleon, who slumped over the steering wheel. Ninny jumped out and fired several shots back. Then he climbed into the car and we took off. I lifted my head off the backseat and saw the jeweler clutch his stomach and collapse onto the front of his car.

Napoleon had been hit in his right forearm. The wound wasn't too serious, although it didn't stop bleeding. Fortunately, nobody passing in their car at that moment had noticed what happened, or they did notice and preferred not to stop.

Napoleon tossed me a bunch of keys and in a commanding tone tinged with pain said, "Keep hold of them." They belonged to the jeweler and Napoleon had taken them to stop him pursuing us. What should I do with them? Why had he given them to me? Why didn't he keep them himself?

I did not pose these questions aloud while he groaned in pain. Once he was assured that we were safe, he stopped and asked Ninny to drive. He got out clutching his arm and sat in the passenger seat. I relaxed when he took the keys back. He looked at the bunch and put them in his pocket.

I suggested going to the nearest hospital for him to get treatment. He refused because he knew that the hospital administration would notify the police station of any case like his. Subsequently I learned that one of his relatives, a retired nurse, had removed the bullet and stitched up the wound.

Napoleon didn't open the briefcase in front of us, on the pretext that it might hold documents and it would be inappropriate for anyone other than those concerned to see them. I deluded him into thinking that I believed him.

The briefcase might have been full of jewels, and he wanted the lion's share for himself. It became clear to me that the mission had nothing to do with any military order issued by a senior party figure. It was a freelance operation. He had surveilled the jeweler and wanted to rob him, while pretending to us that the guy was smuggling spies from our zone to another.

I didn't know why he chose me to take part, given that he had no need for me. The proof was that I had done nothing. The operation could have been carried out with the help of just one person. He wanted to involve me to ensure my loyalty and my silence about what I might hear or see in the days to come. I remembered his words to me at our first meeting that everything that went on in our unit stayed in it, and that anyone who leaked one of its secrets would vanish off the face of the Earth.

I was an accomplice in a crime, perhaps a serious crime. It was possible the jeweler had died immediately, or been wounded and, without treatment, bled to death. A tight spot that would have paved the way for more to come, had Azizi not interceded for me with the barracks commander and persuaded him to transfer me to the snipers' unit. Azizi took the initiative by himself. Perhaps he knew something about the robbery of the jeweler and wanted to save me from what was to come before it was too late. Perhaps he did it to assuage his conscience because he knew Napoleon's transgressions all too well, and it was likely I would not remain immune from them. Maybe he was just afraid for me and intervened.

I was transferred to the snipers' unit despite Napoleon's resentment at the sudden decision. He stifled his complaints, however, and wished me luck, provided I respected the promise I had given him and forgotten all I had seen, heard, and done during my service under his command.

11

My new unit commander, the Godfather, promised me a surprise if my marksmanship produced a good yield. He repeated this in the hearing of a few comrades drinking their morning coffee. He was playing with his mustache—his usual custom when he wanted to keep a promise.

Before I left, he stuffed something small in my pocket, then leaned in and whispered: "Top quality, resin, I swear." He thought I smoked hash like many of the guys. I did not respond, in case he took a refusal as an insult.

I picked up my rifle, fitted with telescopic sights, the pouch of ammunition, and a bottle of water. I rode in a jeep that was taking two comrades to the frontline.

The front was quiet, the only noise the roar of armored vehicles.

I went up into Sardine Tower. Why it was called that I didn't know, but they said a modest fisherman owned it. He had bought it from an Armenian businessman three years before the start of the war.

I reached the tenth floor out of breath and surveyed the area opposite. From a window too small to let a tennis ball through, I could see stores, a butcher's, and a pinball place. I could see a school and part of its playground, and an empty street with cars on both sides, some burnt out, others unfit to drive. I had a view of roofs, water tanks, and clotheslines. In the distance, I could see a cluster of buildings, with what they called Fog Tower on the news in the middle.

From another tiny window, I could see part of a hospital entrance protected by sandbags and a sign standing in the middle of the street with "Beware. Sniper" written on it. I didn't spot anyone going in or out of the hospital. Going in and out took place behind high barriers.

My rifle was next to me. Its sights allowed me to see all that. Through it I could read the names of shops and even know what was in the windows.

While waiting, I inspected the resin and took a sniff. I decided to give it to Softie, then changed my mind. I wanted to burn it. I liked the smell, just as I liked the smell of chicken or hunks of meat being grilled more than eating them. I found an empty can of tuna. I crumbled the hash in my palm, put a small piece on the edge of the can, and played my lighter flame over it. It caught fire. I lifted the can up to my nose and inhaled its fragrance. I did this over and over until I had finished off all the crumbs. I got high, but the intoxication didn't last.

A disgusting smell came carried on a draft of wind. It might have been the product of a dead animal or a forgotten corpse. I followed its trail from room to room. When I passed in front of a window, I took care to lower my head so as not to show myself to the enemy on the opposite front. I still hadn't reached the source of the smell. Perhaps it was in the room I was about to enter. I found a bloated rat sheltering a squadron of flies and scattered piles of dried shit. The smell only came from the dead animal. When it's dry, shit has no smell. No taste either. I say that on Starling's say so. He was kidnapped once and his kidnappers forced him to eat shit. He did. The shit was dry, so he crunched then swallowed it, and smelt nothing. With an iron bar I dragged the rat onto a piece of egg carton and threw them both down below.

I went back to the window. Movement in both the directions I scoped was still paralyzed. People started to leave the shelters at noon and head home after a night of nonstop shelling. I picked someone riding a motorbike, but I was unable to fire when the victim was in my sights. Something made my finger freeze on the trigger and I was unable to squeeze.

Friends and relatives who had been killed by snipers' bullets went through my mind. They had been killed at the entrance to the bakery, at the gas station waiting to fill up, on the way to hospital, on the way home from work, or vice versa, while sipping coffee on the balcony. . . .

Snipers were on the lookout. They sowed terror with treacherous bullets in the calm hours that followed exchanges of shelling.

I often reproached myself for having agreed to such a task. I became one of those most often chosen for it after word got around that I could hit a swallow in flight with my Kalashnikov. That was an exaggeration, and I don't know who spread it. Once, however, I did hit a pigeon on the edge of the roof of some building. That was not news worth spreading. Sometimes a modest act becomes heroic in the retelling. People are inclined to embellish the story until it becomes entirely different. If only I had excelled at something other than shooting, although there's nothing else I do so well.

I went to Sardine Tower when I was on duty, but not to snipe. I often slept. When my duty ended I went back to the barracks. Sometimes I read a novel or did crossword puzzles that I collected from the newspapers discarded by trashcans. The hardest crossword was in *al-Nahar*. Only specialists in Arabic, or those who had memorized the dictionary, could solve it.

If I wanted to shoot, I didn't shoot at people but at a metal sign or cloth banner in the street; or I would aim at the picture of some leader hanging from an electricity pole and try to embroider it with bullet holes; or I would fire at the paper kites flown by children in the school playground. I knew that hitting a kite was next to impossible because they moved constantly with the wind. I did that when I grew bored of reading or solving crossword puzzles.

I amused myself. Nothing goes more slowly than time spent doing a job that doesn't appeal, and in a place that when you leave or return, you can't believe it.

Behind the observation slit, I felt I was a coward. But when I was at the barricades I felt like a real fighter. Panther, the sniper with whom I rotated duties, told me that his greatest pleasure was to shoot someone and watch the passersby gather around the body. He said he would fall about laughing at such moments, then resume picking off the crowd until it dispersed. Then he would keep sniping at the injured man until he was sure he was dead. It was his greatest thrill to shoot anyone who approached the victim. He often bragged that he felled someone giving first aid to someone who had tried to drag another corpse to safety. He told the story as if telling a joke, punctuating it with fake laughter. He would crown his delight with a glass or two of arak whenever he heard on the radio, or from another comrade, that a citizen had fallen to a sniper's bullet in the area in his line of fire. The broadcasting of the news was proof.

Panther was diligent about writing down the name of the dead man on a piece of paper that contained a few names that he claimed were the names of his victims—apart from those whose names were unknown. He picked up the names from the radio and wrote them down along with the name of the station that broadcast the report and the date.

Whenever he wanted to offer condolences to a comrade, one of whose friends or relatives had been killed, he promised him that he would take revenge for him. Revenge meant sniping some passerby. It didn't matter who, what mattered was that he was from the other zone. As soon as revenge was exacted, he would personally relay the good news to the comrade, pre-empting the news broadcast. He would be proud that through his revenge he had done a great service to both his comrade and the nation.

He bragged that once he had fifty victims he was going to celebrate. He would hold a slap-up dinner at his commandeered apartment and invite us, his colleagues; me, the Godfather, and Hudhud. I found it shocking.

Panther thought he was an incomparable sniper, especially after his name spread among the people on the other side. Some young guys put up a large sign saying "Panther Clear Off" on the building opposite. I didn't know how they learned his name and who leaked it to them. I was scared they also knew my name. True, nobody knew my real name, Abir Litani, but it would not be difficult for my nickname, Ittriss, to lead them to me. The war wasn't going to last forever. One day it would end. There was a chance that the family of one of those killed would look for whomever had been sniping from this building on a particular date. It could not be discounted that they would find someone to guide them to the wanted man. Money would buy them what they wanted. Not everyone would disdain giving information for easy gain.

I was surprised when I discovered the secret behind the spread of Panther's name. He had written it in big letters underneath one of the windows of Sardine Tower, preceded by "Snipery." I heard him explain the reason for the name to Godfather. He said he chose it to match bakery, grocery, and laundry. Sniping was his profession, and like most professionals, he guarded the tricks of the trade, and only revealed them to those crazy about the job, like him. He avoided teaching me any of those secrets, and I didn't ask. I hadn't come to Beirut from the village to kill people.

He said that Lard Ass, may he rest in peace, had been his teacher. He had been a highly skilled sniper who was killed behind the trigger. An RPG was fired at him, incinerating his top half.

He often viewed me as his successor. He would follow this assertion with the word, "Mercy on me!" placing his hand over his heart and laughing. He would cut the laugh short and frown as though the thought of death had brought him back to himself.

If he had known the way I felt whenever I looked out of the slit, he would have changed his view of me. Whenever I had a possible victim in my sights, my hands would start trembling and I would lose the target. A haze covered the end of the scope and I could no longer see, and if I did it was blurred. The haze resulted from my lack of conviction in what I was doing, and my refusal to slay a soul whose crime was to pass by at that ill-fated moment.

I did, however, enjoy myself when I played around with the pigeon fancier who would release his birds at sunset and call them back by waving a stick with a black rag at the end. The birds knew the sign and obeyed it. When the flock returned I would shoot at it, so it flew off and dispersed, which made reforming the flight difficult.

The pigeon fancier would go crazy and translate his rage into a frantic waving of the stick, which would only get worse when the birds refused to obey his commands. He was worried they would mix with passing flocks, and that one of his pigeons would join a rival flock, find it amenable, and stick with it. He had often enough added birds to his flock that he had nabbed from other people's. For pigeon fanciers, stealing pigeons was allowed. Those more skilled than others at coaxing strange birds to their flocks would boast about it. Such coaxed birds were not considered stolen and soon found themselves at home. The original owner had no right to ask for one back if he knew the location of the flock that had nabbed it. The fancier might return it out of politeness, and reciprocity, but not because he had to.

I will never forget the day when the pigeon fancier spent hours trying to make his flock come home. Whenever the flock circled over the roof in preparation to land, I fired two or three shots at it. The birds would panic and crash into each other and fly off and up. The man would try again to bring them back together before signaling them to come in to land. No sooner had his effort succeeded and the flock was about to come home, than I would split it up with a couple of shots. The man lost it, kicking things around on the roof, and waving his stick in a way that could only be understood as meaning his patience was over. He looked up at the sky, cursing his birds who were unusually disobeying his orders. What made him lose it completely was that he didn't know the reason why his pigeons were suddenly flying away from their roost. My rifle was fitted with a silencer, but the birds felt the bullet passing among them, got nervous, and soared away again.

He amused me. I often missed him when I went to the building and didn't see him. I looked for him through my sights among the passersby in the neighborhood where he lived, not in order to shoot him, but to check he was okay. If I didn't see him at all during my shift, my mood would darken. I don't know why I thought he was funny. He wore a large straw hat like a Mexican sombrero, and always wore a black shirt, which I thought, like the black rag at the end of his stick, were part of pigeon fancying.

I was worried about him when he vanished. The pigeons flew around and landed, but I did not see him.

Perhaps Panther, or another comrade of mine, killed him.

12

Azizi and I soon became buddies. I felt I had a brother, albeit from a different mother, and I assuaged the aching loneliness in my soul since leaving the village.

We often spent the nights swapping ideas and stories, and listening to music, especially French songs. He loved them so much he had taught himself French, even though English was his second language. His favorites were Jacques Brel, Aznavour, and Edith Piaf. He knew most of their songs by heart. I often heard him humming one of them at the barracks. I listened to them so often with him that I also grew to love them, even though I only understood the lyrics with the help of a dictionary.

We would meet in his modest room, with attached kitchen and bathroom. The building residents and the neighbors called it the janitor's room, but he called it home. When he left the barracks, he would say he was going home. When asked, "Where have you been?" he would reply, "At home." For him, a home was not about the number of rooms, but about the sense of security between its walls, even if only one room. I was struck by how tidy it was, as if a cleaning-obsessed woman lived in it, not a young guy who spent most of the time out. I was also struck by its minimal contents. A small bed that squeaked when you lay down or got up, which was annoying for a guest who slept lightly. Above the bed was an oil painting (it bore the title *Chopin's Lover* and the initials

V.M. in the left-hand corner) that had been given to him by a student at the Engineering Faculty. They had been romantically involved. On top of the bedside table was a radio cassette player and a box of tapes underneath. Opposite the bed was a sofa big enough to serve various purposes that turned into a bed when needed. In a corner there was a square folding table and three chairs. Between the table and the sofa, three piled-up columns of books went halfway up the wall.

In the kitchen, which Azizi called the 'scorpion's nest' because it was so small, were a refrigerator that did not reach the waist and a one-ring cooker attached to a gas canister. Above it was a wooden shelf holding a few plates, small cups, and a coffee pot. At the end of the shelf was a paraffin lamp whose copper plate was covered in green rust. By the right of the door was a table and two wicker chairs. The bathroom consisted of a sit-down toilet that flushed with a chain.

Azizi found his small house comfortable. He took refuge there from the din of comrades and the gossip that enveloped relationships and hurt people. I wished I could live alone in a room like his instead of the room I slept in at the barracks. I wished I could sleep on a carpet spread on the floor instead of a three-tier bunk.

The few times that I slept at Azizi's made me think how important it was for people to have a home. Azizi only invited me to spend the night very occasionally: if shelling started and it would have been unsafe to return to the barracks, or when we drank and the booze went to our heads and we fell asleep. When we woke up hours later, he would get into his bed, and I would sleep on the sofa. Not inviting me to spend the night didn't mean he didn't want my company, but how much he liked solitude. Because of that, only a few comrades knew where he lived. The fact that he welcomed me rather than them I took as a mark of how much he liked me.

With the intuition of a friend, who over time understands the obsessions of his friend and knows his likes and dislikes, I concluded that he sometimes preferred to be alone. I respected this hidden wish of his, and was always careful to return to the barracks if he didn't invite me to stay, even if the evening at his place had gotten late.

We made dinner together. I would peel and crush a few cloves of garlic, chop some tomatoes and lettuce, and squeeze the lemon, then I would mix them all together to make a plate of salad. He would sauté chicken and potatoes and prepare a plate of hummus and tahini, then lay the dishes, a bottle of arak, and some glasses out on the table. At our first dinner I was taken aback by the number of glasses given there were only two of us, but I didn't show that I found it strange. Later on, I learned from him that one of the rules of drinking, arak in particular, required changing your glass after every drink. We would eat dinner listening to music, often one of the musicals starring the legendary singer Fairuz. Azizi had memorized many lines from those plays and would quote them to comment on some situation. The lines were picked up by the comrades and they repeated them too. When they ascribed them to him, he would demure, pointing out they were the Rahbanis' not his.

Leafing through the pages of one of his books—after asking permission—I saw handwritten notes in the margins, his handwriting, which I knew well. Azizi was the only person at the barracks, apart from a very few who were continuing their studies, who read. I often saw him undo one of the shirt buttons over his stomach, pull out a book, and start reading with a pencil in his hand. Most of his books were about politics and history. It appeared he had not finished some of them, as shown by the bookmark stuck into the page he had reached. Sometimes the bookmark was a quarter of the way through the book, sometimes halfway. Another proof of this was the notes that appeared on the pages he had finished reading and were not evident on unread pages. I tried to read one of his books, but I got bored after a few pages. Only detective novels kept me glued until the last page. His hint that he read to educate himself rather than for pleasure annoyed me and I took it as an indirect criticism on my partiality to crime fiction.

He furnished me with biographies of great men after urging me to look at that kind of work. I read Hitler's *Mein Kampf* and Bismarck's *Memoires* and *Thoughts and Reminiscences*.

Perhaps as a result of his penchant for history and the experiences of major politicians and leaders, he kept a diary in a ruled notebook. He hid the notebook under a floor tile after removing a quantity of sand so the spot did not draw anyone's attention. To further camouflage it, he chose the tile under one of the legs at the head of the bed. Whenever he wanted to write, he lifted the side of the bed a little, then the tile, and took the notebook out from underneath. He did the same when he put the notebook back. A clever trick, the likes of which I had not read of in any novel.

Staying over at his place, I got up to use the bathroom after midnight. I saw him writing in bed to the light of the lantern. The next morning, he told me he had been keeping a diary since he was fourteen. He said he had several notebooks-full in his village, which his father had hidden when he came to Beirut. Here, in this room, he had filled up two notebooks, which he kept buried in a place that he did not disclose. He made me curious when he lifted up his notebook with a theatrical flourish saying that its contents were highly dangerous, and we would be wading in blood if they got out. He kidded me, saying that my detective novels seemed flimsy compared with the information in his notebook.

I didn't ask him to let me read it. From the way he was talking about the notebook, and his extreme care about concealing it, I expected a no. If he had wanted to show me he would have. More than once, however, he charged me, in a voice vacillating between reluctance and a desire to confess, to preserve the notebook if anything should happen to him. What mattered was that it did not fall into the hands of a malevolent stranger. "It stays with you or it goes up in flames," he said, giving me a look whose meaning it was impossible to discern.

Yet it disturbed me. He was among those who had been at the barracks for longest, and he knew everyone well. But no one knew any more about him than he let on. Even I did not know him as well as friends should know each other. Perhaps he was reticent by nature, influenced by his father who had served in the Second Brigade of the army until he retired.

After the frisson of fear provoked by my unspoken questions, he wanted to reassure me. He said that he hadn't recorded all he had been through and seen and all the impressions he had formed. He'd been content to write the headings that would spark his memory when he wanted to restore the details. My name, he said, was mentioned more than once. He added no more, waiting for me to ask for clarification, but I met his confession with a smile. I didn't ask him why he had confided that secret to me in particular. Questions like that seemed a bad omen. Once I knew about the notebook, I wasn't just afraid for Azizi, but also for myself.

13

THE FRONT HAD BEEN RAGING since early evening. Bullets, shells, and fires in various locations. Only military jeeps with their lights off moved around. On a night like that, nobody left their house unless it was essential. Medium and heavy shells exploding sent beams of light through the darkness. I reached the barricade, startling everyone with my arrival under fire. No sane person would dare to leave where he was holed up. Shakespeare called me a screwball.

At the barracks I was bored. The power was out and most of the guys were at the frontlines. It was still only nine o'clock, so what was I going to do? I went to Azizi's house. He was out. Pinned on the door, I saw a hand-sized piece of paper with one line in French and no signature. From the handwriting I guessed it had been written by a woman.

Only the Spring Barricade was left, so I headed for it. The name derived from its proximity to a stream. It was my favorite barricade. I had a habit of visiting it even when I wasn't on duty. I saw the usual gang behind its sandbags. Softie, Dali, Captain, Petronella (a Lebanese girl born in Los Angeles who had married a Lebanese guy after a love story and come back with him. A year later they divorced and she sought refuge with the party). Visitors included Azizi, Psycho, Lightbulb, and Zahlawi (he wasn't from Zahle. His love of arak had given him the name). Countless comrades had been killed on the way to or back from the barricade, or inside it before it was well reinforced. More than once, I had almost been killed myself on the way there.

My friends back in the village, and those who knew me, would never believe that the barricade had become one of my favorite places even if they saw it with their own eyes. Me, who refused to take part in guard duty or carry a gun, even when there were reports of an imminent attack on the village, at a barricade.

I still hated guns, although I was used to them and their smell and the smell of bullets. In the early morning I often delved inside the sandbags in search of bullets that had gotten lodged in the night. I collected them in a glass jar, just as I had collected colored marbles as a boy. Picking up bullets became my hobby. Even my comrades saved me every bullet they found.

In addition to that hobby, a number of things drew me to spend nights at the barricade. Mainly it was the deep affection that grew up between the troops, despite their different characters and temperaments. The prospect of death, which could strike at any moment and in any way, dampened resentments and spread affection and sympathy. It was quite unremarkable, therefore, to see a comrade run, in complete disregard of danger, to the aid of another lying wounded. At such difficult moments, the camaraderie of arms got the better of fear and indifference.

Some people thought that one of the rites of the barricade led to the loss of many lives. Smoking hash. They said the young took hashish and went to fight while off their heads. At our barricade, that rite was current, but restricted to Softie, Shakespeare, and Petronella. They passed around a 'rocket' (the usual name for a hash cigarette) with obvious glee. Softie would close his eyes and slowly exhale as if he wanted to keep the smoke in his lungs. Shakespeare would half lower his eyelids then watch the cloud of smoke recede, tracing phantasmagoric shapes in front of him. Petronella would puff out the smoke in bursts and, with a glazed look in her eyes, contemplate its slow ascent over her face.

More than once, I joined in the fun with them, but I didn't feel what they felt. I was content with ordinary cigarettes. I often amused myself by rolling a rocket and letting someone else smoke it. Not that I was much good at rolling. Softie was far better than me and outshone the lot of us in his rolling craft. He would pull a cigarette out of the pack, run the tip of his tongue down it to wet the paper and split it open. Holding a small piece of hashish between his thumb and index finger, he would heat it with a lighter underneath until it softened. Then he would crumble it into the strands of tobacco. He would take a fresh cigarette paper, wet it with saliva and start rolling. A real expert. I watched him to learn the basics. Over time I got good at rolling. They begged me to roll them rockets, and out of kindness I would. Very often, I took the initiative myself. The first rocket I ever rolled looked anything but.

Running out of hash and its effects wearing off made time drag and the night long. In truth, without it, feasible dreams would have vanished from the world of some of the comrades, and the blows of disappointment would have been worse. Without its sweet fragrance, the smell of gunpowder and of our exhausted bodies would have blocked our nostrils.

Rolling and smoking rockets was not complete without the songs of the renowned Egyptian diva Umm Kalthoum playing from a large battery-powered radio. They turned the volume up and nodded their heads as a sign that they were into the song. I didn't understand the connection between the rocket and the voice of that diva, for whom Egyptians dropped everything to hear on air the first Thursday night of every month. I was always itching to know what pleasure they found in the repetition of a line over and over. That kind of singing made me feel sleepy. Whenever I heard it, I heard my dad's voice at the café repeating the opinion of the poet Unsi al-Hajj about Umm Kalthoum and her voice. And he repeated it a lot. According to Dad, Unsi said, "We've been stuffed full of this dreadful monotony, which, like opium, holds sway over the minds of her worshipers. In truth she has exactly the form and meaning of a pagan idol." I remembered how much I hated my uncle's wife who listened to 'the Lady,' as she called her, when she was cooking, sweeping, mopping, ironing, and doing the laundry.

At the barricade next to ours, some thirty meters away, Fairuz was the favorite singer. The volume of the tape player would be turned right up in response to us. Sometimes, I went over there to escape and listen to a bunch of Fairuz's songs while Umm Kalthoum back here was still only a quarter of the way through the first song. One of the reasons I favored Fairuz was I had fallen in love with her sister Hoda in the soap *From Day to Day*. I fell for her, and she fell for the actor Wahid Jalal, whose death I longed for at the time, to leave me without a rival.

Competition between the two barricades was not limited to turning up the volume. It nearly erupted into clashes with live ammunition. This one championed Umm Kalthoum, 'The Planet of the East,' and that Fairuz, 'Our Ambassador to the Stars.' Artistic partisanship trumped party partisanship. If sensible heads had not intervened to calm those fired up, there would have been fatalities.

Weird things often happened because of smoking too much hash and drinking too much, mostly cheap, whisky. I recall an incident that happened on New Year's Eve 1979. We celebrated at the barricade, and it was the first time I'd celebrated the occasion away from my family. Petronella was loading magazines with bullets. She turned up the radio when she heard a song by John Travolta and started dancing by the barricade, sexily gyrating her hips. She went down on her knees and bent backwards until her hands touched the ground. She shook her waist with her legs wide apart and seemed on the verge of orgasm. We applauded when she finished dancing. Imitating a professional dancer, she gave a bow of thanks and blew us kisses.

Softie jumped over to her, grabbed her head, and kissed her on the mouth. She kicked him between the legs and he doubled up in pain, placing his hands over the site of the blow. In an effort to imitate a man when he swore, she slapped her hand over her crotch, and in perfect English addressed Softie, who was groaning in pain: "Mess with me one more time, and this is going in your mom's ass."

We didn't understand a word she said, but we knew she was insulting him. He staggered up the back of the barricade, pointed his gun in the air, and fired a burst of bullets screaming that he wanted to kill the moon. Shakespeare and the Captain were fired up and joined in with his shouting. Their voices rebounded off the buildings and echoed loudly at intervals.

Petronella started to strip. She danced, her long hair streaming loose. She threw her bra at Softie. He picked it up, sniffed it, and hung it on the pole flying the party flag above our barricade. We applauded Petronella, giving shouts of encouragement for her to remove her underwear. Her weak spot was seeing us aroused. Our weak spot was seeing her dance nude. Stark naked, she clambered up the barricade, looked up at the moon, and shouted as she opened her arms: "Enjoy my beauty, gorgeous, before Softie kills you."

We laughed and laughed until tears came to our eyes. With arms linked, we circled around the still naked Petronella, singing martial anthems. With one hand she was covering her breasts, whose nipples were erect because of the cold or in arousal, and with the other hand she was hiding her crotch. She slipped away from us and ran over to her clothes. Captain followed and grabbed her. He threw her over his shoulder with her face to his back. He slapped her lightly on the buttocks while she punched him as best she could.

We begged him to let her get dressed. He carried on spinning around with her in his arms, then brought his face down toward her chest and bit one of her breasts. She pulled his hair and took his nose between her teeth. He was desperately trying to kiss her. Shakespeare cocked his gun and ordered him to leave her alone. He refused. He threatened to shoot him if he didn't let go of her immediately. He ignored him. Shakespeare carried out his threat and fired a bullet between his legs. Captain froze on the spot and released her. Petronella picked up her scattered clothes and ran to the barricade. She got dressed behind the bank of sandbags and left barefoot, carrying her army boots.

Such incidents were frequent. I often replayed them as though they were comedy sketches or had happened elsewhere to other people. Tragicomic incidents marked out our nights at the barricade, which was the only refuge for us strangers to the city and the war. We headed for it to escape loneliness and despair. The time spent among its sandbags and under its roof passed quickly. When the boredom was oppressive, we would fire at the positions opposite to induce our enemies to return fire, expecting that their situation was no different to ours. They never let us down. We also responded to a greeting in kind when required. What started as an isolated exchange of fire would expand to cover the whole frontline.

Sometimes we exchanged insults not bullets, also for fun. Insults against mothers, sisters, and leaders, even the Messiah, the Prophet Muhammad, and the saints were not immune. As a result, the front would erupt. Contagion would spread to the artillery dugouts, which would fire their shells onto the neighborhoods. The shelters would fill up, and the ambulances would wail.

We felt safe in our barricades, which were impregnable as long as a direct attack was, for unknown reasons, ruled out. The orders given in our hearing were to defend, not to capture enemy positions. They said there was a red line that divided between us that had to be respected.

We mostly hated the truce, because it made our days deathly boring. It was a harsh punishment, particularly when

it extended as a result of pressure applied by the major play-
ers on our leaders, and which our leaders applied on us. We
refused to be bound by their conditions, and broke them,
while blaming our foes. Sometimes we relied on them to cause
a breach, and often they did.

Boredom was one of the reasons the war continued.

14

I came back from Sardine Tower and saw trucks and per-
sonnel carriers at the barracks. I had never seen so many
military vehicles on the parade ground. Our barracks' share
of imported equipment perhaps, or the spoils of war. A few
fellas were checking the machinery over, happy as children
with a new toy. One, an art school graduate, was painting the
party emblem on the front of each. I watched what they were
doing from the window of my room. Then I lay down and
fell asleep listening to the news on the radio. I don't remember whether I turned it off before sleep took me or whether a
comrade did.

I woke up at two in the morning to the sound of voices
and the roar of vehicles. My roommates were still asleep. I was
too sleepy to get up and find out what was causing the commotion, while the noise itself stopped me going back to sleep.
With me in limbo, two comrades came in and asked me to put
my fatigues on and come down to the parade ground. Then
they woke everyone up.

We went down, and in a few minutes were all set. The
scent of sleep still clinging to our bodies, we formed ranks.
The chill turned our breaths into foggy swirls, but being
armed to the teeth imbued our spirits with a certain heat. A
mission awaited.

I don't know why most military operations take place at
dawn. They pull the blankets off our hunkered, exhausted

bodies and drive away our dreams with their orders. If it had been up to me, I would have broken ranks and gone back to bed.

The barracks commander, surrounded by the unit commanders, filled us in on the details. In conjunction with allied parties we were going to attack a strategic zone under enemy control. He forcefully reminded us of the rules of engagement. Orders that were frequently given but rarely heeded, discarded as soon as the first bullet whizzed overhead. Killing children, women, and the elderly wasn't allowed; prisoners had to be well treated and the remains of the dead respected; places of worship were not to be desecrated, and so on.

At zero hour, we took off in the trucks. I sat next to Casper, the driver of the third truck, which was full of ammunition boxes. Softie climbed in and sat to my right. It seemed he had come straight from the barricade. He pulled a hash cigarette out of his jacket pocket, lit it, and took a deep drag. He offered it to Casper, who declined with a polite thank you. Softie insisted, and Casper maintained his refusal. "I don't do drugs," he said rubbing something out of the corner of his eye with a finger. Then Softie offered it to me, holding the roach between his thumb and ring finger. I said no thanks, and he did not press.

There were no cars on the streets at that hour. Only cats and dogs roamed for something to eat. All of a sudden, the artillery moved into gear and gave the target zone a sustained pounding. The crash of a symphony orchestra reverberated in the pale dawn.

We arrived. In a flash we left the trucks and spread out. Fires flickered and smoke filled the air. The smell of burning petrol was pervasive. Fierce resistance came from the barricades planted at the tops of streets and alleyways. Bullets ricocheted off the buildings like popcorn popping in a pan. We advanced slowly.

We tightened the siege, sealing access corridors and supply routes to paralyze the enemy's room to maneuver and sap its strength. The siege continued for two weeks. The outcome was a draw. The enemy hadn't been defeated and we weren't victorious.

I wished I would get injured and be taken to hospital. Then I wouldn't be forced to kill anyone in self-defense. My life meant a lot to me, and preserving life was a sacred duty in all traditions. My magazine was loaded. I checked it before making any move. Only two full clips remained in the pouch. Four hand grenades on my belt, and a revolver primed to shoot. There was always a bullet in the chamber. I was careful not to waste bullets needlessly.

I could have left the battlefield if I had wanted. That would be a double loss though: a black mark on my record and being dubbed a coward. I would rather leave as a corpse than be deemed a coward. I had no cause to sacrifice myself for. Many of my comrades were like me: they had been forced into the war but fought for the spoils from houses and stores. Without that enticement, most of them would have dropped their weapons and slung their uniforms in the faces of those who issued them. They were poor migrants and found shelter with the parties, which trained and fed them during the interval before leading them to their deaths. All of them dreamed of escaping poverty. Taking part in battles was the quickest route.

At the beginning of the third week, we gained the upper hand after the enemy's forward positions fell. Many prisoners were taken. This development in the field was accompanied by ever-louder local and international calls for an end to the offensive.

By the end of the week we were on the verge of victory. We hunted down the fighters who were determined to resist and refused to flee with those who abandoned their weapons and slipped away. We patrolled cautiously. This phase was highly dangerous. You never knew when a concealed fighter would jump out and empty his automatic into you. Many comrades survived the assault only to be killed in the sweep and cleanup.

Walking in two lines on both sides of the street, we were fired upon. We took cover, each in our own spot. I crouched with Charno in the entrance of a building. Guevara asked Casper to cover him while he crossed the street. Conger opened fire on a fighter trying to lob a hand grenade at us. He made him dance before he fell, like a gunslinger in a Western staggering after being shot in a duel. We survived. If the fighter had managed to throw the grenade, Charno and I would have died.

We kept walking. We saw Fikamoro go after a lone fighter. The fighter was running in a spiral, which made him a difficult target. I had him in my sights. I aimed at his legs and fired. I hit him. I didn't want to kill him, but to save him from certain death. I thought that capturing him would be useful, particularly as some of our troops had been taken prisoner. Dara went up to him and put his rifle to his head. I begged him not to kill him. I convinced him that the man was more useful as a prisoner than as a corpse. He granted a reprieve. We tied him up, and Conger and I led him to a nearby shelter. I locked him in and we went back.

We explored the surrounding buildings, window by window, balcony by balcony. The slightest mistake might cost one of us his life. We heard a burst of bullets in the alley parallel to our group. We started the plan to encircle them, with great support from an armored vehicle.

A white flag appeared from the last fortification we were about to deal with. Three fighters came out of the barricade with their hands up. Conger, hunkered behind a garbage container, asked them to come toward us. It might have been a ploy, or there were others who refused to surrender. Guevara ordered them to line up next to each other facing the wall. We bound their hands, blindfolded them, and led them off to the shelter.

All the positions had fallen. We could stroll around as if on a day out. Casper and others went through the pockets of the dead. They tossed the wallets aside once they had taken the contents. Not a single wallet was without a picture of a child or a young woman or an old lady. Fikamoro filled his backpack with gold chains, watches, and personal effects that he stripped off the corpses and from the living. Marx ran over to the truck with a bundle of light weapons tucked under his arm.

The Clown, as usual, was graffitiing the walls with a spray can. He got as far as 'The Clown was' but did not add 'here.' An enemy fighter stood up from between the bodies and killed him with a single shot. The bastard pretended to be dead and his trick worked, even though Conger had been charged with firing a bullet into each corpse just to make sure. Charno sprayed the dirty fighter with bullets, making him drop dead as Clown's spray can bounced down the street.

Mobile and fixed checkpoints went up at key points. Women, children, and the elderly were fleeing. Bundles, bags, and things wrapped in blankets carried on backs and shoulders. Trucks and buses were crammed with those fleeing in preparation for their transfer to one of the crossing points. From there they would disperse. Some would settle down in the schools, other would go to their villages, or take refuge with friends and relatives.

There was a rumor that women were hiding their gold between their legs or in their bras. A woman cradling a baby she had wrapped in an old carpet stared at me. In her furious eyes I read that she was ready, if the chance arose, to take off a shoe and slap me and my comrades around the head with it. Charno took her out of the line and quickly interrogated her. It was not possible to be alone with her for a few minutes to make him happy. He said that her big breasts had made him horny.

New orders stressed letting the inhabitants leave in peace. Those came in response to the appeals of religious leaders and human rights groups. The surviving fighters had escaped through bolt-holes we had deliberately left open to the fields and woods. Ferocity reaches a peak with a cornered fighter. When he is sure there is no escape, a soldier will fight ferociously on the basis of kill or be killed. I experienced that myself when I was trapped inside a building with a group of comrades. I kept resisting, indifferent to everything. I was scared of capture and determined to fight to the death. In my jacket pocket, I always kept a bullet to shoot myself in the head when needed, but I survived. My Mum's prayers saved me.

We continued exploring the liberated area. In the street we met first aiders carrying dead bodies on stretchers from the barricades, the streets, and building doorways. A jeep approached from the top of the alley. Fighters on it raised V-signs and were singing. We took a crate of beer off them. I pulled out a bottle, and with the edge of my lighter, prised off the top. I drank it in one go. They invited us to go with them. The time of spoils had come. Before getting into the jeep, Hatchling, who had a stick of miswak in his mouth to clean his teeth, said, "You'll only find TVs and washing machines."

Charno and I stayed behind, leaning against the edge of the barricade and sipping beer. We drank half the bottle and then threw it against a wall. We demolished a quarter of the crate. Charno was drunk and slurring his words. He was singing and dancing with his automatic rifle in his hands. I got his gun off him by deceit. I advised him to stick a finger down his throat to make himself throw up and feel better. He did. He emptied his stomach and soiled his boots. He started stamping on the ground to get rid of the vomit.

At sunset, our platoon commandeered a truck. The guys piled it up with refrigerators, washing machines, chandeliers, and odds and ends. Then they emptied it at a warehouse they also commandeered. I didn't join in. I went looking for novels in the piles of books abandoned in houses.

The number of trucks, pickups, and smaller cars entering the area empty and leaving full kept growing. Some fighters turned into porters and thieves. Greed lay behind the deaths of several. For the sake of a refrigerator or a washing machine, sometimes even a gas canister, some were prepared to die. Those who died stealing were no fewer in number than those who died fighting. They too were called martyrs and shrouded in the party flag.

When the news spread, civilians streamed in and started looting. They ripped out doors, shutters, and faucets. They even ripped out floor tiles and water pipes. They only left family photos, clothes, and bags of lentils and sugar unfit for eating.

At one of the exits, Guevara, Conger, and Charno set up a roadblock. They confiscated stolen goods and made those who had them take them themselves to the truck that Guevara drove to the warehouse. A prominent party leader bought the stolen property very cheaply.

The three of them split the money and held a Dionysian drinks party. After the drinks, they decided to continue the evening at Weeds. They said it was the best nightclub in the area. Most of the girls there were from Aleppo and Damascus, although there was one Moroccan girl who looked like Souad Hosni. They insisted I join them, so I did.

15

THE ONLY REASON I ACCEPTED Guevara, Conger, and Charno's invitation was a desire to get to see a nightclub. I had read about them in novels, seen them at the cinema and on TV, and heard about them at the village café. It was the only place that when I heard its name, I had visions of girls dancing and men drinking and smoking as they watched. Each man would then sit down with a woman for company. The mere mention of the word set my imagination soaring, and I took solace in the fact that life was before me, and the right time to visit a club would come.

Better not go on my own for sure. The first time, I needed to be with a regular. I would get an idea of the atmosphere, and the little details a patron ought to know. After that, I would be able to go alone, especially if a night there proved fun.

The right time had come. There were three of us. Me, Guevara, and Charno. Conger couldn't make it after drinking too much and falling asleep.

As we were getting out of the car, Domino arrived accompanied by two bodyguards. He rarely went out without guards, and if he did, it was in utmost secrecy. Domino had many enemies, though he often invented them to make those around him believe he was important and a source of envy. He had a bad reputation. Rumor had it that he was fighting the war to make money in nefarious ways and to sleep with all the women he fancied. His brain was in his crotch. He had memorized dozens of lines of dirty poetry which he recited in the manner of Saeed Aql. Supposedly, he had been fast-tracked through the ranks because of his political activity when at university. He had participated in all the strikes, and his shoulders still bore marks from carrying leaders of demonstrations aloft. His student glories culminated with two months in prison after he assaulted an internal security officer.

We said hello to him and exchanged congratulations on our victory, then we went in together. He led the way. Anyone seeing us behind him would think we were his men.

The club owner and the waiters welcomed us, him in particular. Their glances at him were full of fear and aversion. Their smiles concealed fangs waiting for the right moment to rip him to shreds. In their faces, I read that they couldn't stand him or the very ground he walked on, but they flattered him to preserve their livelihoods. He could easily close down the club if he wanted—by throwing bombs at the entrance night after night or instigating one of his underlings to start an altercation, which would be punctuated with flying chairs and plates, smashed tables, and gunshots.

He insisted we sit at his table. We tried to decline and escape, but he wouldn't take no for an answer. We sat at the table nearest the stage. It was soon stocked with a bottle of expensive whisky, and plates of carrots, sliced apple, and nuts. As soon as we dropped something in the ashtray, a waiter replaced it with a clean one. As soon as one of us put a cigarette in his mouth, a lighter appeared beneath it from behind our backs. If our glasses were almost empty, a waiter came around with the bottle filling glass after glass with a flourish.

This exaggerated service and hospitality irritated Domino, and he summoned the boss with a click of his fingers. He asked him not to let any of the waiters come near our table. He also asked them to lock the front door and not let anyone else in.

Domino had hardly finished his third glass when the effects of the alcohol became obvious. His cheeks were flushed and he started laughing for no reason. Giggling, he raised his glass and said, "Here's to the time of destruction not reconstruction!" Then he downed his drink.

He pointed out one of the women sitting by the bar, claiming that he had tried her and she had given him a good time. Putting his hand over his groin, he said she knew his worth. Then, he described her attractions in detail, speaking with the highest admiration for her breasts, which were firm and erect despite their size, and the two moles next to each other at the top of her right thigh that had aroused him. He said she always wanted more: he filled her up and she said, "Where's it gone?" She was never satisfied, as if she had been created to stay in bed. He swore she had made him come three times, and that he counted four orgasms for her before he stopped counting.

Domino bragged about his prowess and, from time to time, he looked over at the girls who were getting up on stage. They started dancing, exposing themselves to the audience. None of the few punters present dared to try it on with any of the girls. Domino might fancy one and ask for her. He was known for his arrogance and quick temper.

Three girls came over. Under the strobe lights they seemed like models from *Playboy* magazine, whose pictures we pinned up in our rooms and in our imaginations. The best looking of them, the tall dark one, sat to Domino's right; the blonde, plump one sat between him and Guevara; and the fair-skinned one whose hair hung halfway down her back sat between me and Charno. Domino kissed his two guests as if he had never kissed a woman before.

I felt a wave of disgust when he started lobbing pistachios at the girl sitting next to me. He said he wouldn't stop until he had landed a nut between her breasts, which peeked from the neckline of her dress. He finally hit the target and applauded himself. He raised his arms in triumph, stretched over toward her, and buried his face in her chest in an effort to retrieve the pistachio with his tongue.

She made me angry when she puckered her lips and thrust them forward to take the same nut from his mouth. Power attracted women, for sure. They were weak before it. I had often heard that hookers gave their bodies to johns but refused to let them kiss them on the mouth. A kiss on the mouth was for someone who possessed their soul. Money got you the body, but with love you got both together.

What I saw was the opposite of what I had heard. Domino kissed them on the mouth, and they were amenable, laughing. His arms were draped over the shoulders of the two girls next to him, and his hands ran through their hair and stroked their necks. I noticed his shoe between the thighs of the girl seated opposite him, between me and Charno. I curbed my anger and adopted an air of indifference as if I had seen nothing.

Charno was oblivious, as if not with us. He drank, smoked, and shelled pistachios that he tossed into his mouth. He forced himself to laugh when Domino laughed loudly. Domino was his role model. He emulated him in everything, even allowing the nail of his little finger to extend a few millimeters. I despised him when he confided that Domino's breath smelled sweet. I observed his movements and compared them with Domino's to see how similar they were. A carbon copy.

The second bottle of whisky sat in the middle of the table accompanied by refreshed dishes. That night the girls were allowed to drink whisky. Normally they made do with fruit juice. Drinking alcohol wasn't allowed in case they got drunk and lost control of themselves. The opposite was supposed to happen. The punters got drunk and the girls pulled the strings. Off shift, they were free to drink what and how much they wanted, but here at the nightclub, rules had to be followed to keep things running smoothly.

The loud music stopped us hearing the sound of neighboring areas being shelled. If the two bodyguards hadn't come in for safety, we wouldn't have known that a shell had fallen next to the nightclub. Domino ordered the music turned up so as not to spoil the atmosphere of the evening, which was still going strong. The nightclub was safe because it was on the ground floor of a tall building. Originally a bomb shelter, it had been requisitioned by a relative of a party leader and turned into a nightclub.

Hiyyam, Samira, Nada, and Fadya climbed on stage. Their bodies turned into snakes writhing to the rhythm. Then slowly, piece by piece, they took their clothes off. The spectacle, the likes of which I had only seen in films, entranced me.

Charno stirred the ice in his glass with a finger, as he eyed the dancing girls. Domino shook his shoulders to the music and clapped, missing the beat, to encourage the girls to go further. His two companions stole glances from behind the bead curtain hanging between the entrance and the room. The waiters were blown away too, even though the scene was nothing new.

The girls' dance went on without them getting tired. One song ended and another began, and they changed their moves to fit the new rhythm. It was as if dancing was their way to escape their fates.

The sweat on their chests glistened under the roving lights, and some flew off their waists as it continued to drip downward. Its hot spray landed on our faces making our hearts tremble and a chill wave pass through our bodies.

Hiyyam went up to Domino, shimmying her shoulders with her arms outspread. He raised the bottle and poured the rest of the whisky over her chest. He started lapping the whisky off her breasts while she pulled him to the stage. She and the other girls surrounded him, and the four of them danced around him.

The looks they exchanged did not hide the intention to humiliate him. Drunk in the middle of the stage, he lost his balance and fell to his knees. He started crawling on all fours and Hiyyam mounted him, imitating a rider on horseback with the movements of her hands and body and leaning forward.

He slowly wheeled her around. Whenever he stopped, she slapped him on the ass and he resumed turning. The other girls followed them, dancing and snorting with laughter. They took turns to ride him. He kept spinning around and around until he threw up.

The girls left the stage and the two bodyguards, horrified at the sight of him lying on his back with vomit around his mouth, hurried to carry him back to his chair. Their real sympathies lay with girls however, and their faces betrayed a veiled pity.

I turned to Charno to see his reaction. He was propped up on his arms on the table and snoring fast asleep. The whisky had sent him to sleep. I remembered Azizi saying that the best drunk falls asleep after drinking and is spared the gloating of others. I woke Charno up. We said goodbye to Domino, who replied with difficulty. In his eyes, I discerned an unspoken warning as if he wanted to make us understand that we had better forget what we had seen if we valued our lives.

Under bombardment, we returned to the barracks.

16

WE WERE SITTING ON THE sidewalk outside the pinball arcade opposite the barracks sunning ourselves. The warm winter sun made us sleepy and our bodies languid. The joint's generator hummed and disturbed our morning calm. It was really annoying and made you think it was right over your head.

Charno, with his automatic between his thighs, was rolling a rocket.

Guevara was sprawled out reading the paper. He pursed his lips every now and again or thrust out his head and spat. Sometimes the spit went as far as four meters. For us relaxing near him, it was a puzzle. Was he doing it to expectorate, or as a commentary on a political opinion piece? If a journalist's views infuriated him, he jabbed his middle finger at the article, swore at its author, and accused him of being a foreign agent. The paper was unreadable afterward because of all the holes.

Bonanza watched the pedestrians as if counting them. He played with his beard, twisting it into strands, unpicking them, and then twisting them together again.

Lightbulb was listening to a transistor radio pressed to his ear. The tapping of his feet suggested he was in another world.

Casper had his face in the sun to get a tan.

I was stood in the doorway of the pinball joint, back to the road, watching two people play pool. An observer would think the game had grabbed my attention, but I was staring at the colored balls without seeing them or hearing them cannon together. My thoughts were elsewhere. I was replaying scenes from the area we had liberated the day before and the evening out at the nightclub. The scene of Hiyyam riding on Domino's back was as good as happening in front of me. I recalled the way he had looked at me when I said goodbye. Looks that did not inspire confidence. God alone knows what they implied.

I was about to leave when I spotted Conger coming up in a covered jeep. He was driving overly fast. He stopped by the pinball place, and from a motion of his head, I understood he was asking me to get in.

I climbed in and sat next to him. "They've killed Azizi," he said.

The news hit like a pistol whip. I didn't believe it. I asked question after question without leaving him time to answer. I was in shock.

From Conger's silence, I inferred he didn't want to talk. All he said was that they killed him in his house. In such cases, 'they' usually implied that the killer wasn't a stranger, that is 'one of us' echoed unspoken in people's minds. Nobody would dare express such thoughts out loud, fearful of meeting the same fate as Azizi.

'They' could also imply the enemy. They had agents that carried out operations in our area and helped transport car bombs. Azizi's killing could be blamed on a spy; a narrative could be constructed around a motive and an MO, and the victim declared a martyr. Lots of crimes were wrapped up like that. Lots of comrades and people resorted to that 'they' and spared themselves doubts.

In the case of Azizi's death, suspicion only pointed one way. Who the hell was he that our enemies would try to eliminate him? Conger's saying, "They've killed him" only increased that possibility. If it really had been them who killed him, he would have said so without reservation.

Tons of possibilities flew around my mind before we reached Azizi's house. I prayed to God that the news was wrong, just a joke.

A crowd of neighbors in front of the building and in the entrance confirmed the worst. Nobody said a word when they saw me. Not one of the men or women neighbors who knew me offered me a word of consolation. It was as though grief had rendered them speechless and immobile. I passed between them and felt ashamed as I sensed all eyes were on me.

The door to the room was open. I went in and looked over at the people within: two policemen and three comrades. The body was prone on the bed, covered in a blanket that I had often covered myself with as a guest under his roof.

Haltingly, I approached the corpse. One of the policemen tried to stop me but I insisted, and, when he knew who I was, he raised the blanket. I wished I had not seen what I saw. The right side of the skull was bloodier than the left. Patches of blood stained the pillow.

I could not look for long. I almost fainted and was unable to keep standing. I sat down on the couch, buried my head in my hands, and cried. I cried in a way I never imagined possible. Where did all the tears come from? Two eyes alone were not enough for such an outpour. The heart must have added its tears too.

Wherever I glanced, I saw Azizi. I saw him coming out of the kitchen, with the coffee pot in one hand, and two cups in the other, which he was clacking together in imitation of street coffee sellers. I saw him set the plates out on the table, cut four slices of bread, and put them next to the plates. I saw him dilute the local arak with a precise measure of water and, after holding the empty glass to the light to make sure it was clean, pour a drink. I saw him reading in bed, or writing. I remembered the notebook. I glanced at the floor tile under the leg of the bed that concealed it. Absorbed in my private grief, all those images and more passed through my mind in a few seconds.

Out of a comrade's mouth flew an unanticipated piece of news. It was the last thing I would have expected. While he was commiserating with me, the comrade said he had never expected Azizi to kill himself and that he still couldn't believe it. He said that Azizi had used his own pistol to kill himself. The investigators had taken it for fingerprinting.

I stood up with difficulty. I didn't want to leave the room. I might be able to take the notebook without anyone noticing.

The CID investigator, once he knew I was a close friend of Azizi's, summoned me to give a statement. His questions were premised on the cause of death being suicide. I explained that I knew Azizi very well, and that he was the last person on earth who would think about killing himself. He didn't have any problems to make him suicidal. I told him all that so he didn't exclude other possibilities. I considered it likely—not wishing to say certain—that Azizi had been killed. He was killed like that (shot in the right side of the head—as normal for those who kill themselves with a revolver) in order to mislead the investigation and make people believe the opposite to the truth.

The killers missed the fact that Azizi was left-handed. If he had killed himself, he would have fired from the left-hand side of his head. I pointed this out to the detective to sow doubts in his mind. I didn't put it to him directly. I whispered it to myself when he was close to me: "But Azizi was left handed." I preferred to hint rather than state. He might have been in league with the killers, and on their orders was trying to erase the evidence. Equally possible, he didn't need it pointed out to know the truth. Perhaps he knew, but avoided admitting it, because he was scared for himself and for his family.

Once he had finished taking down my statement, he ordered the room to be cleared and went to take a statement from someone in a neighbor's house. Everyone left the room except a policeman and me. I stayed on the pretext that I was going to accompany the body when the time came to transport it by ambulance to the hospital morgue, and from there by hearse to his village.

The policeman sat on the couch, took a pack of cigarettes out of his pocket, pulled a cigarette half out of the pack, and offered it to me. I took the cigarette with thanks, lit it, and lit another for him. I tried to humor him and so gain his sympathy and trust. If he relaxed, getting hold of the notebook would be easy.

I went to the bathroom, not to use it, but to make him want to use it after me, allowing me to carry out my task. It worked. As soon as he locked the door behind him, I lifted up the bed, shifting it slightly sideways, then putting it slowly back down. I removed the floor tile. I got a shock. The notebook was gone. I noticed that a quantity of dirt had been put in its place, so that the floor would be level when the tile was replaced. I did all that and the man was still in the bathroom.

Where was the notebook? Who stole it? Had Azizi taken it before his death and hidden it somewhere else? Those questions took me back in time to the dawn of a day I slept here, on the same couch I was sitting on. I woke up to use the bathroom and saw a hand-size piece of paper in the middle of the floor. I picked it up and carried on to the bathroom. Once inside, I read it. The contents horrified me, and I was at a loss as to what to do with it. Should I put it back or keep it? If Azizi woke up and saw it while I was putting it back, it would be awkward for him and for me. If I kept it, I would break one of the rules of friendship: trust.

He must have written it at the barracks, hoping to copy it in the notebook, but he had put it off and left it between the pages. It then fell out unnoticed.

After some thought, I left the bathroom, intending to put it back if I found him sleeping, and to keep it if he was awake. Fortunately, he was asleep and snoring. I put it back where I found it, but I was unable to doze off.

The paper read:

115

There are plenty of reasons not to disagree with anyone. They might betray you in battle, then claim they found you dead and carry you to the ambulance. You must always be circumspect; don't trust even those closest to you. This world is based on plots and backstabbing. Grow eyes in the back of your head. It's in your own interest. If you haven't died through betrayal till now, you've seen how others met their deaths. Comrade B.D. killed his comrade H.S. during an attack on a hostile position. He watched him until he went inside a house, approached the window, pulled the pin on a grenade, and lobbed it inside. I didn't see comrade H. exit after the explosion. The next day, they found his body covered in debris. They said he was a martyr. He was killed because he sold comrade B.'s share of some stolen goods and lost the money gambling. They had buried the stuff somewhere only they knew about.

Whenever I recalled the contents of that piece of paper, I remembered the time he instructed me to keep hold of the notebook should anything bad happen to him. I hadn't foreseen that he was afraid of something being planned for him in the shadows.

It was the first time I felt such fear. It could not be compared to the fear that had struck me when the teacher chased me at the village garbage dump. The notebook, as Azizi had said to me, contained information more exciting than the detective novels I read. Of course, that information wasn't about people living in another country, but about people, a number of whom I knew. They did what they did under the wings of the party and the party either knew and turned a blind eye because it needed them, or it didn't know.

That Azizi had fallen victim to one of them couldn't be discounted. He was one of the longest serving at the barracks. He had started out there when half of it was still a school. What he knew, and his ability to keep what he knew a secret, secured him a certain status, even though he held no official position.

Like me, he had been forced to leave his village. He had received direct threats, sometimes of death, sometimes of kidnapping. Behind these threats were the political views he expressed in the speeches he gave at student events. He was nicknamed the 'High School Mirabeau' by his friends and acquaintances. He spoke without notes. He learned every word by heart, and his audience thought he was speaking off the cuff. He had a very good memory. Two or three readings of the text were enough to memorize it. He was bold and called things by their names. Often he stole the limelight from other speakers, especially if he went first, even though he was the youngest of the lot.

The high school principal was reputed to have said that speaking after Jihad al-Arif (that was his real name) was like speaking after Saeed Aql. With his sense of oratory, he knew which passages would inflame passions. He included directions about applause and cheers in advance, and his response would reignite the applause. There wasn't a party cell—and in high school you couldn't count them on the fingers of one hand— that would stage an event without ensuring his participation.

He wasn't a party member, but he did lean toward one party, whose ideas he found close to his own. His affiliation was in his heart, not openly declared, not out of fear for himself, but for his family. The village where he was born and raised comprised a mix of confessions and opposing party currents. For that reason, he kept it under wraps.

Their neighbor, a lieutenant in Public Security, told his father that his son's file at HQ bulged with reports on what he said at high school events. The neighbor had been assigned to attend one and write a report about what happened and who spoke. He did so and felt proud when Jihad's speech was inter- rupted by applause and cheering. He had not expected the lad, whom he saw every day, to be an eloquent speaker, beloved and listened to. Out of loyalty, he wrote in his report that the student Jihad Fawzi al-Arif had a rebellious streak and was able to mobilize the high school with his incendiary speeches. This impression overlapped with the impressions of Public Security men who had heard him on previous occasions.

After high school, he had shone on platforms at the Faculty of Law and Political Science (a branch opened in his region), and eyes remained on him. Still in his first year in the law department, he was bombarded with reports that there were those who sought to harm him. He left the village and escaped to Beirut.

In Beirut, he had neither relatives nor friends to stay with. He joined the party, at this barracks specifically, for board and lodging. He continued his studies during the day and manned the barricades at night.

I remembered all that sitting next to his dead body in the ambulance.

On the way to the hospital, I decided to quit the barracks and the war, and look for a job, any job. I would leave for a place where no one knew me, and I knew no one. I was always destined to flee because of fear, and because of things that had nothing to do with me.

17

I HANDED BACK MY GUN, took my possessions, and left the barracks.

I didn't tell the commander the real reason motivating the decision. I said I was going back to the village because I'd been cleared of involvement in the teacher's kidnapping now that the perpetrators' names had come out. He wished me good luck and asked me to pass on his greetings to the guys he knew.

I felt freed from a host of restrictions, but, at the same time, I felt on my own again. The manner of Azizi's death made me extremely wary. I constantly thought someone was behind me, following me, watching me, waiting for the chance to kill me.

I moved to a crowded neighborhood after attempting to lose my tail. I assumed that the mastermind behind Azizi's murder would have assigned one of his men that I didn't know and that didn't know me to tail me and keep tabs on my movement, and so keep me within his grasp.

I put what I had learned from relevant novels to use. I took a taxi; I got out on a busy street, walked quickly until I reached a side street, and waited at the beginning of the street scanning the eyes of passersby for a look that betrayed someone on surveillance however hard they tried to appear innocuous.

I made sure I was safe. I had to be on guard, seeing as anything was possible in wartime. They would kill you and attend your funeral.

If you didn't protect yourself, nobody would.

I toured every shop in the area asking the owner if there was anywhere for rent in the neighborhood. I also asked the mukhtars. One said that finding a house for rent those days was really difficult. Landlords were afraid that tenants had party affiliations. They would move in, then refuse to pay the rent or vacate, even if the landlord paved the sea over trying. It had happened often.

Another mukhtar urged me to go to the local party HQ and try to obtain its consent to requisition an empty apartment. Plenty were available: the residents had been forced out less than two months before. The party took control of apartments to stop people moving in and selling them, or to stop those who already had an apartment from grabbing another. The thought of requisitioning did not appeal. It was against my upbringing to filch people's hard work and live in houses they had been forced to abandon, and whose keys they still had in the hope of return. Besides, I was not running away from the party to go back to it or any other.

I preferred to return to my old ways rather than living in a house with an owner and begging the party for permission to stay in it. My old ways were sleeping in the entrances of buildings and in cars. I was nostalgic despite the painful memories. It had been full of adventure. I missed that in the first few days at the barracks, where I had a bed and bedding. That feeling of excitement soon came back though once I started going to the frontline. Getting to the barricade during clashes was an adventure unlike any other. As was running to a safe place when a 120mm mortar shell was fired and waiting for it pass overhead and hear the sound of the explosion.

While I was thinking about where I was going to sleep that night, I remembered my cousin. She had started working as housekeeper for a surgeon and as nanny for his child after the death of his wife. I had heard about it from one of my mother's relatives—I had bumped into him outside a cinema that showed double bills. That relative told me the doctor's full name and the suburb he lived in. He also said that my uncle had made a huge fuss to stop his daughter working as a domestic servant, but acquiesced to her decision, provided she help him with a little money. He had lost his job when the company he had been with since its incorporation went bankrupt and had fallen deeply into debt after gambling away his lifesavings. She wanted to get away because life with her father was unbearable, and because she was bored of the village. She wanted to move to another area to work and study until she met her Prince Charming.

I went to their suburb in the middle of the day. It didn't take long to find the doctor's residence. I asked a worker at the gas station on the outskirts of town and he gave me directions. It wasn't a house. It was a two-story villa with a big garden full of almost every kind of flower and plant.

As soon as I approached the gate, a man appeared behind it. "How can I help you?" he asked. I said I wanted to see my cousin and gave her name. He welcomed me and opened one side of the large gate. I went in. He escorted me along with a dog that started sniffing me and licking my shoes. My cousin greeted me warmly. She couldn't believe her eyes that I, the son of her father's sister, was standing there in the flesh before her. After a cup of coffee and swapping our news, she took me to the dining table. I ate lunch while she sat next to me. The lunch was delicious. Okra and rice. For dessert there was fig compote her mother had made.

I didn't realize that my cousin was a great cook and an excellent housewife until after she left the doctor's house and went to Syria and from there to Nice in the South of France. She got married there, had children, and opened a Lebanese restaurant. After word of her food spread, the restaurant opened a second branch in Cannes.

She invited me to spend the night at the villa once she knew I was homeless. She called the guard and told him that he would have a guest tonight and asked him to take care of me.

In the evening, the doctor came home and she introduced him to me. She asked him if he could find me a job at the hospital where he was in charge of the surgical department. He promised her and promised me that he would do his best. He had great respect for her because she ran his large house so well, and also prepared tasty dishes. Luckily, he loved eating and knew what he liked. More importantly, his son loved her and was attached to her, and she too loved him and was attached to him. So much so that she cried a great deal when she had to leave. She even named her first son after him.

I don't know why I had a feeling that the doctor would bring me good news the next day. His face, whose wrinkles made him look older than he was, instilled confidence, a sense that life had his back. After the death of his American wife, whom he had met while doing his internship at a Boston hospital, he lived for his son. She had also been a doctor, a pediatrician. It was love at first sight for him, and they got married before graduation. She discovered late that she had cancer, had treatment for two years, then left this life. Her premature death marked a turning point in his life. He took to seeing the world from the perspective of his only child.

As I was sleeping in the guard's room, the Devil started whispering that the doctor, who was twenty-five years older than my cousin, could not be immune to a young woman, almost twenty, who was attractive, plumpish, well proportioned, and with irresistible eyes. I suspected, no, I was positive, that he was sleeping with her. They might have been in bed together right then. I could not believe that nothing was going on between them. If things were like that, he was either a fool or still faithful to the memory of his wife. Assuming fidelity girded his chastity, what was to stop my cousin seducing him with her feminine charms in the hope that he would marry her after she had made him fall in love with her? When it came to love, taboos were demolished and social divides vanished. He could marry her and throw all the gossip that might accompany his second marriage over his shoulder. Perhaps the harshest that could be said was that he had married his servant.

My cousin, it's true to say, when asked what work she did for the doctor, would reply that she was his housekeeper and nanny for the boy. But the doctor's friends and neighbors shortened those two descriptions into one word: servant. Some of those with ill will added another epithet between themselves: his mistress, or, as they put it, girlfriend.

I wished the doctor would marry her. He was still young, and the age difference was no obstacle. If that didn't happen, she could do what she wanted. Everyone's free to lead their own life. All the talk about the family's honor and reputation when it came to womenfolk was backward and mostly put about by men who rubbed their mustaches between the thighs of hookers, but who, nonetheless, trumpeted the family's good name if one of their women so much as smiled or glanced at a passerby, then disowned her and expressed the wish that she had never been born.

I tried to engage the guard when we were drinking tea in the hope of deducing something, but I didn't get a word out of him. He was like the three monkeys, a likeness of which the doctor had in the living room, one covering its eyes, one sealing its mouth, and one blocking its ears. Every question I asked, he answered, "Don't know." He was only averse to speaking when it came to the doctor and his house. He told me all about his father, the policeman, who had been present at the execution of Antoun Saadeh, the Lebanese intellectual, and about his own trip to Turkey in a truck carrying sheep, and his return the same way, to save the fare and blow it in Istanbul, and how he had made a profit in a casino and spent it at a nightclub.

That first night without the smell of guns, military uniforms, and sand, I slept peacefully in a room in a corner of the garden. Even the wind stirring the leaves on the trees seemed afraid to annoy the residents and the sleeping birds.

I didn't see the doctor leave, although my eyes were glued to the entrance from the moment I woke up at exactly seven o'clock. He'd probably had to leave earlier for some reason. Perhaps the hospital had called him in to attend to a patient in critical condition. Doctors are bound to respond to a humanitarian need whatever the time, and the doctor for whom my cousin worked was humanitarian and compassionate. That was her opinion. When I met him, I found him pleasant. He seemed to take an interest in me. He didn't have to write my full name and qualifications on a scrap of paper, but he did. He put it in his pocket, then said, "It'll work out, God willing," and patted me on the shoulder.

I spent the day waiting for him to come back. I went to the market with my cousin and helped her carry the shopping from the supermarket to the car, and, back home, from the car to the kitchen. On the way, I learned that the doctor had bought a car specially for her so that she could go to university twice a week and take his son to and from school. He could not stand buses and did not trust their drivers because they drove crazily.

While I was strolling in the garden, the dog came up to me. He was called Mortred, and, as a precaution, I was nice to him. The guard, however, asked me not to be. He said that the dog was still being trained and shouldn't get used to strangers so he didn't fail in his duty as a guard dog. Looking over at the villa, he said that only the residents had the right to play with him, so that he would get used to them and not bark when he saw one of them.

When he noticed that I was listening to him, he told me with some pride that he had taken a two-week workshop on the basics of dog training. He called Mortred over and started training him. He seemed delighted, like he was playing with one of his children, or as if the doctor had seen him, been pleased, and rewarded him. He started teaching him how to sit. He pressed on his rear with his left hand and placed his right hand on his chest or pulled the lead upward, making the dog sit. He repeated this movement a few times until the dog sat when the guard's hand merely touched his rear. I observed the dog's movements and was amazed by his intelligence and how fast he caught on.

In the evening, I waited for the doctor to arrive. I prayed he would bring me good news. I wasn't a beggar or making impossible conditions. I was willing to do any job, on one condition: that I be safe. Peace of mind is a boon whose value is only appreciated by someone who has lost it, and I had lost it since Azizi's death. I slept with my eyes open. As soon as I fell asleep, I awoke in a panic. I was afraid of being double-crossed and killed in a way I hadn't bargained for. Azizi's killer was quite capable of devising a means to get rid of me without leaving any clue to his identity.

The clock showed two a.m. when I heard a hoarse yelping. I glanced at the clock, then at the guard, who was fast asleep. Sleep flirted with me. The dog was giving a strange growl, a mix of pain and a call for help. Perhaps somebody had thrown him a piece of poisoned meat to kill him for some purpose. The dog had wolfed it down and the poison was taking effect. That somebody might have been drafted to kill me. True, I had taken the utmost care when moving, but it was still possible that an informant had seen me and my cousin at the market and told on me. That possibility loomed larger whenever I heard the low growling. That was followed by another, less significant, possibility: a thief had sneaked in to steal whatever he could get his hands on, after having staked out the villa and obtained the knowledge that allowed him to get in and out safely. There was a third, if very slim, possibility that the infiltrator was out to get the guard. I discounted that option, since the guard seemed peaceable to me and without a criminal past. I did not disregard the fact that people disguise themselves: wolves in sheep's clothing. The guard might have been one of that sort.

I remained in bed, watchful and vigilant. If the intruder wanted to harm me, or us, given that I was now part of the household, I would be doing him a favor if I made any audible movement. He would be alerted and on guard, either to run or for a confrontation.

The growling grew sporadic. That convinced me that the dog was slowly dying. His growls were like a wail from the depths of his heart to let us know that something out of the ordinary was happening, and that we had to beware. He was performing his role despite his bad state and affirming that he was faithful to his master. Such qualities were almost extinct for the species called man or humanity.

Suddenly the barking stopped.

After much suffering, the dog had died. I listened closely, hoping to hear a low groan or a movement indicating that something was happening outside. Without the snoring of my companion in the room, which was also sporadic, I would have believed we were living in the clouds and not on the ground.

Calm prevailed. Even the wind seemed to have swallowed its tongue and left its gentle breath free to meet the dawn and play with the birds getting ready for the morning chorus.

Without prelude, the howling started. Then the gate opened. The guard got up and said good morning to me as he yawned and rubbed his eyes. He said the "doctor" was back and that the dog was welcoming him in his way. I told him that the dog hadn't stopped whimpering, and that I hadn't slept. He slapped his head like someone who had forgotten something important he should have done but overlooked. He said that he had forgotten to feed the dog. A hungry dog cannot sleep, and whimpers reflexively as Mortred had done all night.

I didn't see the doctor in the morning. He came back tired out and slept. The operation he had performed overnight had exhausted him. The patient was a fighter on the front-line and a bullet had hit him in the spine. That was what my cousin told me over breakfast. I asked her whether she knew the name of the fighter. He might have been one of my old comrades. She said no.

I cannot describe my happiness when she gave me a small piece of paper with two words on it: Sister Christine. The name was written in French. If she had not pronounced it, it would have been impossible for me to read. Doctors' handwriting is strange. They write as if they don't want anyone to understand them except their colleagues and the pharmacist.

18

THE LADY AT INFORMATION DIRECTED me to the emergency department as soon as I asked her where I would find Sister Christine. Emergency was crammed with people, unlike the departments I passed through on the way.

I saw one nun among the male and female nurses. Tall and pretty. Her blue nun's habit was crisply ironed, as if she was going to Mass, not working at a hospital. Strands of her auburn hair showed at the edges of the white cap covered by a navy blue wimple. She was about thirty years old and would have made a good actress or model rather than a nun. She was taking someone's blood pressure and giving a nurse instructions in French. I stood near the doorway waiting for her to finish her work. She took the strap of the pressure gauge off the patient's arm and hurried to take a look at another patient lying on a trolley, so I didn't get to speak to her.

I sat on a seat big enough for two with a view of the room where the nun was working. I did not take my eyes off her, so that when she took a moment's break, I could go over and introduce myself. In my imagination, I acted being a nurse like the one who was bandaging a boy's finger while joking with his female colleague, or the one who stuck a needle into the forearm of an old woman, then swabbed the spot with a piece of cotton wool, or the one helping a man get on a trolley.

But I knew nothing about nursing. Could I learn fast and do the same? Nobody is born educated. My mind wasn't slow.

If I liked something, I was good at it. What counted was liking it. Giving injections, bandaging wounds, and measuring blood pressure were certainly not difficult things to do. I could learn the basics in an hour, then do them under the supervision of the nun herself or any nurse she delegated. I would be extremely cooperative. I wasn't going to disappoint her or the doctor who had recommended me.

The moment the nun took off her gloves and lowered her mask, I leaped over. I said hello and told her my name and the doctor's name. She welcomed me and asked me to wait for her in the next-door room. I didn't wait long. I anticipated that she would ask me a number of questions, but she didn't. Perhaps the doctor had told her about me, or she trusted him enough to get straight down to the matter in hand. She said that she needed someone for the morgue during the day and to help out as needed in surgery at night. She fell silent awaiting my response. I met her silence with a silence that she took to mean I needed time to think it over. As if she had read in my eyes what was worrying me, she said that I would be able to sleep in the room for the doctors' assistants. She fell silent. When she realized that her last statement had caused me to relax, she gave me two hours to think about it before answering.

Working in a morgue, me, Abir Litani? Impossible. I'd never agree. Let her find someone else. True, I was willing to do any job—there's nothing wrong with working—but working in the morgue was objectionable. I remembered the story *The Gravedigger* by Gibran, which I had read at school. The title had frightened me, and I remembered only that and forgot the contents.

What was the difference between gravedigger and guard or porter of the dead, or whatever other work lay in store at the morgue if I agreed? Wasn't there any other work? Why couldn't my job just be in surgery? She was exploiting me. She wanted me to work night and day. When would I rest? Didn't I have the right to my share of rest, like the rest of God's creatures?

What made me hesitate, or inclined to accept in the end, was the chance of spending the night at the hospital. Perhaps she knew that was my weakness and scratched it.

If I found a house to rent, I wouldn't take a job like that. I would work in the morgue and look for a house. When I found one, I would quit the job and look for another. That was the logical thing to do as long as doors were shut in my face. Right now, the only open door was that of the morgue. It would be stupid to waste that opportunity. I would try it for a month or two. We'll cross the next bridge when we come to it.

I sought out the nun to tell her I accepted. I didn't find her. They said she was having lunch. I went out to the park nearby and sat under an old willow tree. On its trunk were carved party emblems and hearts with an arrow through along with the names of lovers who might have parted, yet the tree continued to bear witness to the love that was. I looked up. I didn't see a leaf shake as one bird came and another went. There wasn't a single bird in its branches, not a single nest of chirping chicks. Trees abandoned by the birds were so miserable. Only dust and flies resided.

Back in the village, during the hunting season, I often liked to doze under a willow that cast its shade over a tiny spring. My snoozing was often disturbed by a bird letting its droppings fall on my face or head. It would enrage me at the time and make me laugh when I remembered later. I didn't seek revenge. I swear I never shot at a bird perched on a branch. The pleasure, all the pleasure, came in hitting it in the air, turning and wheeling. A real hunter enjoys hunting birds, not eating them. On a taxi ride once, I heard a poet on the radio. I think his name was Shawki Abou Shakra. He was condemning bird hunting. A sentence he said stuck in my mind and made me regret every bird I had killed: "Does anyone eat music?" I swapped 'kill' for 'eat.' Yep, I killed music.

Hunting trips and memories of the open country were still on my mind when I went into emergency and saw Sister

131

Christine conversing with another nun in the corridor leading to the administration department. I stepped back and turned aside. I didn't see her look directly at me, but I sensed her looks following me when I turned my back and withdrew. I became certain of it when she finished her conversation and came over. "I want to work," I said right away. She welcomed my decision: "You have three months' probation. Either you're up to it, or . . ." I didn't let her finish: "I won't disappoint you."

She called a nurse and asked him to take me to the mother superior's office, for her to be introduced to me, and then to the employment office, and to one of the nuns to pick up two white coats. The nurse also showed me the room where I would sleep and the locker where I would put my things. He was very friendly. It must be rare for someone starting a new job in a place where he knows no one to have the benefit of a person like him.

In a clean and pressed white coat, I stood in front of the mirror. I didn't recognize myself. I was only missing a stethoscope to appear a doctor. Whoever saw me would never have any doubts about me. I marveled at the change clothes could cause to people. A few days before, in military clothing I looked like a fighter. I felt strange in my new outfit. I wasn't used to wearing clean clothes. I was scared that my hands would touch the coat and make it dirty.

I walked around looking at people. I hoped I might discern looks of surprise in their eyes, as if to say they knew what I was about, and also sensed that my new situation was weird. It was only once I got to emergency that I felt ashamed. The looks of my colleagues, male and female, punctured me like needles. I was embarrassed and almost took off the coat to throw in their faces before leaving. I could hear their voices coming out of their eyes: *he's* going to work in the morgue? One nurse was immersed in her work. She didn't look at me and give me the same fake smile of her colleagues. She was the best looking of them. Her disregard irked me, although I found excuses for it.

Sister Christine introduced me to them using my full name. When she had introduced them to me, she was content to mention just their first names. I felt discriminated against.

She didn't tell me what I had to do. She waited until she had finished writing in a thick ledger like a school register book with ruled paper. She asked me to follow her. I followed her, contemplating the way she walked. Before we reached the morgue, she said that today she would teach me what I needed to know tomorrow, and that Robert, my colleague in the morgue, would also assist me.

She opened the morgue door, went in before me, and I caught up with her. The cold was nothing special, contrary to my expectations. I had expected that the morgue would be very cold. Two metal beds each with a corpse on and four more corpses on the floor occupying half the room. The nun said that bodies sometimes covered the floor, particularly during battles and incursions and after car bombings.

She talked and explained, looking at me in an effort to gauge my reaction and how solid my position was. A job like that took rare courage and a strong heart. She didn't know that I had been a fighter. I was used to seeing corpses, dismembered, charred, crushed. I had often carried on my back, or with others, the corpses of my comrades and of strangers to ambulances and hospitals.

She continued explaining so that I would have an idea about the work I would start the next day. She stressed the need to respect the sanctity of the dead and to deal with the bodies of the dead as though they were of the living. She said there were other essential things she would teach me later.

While she was closing the door, she wished me good luck. I nearly laughed when she said *bonne chance*. I suppressed the urge to laugh so she didn't misinterpret it. What good luck lay among the dead? What success, when the sight of the six corpses brought to mind every similar scene, worst of all Azizi's body on the bed covered in blood?

We went back to emergency the way we had come, with her in front and me behind. I watched the way she walked, the movement of her fine ass. I watched her surreptitiously, as though she had a magic eye in her back observing me. All that sticks in mind from that day are the way she walked, the purity of her voice, and the press of her femininity under her navy blue habit.

19

THE ROOM I SHARED WITH three others was on the top floor next to the interns' room. The floor's only bathroom made it quick to get to know everyone. Waiting in line for the bathroom to become vacant, especially in the morning, let us swap small talk and news. Talking was fun and helped us forget the need to go, which, as soon as the urinal became free, was translated into a sigh accompanied by pleasant relief, and sometimes the trace of a smile.

I was struck by the presence of French and English medical textbooks in the bathroom, as well as men's and car magazines. As a result, anyone who went in only came out again after being begged by those waiting in line. Reading was a diversion that caused you to forget yourself and your colleagues. When their patience finally ran out, they used the bathrooms on the floors below.

I often emptied my bladder into an empty mineral water bottle I kept for the purpose. I would stand behind the door of the room, urinate into it, then put it in a bag so that nobody would notice what I had done. On the way to the morgue, I would throw the bag into the nearest receptacle.

My roommates alternated night shifts. Two stayed at the hospital for emergencies, while the third slept at home. That arrangement changed once I was qualified to work in surgery. Then only one of them stayed the night. During an operation, the surgeon didn't require more than two assistants.

The three of them competed with each other to teach me the rules and procedures to be followed. The most difficult thing was learning the names of the implements the doctor used. I had to hand him the requested implement as soon as he said its name, which was usually in French. The three devised a way to make it easier for me to remember. They sketched each instrument onto a separate piece of paper and wrote down its name. Then they gave me the pile of papers and asked me to memorize the names and shapes of the implements. It would be no use learning the names without knowing their shapes, and vice versa.

They kept testing me and I learned the shapes and names by heart. They were impressed by my rapid progress and I started accompanying them to surgery, watching what they did and how they handed instruments to the doctor. Hardly ten days had passed before I gained their confidence and they told Sister Christine that I was ready. A friendship developed between us, which went as far as covering for each other to avoid any blame from the administration.

One of them was crazy about racing and cars, and he had a pile of auto magazines in a corner of the room. He bragged that he knew the location of every screw in the chassis of this or that model. He was a fan of Mario Andretti, who a year before, in 1978, had won the Formula One championship. I nicknamed him Andretti. Everyone adopted the name, and he answered to it without grumbling.

The second roommate loved poetry. He idolized Moussa Zagheeb, who, in his opinion, was unbeatable. He owned his books and cassettes of performances with his band, the Fortress Chorus, which he listened to before going to sleep and in the morning when shaving or ironing a shirt. I heard those tapes so much that I learned many lines by heart and, without intending to, crooned them during routine tasks. I sang them in the style of Moussa Zagheeb, preceded with the "Aaach" with which he opened all of his improvised responses, but as soon as I caught myself singing, I shut up and carried on silently. I called him Bou Moussa: he wanted, after getting married and being blessed with a son, to call the boy Moussa, after his favorite poet.

The third roommate was mad about fishing. He had a collection of rods standing in a corner of the room. The rest of his tackle he kept in the trunk of his car. Even when the weather was bad he went fishing. The fish would be hungry then, and it would be easier to catch them. He was exactly like a professional bird hunter, and like me too took pleasure in catching fish, not eating them. He gave his catch to friends and relatives, and often singled out the mother superior to eat fish, which the nuns also partook of, and sometimes the metropolitan, if he happened to be at the hospital at lunch-time. Because of that, he had considerable sway with most of them. As a joke, I nicknamed him Minnow. To begin with he objected, and begged me, Andretti, and Bou Moussa to call him by his real name. Then he changed his mind and agreed to the new name provided only the four of us knew it.

Just as I gave each of them a nickname, they called me Haris al-Mawta, Guard of the Dead. I didn't protest, but deep down, the name annoyed me. They could have chosen any other nickname and I wouldn't have objected. They adopted it even though they knew I couldn't stand working in the morgue. They often counseled patience, saying that nothing in life is fixed, especially in a hospital.

Of those nicknames, only mine inspired Bou Moussa to compose a ditty that quickly made the rounds of the hospital:

His shade if seen is dread
resting on the wall ahead.
Working hard to guard the dead?
Better guard himself instead!

Of the three, Bou Moussa was closest to me, perhaps because we came from the same region, although our villages were a long way from each other. He would say that we had drunk the same water, and that water was thicker than blood, as opposed to blood is thicker than water.

During his shifts, we would stay up together. We mixed vodka with juice and drank listening to one of the poetry performances. We prayed that the security situation remained calm. For sudden shelling at night rarely passed without the injured being brought to the hospital, and we would rush to prepare the operating theater and get ready to admit those in need of immediate surgery. To hide the smell of vodka on our breath, we ate chocolate and wore an extra mask. We could be fired if it was proved we drank at the hospital, even when off duty.

We avoided standing close to the anesthetist, who had a very good sense of smell, which the camouflage did not fool. He exploited our fear of him snitching and would order us to fetch him a bottle of water, or anything else he could perfectly well have fetched himself.

The cardiologist sometimes turned up drunk. He would be called in suddenly, leave behind his drink and his friends, and come in. He would fulfill the humanitarian duty that he had sworn on his honor to uphold. After two cups of coffee, he would start operating. I remember him saying that however much he drank, he sobered up as soon as he was behind the wheel of his car and as soon as he entered the operating theater. There was something in his subconscious mind that rang the alarm and reinvigorated his mind so he didn't die in a car crash or kill the patient under the knife.

The most annoying thing was when the surgeon asked me to drop everything and wipe the sweat off his brow. That happened when the operation required extra concentration and effort. I would be standing close to him, switching my gaze between his hands busy operating and his face and eyes. Whenever I saw sweat beading on his forehead, I quickly mopped it up with a sterile cloth.

Sometimes, he asked me to scratch his nose, or cheek, or chin. When the operation lasted a long time, he would ask me to rub his cramped shoulders, and I would do it. I would carry on massaging as he moved his head left and right, during which the cracking of his neck vertebrae was audible. After that signal, he did not need to ask. I stood behind him working the tense muscles until they relaxed.

The doctors asked me in particular to do that, because I was the only new staff member in the department. It was not on for a longstanding member of staff, someone with experience that made his presence by the doctor indispensable, to do such peripheral tasks. I worried that my work would be limited to wiping the sweat off doctors' faces, rubbing their shoulders, and scratching their cheeks, noses, and chins.

Work in surgery was enjoyable if the operation took place before midnight. At dawn, however, it was worse than hard labor since we had to wake up and rush to get dressed for the next shift and wash our faces. We worked nonstop for three hours, the usual length of an operation, and longer if the operation was complicated.

I often went straight from the operating theater down to the morgue, where other work awaited. I could hardly believe it when my shift ended and I could go up to my room and sleep. My legs were barely able to carry me, my hands would start shaking, and I had no taste for food, drink, or life.

20

I FOUND THE SPACE OF the morgue weird: a square room, four meters by four meters. I thought it would be bigger, like the morgues I had seen in films and TV serials, with walls full of drawers for the dead to lie in. These were guarded by a police-man or an employee, whose role was often played by an actor who gave the impression that he had just come back from the dead himself and was no ordinary guard. He would always be bristling with gear: a flashlight in hand even during the day, a bunch of keys hanging from his belt, and a permanent scowl on his face. The morgue keeper had to be like that. Imagine a guard of the dead whose appearance or behavior made you want to laugh, or just smile, in the presence of death. That might happen in comedies, but the solemnity of the place was still respected. It was the one place where people were equal. There were no young or old, no rich or poor. Nobody was exempt from visiting when their time—known to God alone—came.

I didn't know on what criteria Sister Christine picked me, or whether there even were criteria. I wasn't going to trouble my mind with such thoughts. I wanted to work at a hospital, not act in a film. I didn't think she matched my appearance to the work. If she had placed her hand on my chest when she was telling me about the work awaiting me, she would have reconsidered and asked me to tell her how broad my shoulders were. While she was talking to me, my heart wasn't beating as normal. I could hear the rise and fall of its beats as I imagined myself doing what I was hearing.

My inner reaction was not the same when I saw the room they called the morgue. At first glance, I thought it was the entrance to the morgue whose image I had in mind. I was startled when the nun said, "This is the morgue," stretching out her arm as if giving someone something. I followed the arc of her arm in astonishment.

I was happy the room was small, and also happy that it didn't resemble the morgues of TV and film. I didn't ask where the drawers for the dead were.

There were only two slabs. A corpse on each, and four bodies on the floor. The slabs were about two meters long, less than a meter wide, and a meter high, and supported on four legs. Between the legs at the head end of the slab nestled an electric motor supported by two iron stands, and with two buttons: one to turn it off and the other to turn it on. Its job was to chill the stainless steel slab where the corpse was stretched out. It was likely that its parts had been assembled at a local plant. I found out that was correct subsequently, when a body became bloated despite being on the slab. Bloating was not supposed to happen. The cause was the sudden breakdown of the motor. Repairing it meant detaching it and taking it to the maintenance department. If they could not fix it, it had to be sent to the plant, and it might not be back at work for a few days. I was designated to detach it from its base plates and put it outside the room, even though that was not part of my job description. No one from maintenance had the balls to enter the morgue. An abject excuse that allowed those armed with it to foist work they should do themselves onto others. The nun turned a blind eye to the issue, evading responsibility. Someone assigned to enter the morgue for some job might have a weak heart that could not bear the sight of corpses, and they fainted. They might never come out of their coma.

The room had two doors. One door had a bottom half made of iron and a top half of dark glass set with two thin iron bars. It was impossible to see through. That door opened onto the corridor connecting emergency to the hospital entrance where the reception office, the waiting area, and the administration offices were.

The second door was tightly closed to prevent smells and germs leaking out. It opened onto a lot filled with broken-down cars, the hospital water tanks, and two diesel generators that supplied the local residents with power when the electricity supply was cut.

The walls of the morgue were painted cream. The color had changed because the room was cleaned so much with insecticides, germicides, and air-fresheners.

Against the wall opposite the door onto the vacant lot was a cross. It stood on a small metal tripod resting on a formica sheet held up by two L-shape supports. On the sheet were two candle-shaped lamps that were always lit. To the right of the sheet, a short cord ending in a button hung down to turn the lamps on and off.

It was not only the color of the walls that changed. The floor tiles did too as a result of being sprayed with disinfectants containing a potent mix of chemicals then rinsed with water, which lacked the power to remove the smell of the disinfectant. A smell that could cause headaches and nausea. Some visitors and nurses felt dizzy when they smelled it or threw up. Even so, that smell was less disgusting than the smell given off by bodies after a few hours in the morgue.

The smell of a dead person is possibly the most disgusting of all smells. In my hunting days, I had passed close by dead animals: an old horse, a sick cow, a useless donkey, a mange-eaten dog, a cat run over by a car. . . . But their smell was less intense than the smell of a human corpse.

I figured that the smell of a corpse did not result from putrefaction but was a mixture of its discharges and the foul deeds committed by the person whose corpse it was when they had been alive. All corpses smelled the same though, which disproved that idea. It was unreasonable to assume that all their souls had been corrupt. There were still good people out there.

Smells got through the mask. I wore two masks when the smell was very pungent. As a precaution, I always had a supply of them with me. Working without a mask was impossible. Many times, I had been forced to go into the morgue with my face exposed, because there were no masks. Shelling could continue for a week, or more, and the routes and crossings between East and West were cut. That stopped the supply of medicine and other essentials. Doctors were often ferried under fire from their homes in a tank or armored car.

For such eventualities, I stockpiled masks. I supplied them to Sister Christine after claiming that I had found a forgotten pile of them by chance. I avoided letting on that I stashed them away for times they weren't available. I hid them in places that did not arouse suspicions: in the garden for example. I would wrap a bundle of masks in a plastic bag and bury it in the ground. I would put a piece of wood over it, or anything else to protect it from the rain and sun. I avoided hiding them in the cupboard in the room, so that nobody would think I had stolen them if they came across them. Once, I hid a batch in the vacant lot. I did not repeat the attempt after I saw a man urinate on them. The vacant lot, from the evening onward, was the meeting place for those who needed to relieve themselves. The signs on the walls saying, "Please, no urinating" were useless. Also useless was pelting them from the balconies of homes with tomatoes, water bottles, and other objects that could kill someone if they hit him on the head.

I liked the way I looked in a mask, with my nose and mouth covered, or leaving it hanging around my neck. I got used to it and took to leaving the morgue still wearing the mask. I didn't realize it was still on until I tried to drink from the water cooler at the beginning of the corridor by the emergency room. I some-times chatted with a colleague without removing it, and only noticed when I read in their eyes that they thought I was doing it obsessively, or to avoid their breath. Then, I would take it off and put it in the coat pocket or leave it dangling on my chest.

Just as I grew fond of my appearance in a mask, I grew fond of the morgue. Deep affection always developed between me and places. The place became a part of my being, and I took it with me wherever I went. I compared it with other places and found it preferable to them because it was my place, of my concern alone. I belonged completely to it, just as it belonged to me. My sense of loss would be enormous when I was forced to leave, and that sense of loss persisted as long as the place was still present within me. I would only be cured after I had adjusted to somewhere new. That happened when I fled the village, and to a lesser extent when I left the barracks. Once I was at home with work at the morgue, the affection started to grow. The sense of being at home with it was necessary to deal with expected difficulties.

Just as every trade has its secrets, which you have to know to succeed at it, handling corpses had its own rules too. It was a trade just like any other, but the highest-ranking of them all, because it concerned dead human beings. I was determined to become an expert at this trade and prepared to start acquiring the first of its rules.

21

THE HARDEST PART WAS LEARNING how to get a body ready for collection by the family. This consisted of stuffing and washing. I hadn't heard of these procedures to which corpses were subjected before burial. Before coming to Beirut, I hadn't seen a dead body.

Back in the village, when I saw a funeral procession with a bier at the front, I walked the other way. When my uncle died, I avoided seeing him laid out on the bed despite my mother's insistence that I have a farewell look. I did see the coffin when leaving the house. On the way to the cemetery, his friends raised the bier on their palms, and made it shift around, dislodging the cover of the coffin. That usually happened when someone died young and fit. The elderly were carried aloft on shoulders.

Here in the morgue, I got used to seeing corpses from day one.

I listened to the nun's explanations like someone listening to an exciting story whose chapters unfolded in only one place: the morgue. She explained the importance of preparing the corpse. It was essential, she said, because some corpses remained for days until the next of kin found out that we had the body.

She taught me the basics of stuffing on the corpse of a man in his sixties. He had been hit by a speeding car crossing the highway and died instantly. During the practice, I almost said to her that I wasn't up to the job, but I held myself together and didn't say a word. What made me hold back was the way she looked at me with the mask over her mouth and nose. At those moments her eyes were so beautiful. During the explanation, she gave me looks that I interpreted—I don't know why—in a way that had she been aware of, she might have fired me. Apart from the looks, I was also drawn to the way she used her slender hands. Hands that hadn't been created to stuff the dead and wear gloves for hours.

I tried to take in the information that streamed out of her mouth because she had said it so many times to those that tried out the job in the morgue but had been unable to continue. I was embarrassed to ask her to slow down, lest she conclude that I was dumb.

She moved on from one point to another once confident that I understood, then she went back to the previous points to make them stick. From time to time, she asked me specific questions to test me. I didn't tell her that I wanted to write the details down so I could refer to them if my memory let me down. If Bou Moussa, Minnow, Andretti, and I had not resorted to pen and paper, I would not have learned the names and shapes of the implements in surgery in record time. I found working with those guys easy, for they were understanding and helpful.

The nun was also understanding and helpful, but there was something that made me wary and reserved during the demonstration. Natural feelings for a subordinate toward their boss. I was willing to do my very best to please her. I avoided asking questions. Sometimes, asking questions didn't mean that you didn't understand, but that you were slow to understand. It wasn't a new habit. It had been with me since school. I often quashed the questions on my mind so that the teacher, or my classmates, didn't think I was stupid.

I had never imagined doing what the nun, who treated the dead body as though it was alive, was doing. I heard her say, "Open wide!" when with one hand she opened the jaws and with the other hand placed cotton wool between them, and with her fingers (or a long metal spatula) pushed it down inside toward the throat until the mouth was filled. Whenever she completed a task, she thanked the dead person for their assistance. "Bravo," she said, with a pleasant lisp to the 'r,' and moved on to another place.

For the other places, she remained silent. Perhaps because stuffing them was easier than stuffing the mouth. Or because she was used to speaking to the corpse when she had to prepare it on her own. A voice, her voice, kept her company at those somber moments. Hearing her own voice might make her believe that she was not on her own among the corpses. She needed a sign of life in a room haunted by the solemnity of death to conquer her fear, especially when the delivery came at night. Sometimes she hummed a song that took her far away, but did not disturb her concentration, although a mistake was not a problem, as long as the corpse was being dealt with. No one would believe that a beautiful and elegant nun like her might stuff a dead person and wash their body.

The lesson in stuffing took less than half an hour. Stuffing the mouth required precision and patience. It had to be filled with cotton wool all the way back to the throat. The mouth was then taped shut with a piece of clear tape. Stuffing the ears and nostrils was easy too. As was the asshole.

Binding an uncircumcised penis was easier than binding a circumcised one. The former only required a thin, strong thread to tie up the foreskin after drawing it over the head. A circumcised penis, however, had to be wrapped in a piece of gauze and tied tight.

I cannot describe my feelings when I helped her tie up an uncircumcised one. I grew aroused when she did it, and my arousal continued after she had tied the knot. I excused myself and hurried to the bathroom for relief, otherwise I would have had a terrible pain in my balls that felt like my soul was coming out from between my thighs when I moved or walked.

The afternoon was exam time. The nun asked me to stuff a corpse riddled with bullets. For someone working in the morgue, the job was equivalent to a military baptism by fire. Stuffing the body's orifices took about an hour. She observed me without saying a word. She looked at the corpse then went out, returning after a few minutes to stand opposite me, nodding her head, and then go out again. Robert, the other morgue assistant, did the same as her, with one difference. She wanted me to make quick progress and fill the gap in the morgue, while he wanted me to make a mistake, in the hope that a pile of mistakes would get me fired, even though I would share the hard work with him if I passed the exam.

Stuffing this corpse was difficult. I wished one of them would help me.

I was plugging a wound and the cotton wool dropped inside. The bleeding continued as the blood was still liquid and hadn't yet coagulated. Dried blood stopped the bleeding, but it did not prevent other secretions passing through. The wound kept busting open when the dried blood broke up. Blood surged out again and I swabbed it up with a few paper tissues. Then I continued stuffing the hole with cotton wool and covered it with gauze that I stuck down with clear tape.

Stuffing a corpse like that without making a mistake, prompted the nun to pat me on the shoulder, as a sign of encouragement. When Robert saw her do it, he could not hide his resentment and busied himself with a minor task, pretending not to have seen anything.

If the nun had given me a grade, I would have scored an A. It made me happy that she praised me in my absence in front of several nurses. Nurse Nahla told me the good things Sister Christine said about me.

I had passed the lesson in stuffing. The lesson in washing still remained.

22

WASHING WAS A HUNDRED TIMES easier than stuffing.

I figured that out when Sister Christine poured some disinfectant from a clear bottle onto a piece of gauze and wiped it over the body of a woman who had died during a C-section. The fetus had survived. Whenever the piece of gauze dried out, she passed it over; I poured out some more fluid, and she continued painting the body. She rubbed the gauze over the same spot a few times. Arms and neck first, then chest and stomach, followed by thighs, legs, and feet.

She didn't explain what she was doing. Watching her was enough to understand. From time to time, she gave me a quick glance. When she was reassured that I was following, and not daydreaming, she carried on swabbing. She gave me the bottle to involve me in the task—she could simply have placed it by the corpse's head or between the dead woman's slightly parted legs.

Robert came in, and she asked him to help her turn the body over to let her coat the back and other parts. He did it, then she asked him to take over and finish the job. He took the piece of gauze from her and proffered it to me. I dampened it with the foul-smelling fluid, and he started cleaning.

She painted the body crosswise, while he did it up and down. He wanted me to understand that he didn't adhere to the nun's technique but had one of his own. That behavior mixed arrogance with fear at a rival who might outshine him.

The spectacle of him speaking French to the nun with his eyes fixed on me was too funny. He wanted to let me know that he could speak a foreign language. Sister Christine was wise to his trick and replied in Arabic. He realized that his ploy wouldn't work, so he lowered his voice when explaining the details to me. The nun had thwarted him in his presence. He gave no sign of annoyance but was fuming with anger. His shaking hands betrayed him when he wiped the blood away from the wound.

I learned the basics of washing in twenty minutes. Only the name of the disinfectant did not stick in my mind, even though it was easy: formalin. I wrote it down on paper and kept saying it in my head until I memorized it.

Under Robert's supervision, I cleaned a fresh corpse, with Sister Christine popping in just to make sure. The corpse belonged to a soldier who had taken a sniper's bullet in the chest. Impossible to retrieve, the body had been left for hours lying in the street. Finally, some guy had gone and dragged it to safety with bullets flying around him. He accompanied it to the hospital. I saw him crying at the entrance to emergency and thought the deceased was a relative of his. He asked me to show him the body. I let him in, contrary to the "Staff Only" sign hanging by the door. He studied the face of the soldier, turned around and didn't come back.

The third corpse I washed on my own without supervision. A man who had died of natural causes. He had had a heart attack in the nearby vegetable market and been brought to the hospital by some Egyptians working at the gas station there. I worked with Robert to take the clothes off the corpse, and we put them in a small bag. Robert wrote the dead man's name on the bag and took it to the property store. He didn't bother coming back, seeing as there was someone to do a job he usually did by himself.

When the nun stressed the need to wash and cleanse the corpse as soon as it arrived, I did not realize the significance until later. A corpse, a few hours after death, went stiff, and removing clothing became impossible. The hands locked, and if one was lifted, its bones fractured, at the wrist in particular. Half of it would dangle down and spoil the appearance of the body. Sometimes, if something like that happened, we wrapped the break in a bandage, to make the arm look like it was in a cast and hide it up the sleeve. The next of kin rarely objected to the measure if they found out. The dead have no need of a functioning hand to shake hands with their greeter at the gates of Heaven or Hell. Besides, after burial, the hands and the rest of the body would not remain as before. Worms would finish them off from the inside, and rats from the outside.

It was a rule of washing to cut the clothes and keep the body intact. We cut shirts from the cuffs up to the shoulder, then undid the buttons and freed the dead. The same method applied for cutting sweaters or blouses, with an additional slit down the front. We removed trousers after cutting them from the bottom up to the waistline. We pulled them from under the corpse. Underwear we dealt with in the same way.

I confess that on many occasions I broke the rules. I didn't cut the clothes, but pulled them off the corpse, which risked breaking one of the hands, as happened when a black leather jacket, whose feel suggested it was expensive, caught my eye. I could not free the first sleeve, and I handled it quite forcefully, breaking the arm at the shoulder. Freeing the other sleeve was easy after that. I raised the body slightly, so I could push the jacket over to the other side and get the hand through the sleeve.

I tried to take the jacket without causing fractures, but I couldn't. I put it on under my coat and left the morgue for the bathroom. I went quickly to give the impression that I was about to wet myself. As soon as I locked the door of the cubicle, and felt safe, I started thinking where was I going to hide the jacket. I was panicked. It was the first time I had ever stolen anything. And not just from anywhere. I stole from a dead man. And not just anything. I stole the jacket he was wearing. The smell of his body clung to it.

Whenever I heard a voice nearby or footsteps, I grew more agitated. I thought about going up to the room where I slept and hiding the jacket some place. Then I discounted the idea because the few things in the room did not allow for safe stashing. I reckoned that the next of kin would notice that the jacket was missing and ask for it, and that after a search it would be found in the room. I would be caught red-handed, then I would get fired and have to return to life on the streets.

So as not to remain flustered, I decided to hand the jacket in to the property store. I hesitated before taking the decision, but the voice of conscience only quieted down once I made up my mind. I went toward the morgue with the jacket on under my white coat. I prayed in my heart that I would not run into anyone in the corridor who might discover the reason for my agitation, which I was trying so hard to keep under control.

As soon as I entered the morgue and started taking off the coat, I imagined the nun coming in and seeing me wearing the jacket. How would she react? Would she think I was just trying it on, or that I intended to steal it if it fitted? I would tell her that I liked it and wanted to try it on, and joke, "Does it suit me?"

I took off the jacket and put on the coat, and the nun didn't come in. I felt an enormous sense of relief when I handed it in to the property store. The worker picked it up and looked at it. I was sure he secretly wished it was his. The proof was his nonchalance after having stared at the jacket. He tossed it on to a shelf, like he was throwing away a worn-out item of clothing or an item that had no place there. With his nonchalance he wanted to make me believe that he wasn't interested in the jacket.

That wasn't the first jacket I wanted to steal. Previously, we had cut one open (at the back only) that a guy in his thirties, who reached us as a corpse, had been wearing. I threw

154

the jacket in the trash. After the nun had left the room, I took it and put it in a bag. I went to a skilled tailor and asked him whether he could sew it up well enough to be wearable. He said he would do his best. I left it with him for collection after two days. I didn't go back, but let him keep it. I don't know whether he mended it and waited for me to pass by and collect it, or he ignored it after giving up hope. Perhaps he sold it and allowed himself to keep the proceeds in exchange for his labor.

I let it go because I couldn't imagine myself wearing it. I was afraid I would remember its owner when I wore it. I took it as a bad sign and regretted what I had done. I had planned to have it dry-cleaned after mending, so that no trace of the man remained, particularly the cologne that wafted from the jacket whenever it moved. The jacket should have been left with his possessions, not stolen by me and smuggled out like I was shoplifting a new jacket from a smart store.

Sometimes I could be really sneaky and reckless.

23

I HAD BEEN WORKING IN the morgue for three months and was still embarrassed to admit it. When asked what I did here at the hospital, I replied that I covered for absent nurses during the day and worked in surgery at night. I rarely revealed my main job, although at heart I was proud of it. I was the only person to have stuck it out for so long and I had perfected the stuffing and washing of bodies and also excelled in surgery. The testimonies of the nun and my colleagues were the best proof.

I avoided getting to know new people so as not to be asked what kind of work I did. I was afraid they would change their opinion about me if they knew.

When I agreed to work in the morgue, it did not occur to me that I would still be here today. I had decided I would quit when I found another source of income. The idea stayed with me until I got used to the work and the place and leaving them both became hard. They ensured me food, a bed, and safety. Above all safety. Azizi's killers, if they knew where I was, wouldn't come to kill me in a busy place like the hospital.

Those three reasons made me invent excuses for my embarrassment so as to lighten its impact. Fortunately, I did not encounter anyone I knew and who knew me.

I was very surprised when I heard that my cousin was asking for me. She had come with the doctor, whose son she looked after, to do some lab tests. They directed her to the morgue. She asked one of the nurses to call me. When I saw her, I hoped she wouldn't ask me what I was doing inside. We hugged and agreed to meet in the cafeteria during my lunch break. We had lunch, then coffee. She asked about everything except my work. That worried me. If she didn't know, she would have asked. It was possible the doctor had told her. I didn't remember seeing the doctor in emergency, but I always met him at night in the operating theater. He was content with a single question from time to time: "How's work?" I would reply with a nod of the head accompanied by my familiar response: "It's fine." I rarely asked him about my cousin, not because I wasn't interested to hear how she was, but so that he didn't think I was ingratiating myself.

If she knew I worked in the morgue, it was likely she would tell one of our relatives, and the news would spread in the village. She was a woman after all, and women choke on other people's secrets if they don't blab.

I didn't know how Mum and Dad would take it when they heard that their only son was stuffing and washing corpses by day and assisting the doctors in surgery by night. They wouldn't believe it even if they saw me with their own eyes. They knew me well and knew that I rarely went to funerals. If I did, it was because of kinship or social convention, and I would walk at the back of the funeral procession. When our neighbor the policeman died as a result of losing control of his motorbike, my father sent me to fetch my mother who was with other women hovering around the dead man laid out on a bed in the middle of the living room. The women were wailing and lamenting and sobbing over the loss of the departed.

I didn't see the corpse of our neighbor. I saw women hovering around the bed it had been laid on. I heard the sound of mourning, followed by heart-wrenching wails and sobs. I went back to my father and claimed my mother wasn't there. Really, I didn't see her. All the women were dressed in black and had black veils over their faces too. They all looked the same. For a week, I was unable to sleep before dawn.

Whenever I shut my eyes, I saw a mass of black-clad women sitting and standing around the bed, and heard moans, sighs, and wails.

My cousin knew that about me. That I ran away from funerals was a topic of amusement to her and her siblings. I was happy that she had nearly finished her coffee and we had talked about loads of things apart from the hospital. My happiness was cut short when she asked me as she was saying goodbye, "You haven't told me what you do here."

"Surgical department," I said and left. I was certain that if I told her the truth her response would be no different to the responses of strangers, and might have been crueler. Some visitors who saw me coming out of the morgue or inside it avoided even looking at me. They stuck to the wall if they chanced to pass me in the corridor, like they would catch a fatal infection if we brushed shoulders.

Some of them had an annoying curiosity that made me avoid talking to them. One could not stop himself asking whether I had tried to have sex with a corpse, and what my feelings were when I did. I didn't reply. He asked the question again. I told him to behave himself otherwise he would see something he'd never seen before. He arched his eyebrows and accused me of sleeping with the corpses. He made me angry. I punched him, making him sway before reeling over. My courage inside startled me. I normally avoided fistfights, because I had never once escaped unscathed.

That kind of intrusion I got over, but I couldn't get over that look which sometimes categorized me as a butcher, and sometimes as a war profiteer who made his living from its victims. In the eyes of some next of kin, I found myself implicated in the crime. That kind treated me badly, but I soaked up the insults and put their hostility down to the horror of the calamity that had befallen them.

How could I respond to a man who came into the morgue and saw the leg of a dead person touching the corpse of his brother? He would accuse me of insulting his brother and then curse me. What should I say to a mother who spat in my face because I did not allow her to see the body of her son, so that she would not collapse when she saw the state of the corpse days after death? How to reply to a young woman who described me as a vulture because I called her fiancé a corpse? She did not want to believe he had died from a sniper's bullet on the way to her house.

I always had to face insults like that. To begin with, they annoyed me, then I got used to them. Close contact with many people who had lost a loved one taught me that there were people who could not control their temper when they lost a relative and they mouthed rude words, cursed God and his saints, or physically assaulted someone in their path.

Direct contact with death for eight hours a day—the length of my shift—wasn't easy. Sometimes, when surgery was quiet, I worked the morgue at night too, helping the nun to expedite a body.

I often spent the day consoling the wife of this dead man, comforting the father of that martyr, and commiserating with a mother who had lost her only son. It was forbidden for my lips to form a smile, or the ghost of a smile, so I wasn't accused of having lost my humanity through familiarity with the dead, and that my heart had become callous and indifferent. I tried to lighten things for them with stories and cases of other people's casualties that equaled theirs or were worse. The morgue taught me that people accept their calamities when they are compared with the calamities of others.

I often recounted imaginary tragedies or embellished a real tragedy when I felt it would have a positive effect on the traumatized person. I cited the words of Jesus Christ and others like him that instilled grieving hearts with a spark of hope; sayings and proverbs that the nun repeated, which I memorized and repeated, but avoided discussing or explaining. I just said them exactly as I had learned them. Whenever I quoted them in the presence of Sister Christine, she looked at me and gave a smile overflowing with satisfaction.

In the evening, I would take refuge in my room, depressed. Bou Moussa (when on night shift) would change the atmosphere, especially when he was enjoying a new zajal contest, which he would keep listening to until he acquired another one. When he was absent, only a glass of whisky lifted my mood and rocked me to sleep.

24

SINCE AZIZI'S MURDER I HAD lost my sense of security.

Whose hands had his diary fallen into? I didn't know, but I knew my name was in it. Azizi had told me himself. True, Azizi only used initials, like the newspapers when they printed the names of those who had run afoul of the law, but in a closed world like the barracks it wouldn't be hard to work out who was meant. As soon as I read the initials on that piece of paper I found by chance that night at Azizi's house, I knew who the two comrades being referred to were. Even if my name didn't appear in the notebook, would that convince whoever was behind Azizi's murder that I hadn't read its contents, or that Azizi hadn't told me? If the killer believed I knew what was in it, or some of it, he might not let me off the hook.

Nobody would believe that Azizi hadn't shown me anything or told me stuff that ought to have been classified. I was practically his only friend. Our friendship was in the open, and the whole barracks knew we were close. A friend would open his heart to a friend. That would be a logical deduction, although not true when applied to Azizi and me. All he admitted was that the information in the notebook was dangerous, and more exciting than the Agatha Christie novels I read.

After he died like that, I understood why he didn't want to tell me his secrets. He wanted to keep me out of danger. He knew how shocking his secrets were and that someone who knew and kept them risked death, as did someone who received them and kept quiet. When he asked me to look after the notebook if anything bad happened to him, I didn't give much importance to it. I thought it was a measure of how much he trusted and liked me, but he knew that by letting me in on the notebook, he was tossing me a ball of fire. He wanted his secrets to live on with a trusted person as testimony to senseless events that happened during and around the war. He chose me for the task because he didn't have another friend he could trust with his little cache.

When he died, I thought about his request. Whatever it took, I would carry it out. I had promised, and I wouldn't break the promise even if it cost me my life. I can't describe the thoughts in my head when the notebook wasn't under the tile. Thoughts that made my head spin for hours.

I prayed that Azizi himself had taken and hidden the notebook before his murder. That was a possibility. Perhaps a sudden inspiration had driven him to change the hiding place. Possibly, the notebook had been filled up, and he had stashed it with the other two, to make space under the tile for a new one. Perhaps the notebook had been stolen and he had been murdered, or the other way round. In either case, the result was the same. Azizi had fallen victim to his secrets.

There was a chance that the discovery of the two buried notebooks led to his murder. But how had they been found given that they were hidden in a safe place? Perhaps it was chance. A child playing in the dirt had found them, and not torn them up and thrown them away, but taken them home. At home, his father read them, freaked out, and handed them over to a party member, who handed them over to someone more senior. As a result, the information they contained got out and reached those concerned, one of whom, or a number united by the same concerns, decided to take revenge and eliminate the author.

I couldn't exclude a dog having dug them up. By instinct, hunger had led the dog to a bone near the two notebooks.

It had scrabbled away the dirt, and a passerby had stumbled across them.

Perhaps the landowner had needed to plow the land and found them. He read the contents, took them to the nearest barracks, and, hoping for gain, handed them over to the commander.

For sure the two notebooks hadn't been buried without something to shield them from the rain and damp that would destroy them if left exposed. Being in a box or wrapped in a plastic bag would draw more attention than being unprotected. No way would Azizi have buried them randomly. He was inexpressibly careful about them.

Sensibly, he wouldn't have written his name on the cover like a school pupil. I reckoned that his name didn't appear inside, but the details they contained might lead to him if they fell into the hands of those mentioned. Recounting an event that he knew of by chance or had participated in and whose protagonists were few in number would be enough for one of them to realize that the author was Azizi.

I could be sure that my name wasn't mentioned in those two notebooks, because they had been written before I came to Beirut. I didn't think that Azizi referred to them, or their hiding place, in the third notebook. He was too smart to make a mistake like that, particularly as he did not exclude the possibility of the notebook somehow getting lost. So why didn't he keep them safe?

They might have included the musings about life and people that Azizi liked to write down on scraps of paper and cigarette packs when on guard at the barracks and the barricades and in his free time. He often read to me and others some of his ideas in an attractive dramatic tone. But if they were limited to that kind of writing, why bury them? It was possible that in addition to his thoughts, they included his testimony about the war and his missions, and other information he had obtained I know not how.

If only I could find *them*, given that finding the last note-book was impossible, then I might find a clue to lead me to the perpetrator. Not to avenge Azizi, and not to threaten the guy. Someone like me, who kept his back to the wall for safety, wouldn't embark on that. No, it was to try to find out things about him that would help me protect myself. I was in the danger zone as long as there was no proof that Azizi had been murdered, and that it was his secrets that had killed him. No one believed he killed himself. That rumor had been spread around to cover up the truth. But the rumor itself proved the crime was premeditated. Floating it after the killing was deliberate.

Fear made me shave my mustache and crop my hair very short. "Zero guard," said the barber as he wrapped my neck with two strips of towel. Perhaps changing my appearance would make it harder to recognize me.

Fearful of meeting a comrade in touch with those looking for me and who would give me away, I didn't roam the floors and corridors of the hospital unless it was unavoidable. The boundaries of my movements were precisely drawn: morgue, emergency, cafeteria, bedroom. If I was forced to go for a walk in the streets around the hospital, I walked looking around. I grew suspicious if I saw a passerby staring at me. I would quicken my pace to overtake him then duck into one of the alleyways or go into a store and start haggling with the shop-keeper over something I had no intention of buying until it was clear that no one was following me.

Caution, suspicion, and nervousness became part of my character.

Tortured feelings darkened my life and I couldn't get rid of them.

In my view, everybody was guilty until proven otherwise. Everyone who entered the hospital was a detective come to investigate me. Everyone who exited concealed a report about me, my work, the time I went to bed and woke up, and every-thing else about me.

I doubted everyone, especially for the first few weeks. Even Robert did not escape my doubts. I thought he was a talented actor playing the part of an antagonist or enemy to dispel any suspicions of his being an informant by seeming to be a long-serving member of staff treating a new employee badly for fear of his own position. I gave false details about myself if I should be in the company of nurses close to him. My colleagues on the night shift didn't escape suspicion either, apart from Bou Moussa, who lived in a world of his own—the world of zajal poets and alcohol.

I slept with my eyes open. I woke up at seven, or I would be woken up by the commotion in the street or the commotion of the guys in the next-door rooms getting ready for work. I rarely got enough sleep. When I didn't get enough sleep, I spent the day in a funk. A joke or an unkind word could make me lose my temper. I was like that for a long time before sorting it out.

Suffering, once you get used to it, is less harsh than at first. You become familiar with it until you are amazed that your exasperation with it has disappeared. Over time, you resign yourself to fate and convince yourself that the people who want to harm you or kill you have more important things to do than keep tabs on you and enlist men to write reports about you.

You are comforted by the thought that they have forgotten you or become confident that you will not reveal the secrets that they think your friend entrusted you with. If they saw you working in the morgue with corpses, they would forgive you and take pity. If they knew that you worked, ate, and slept at a hospital, and that the furthest place you went was the manoush bakery across the street from the entrance, they would take you off their list.

If they wanted your head, they would reach you. The city was small, and everybody knew everybody. You weren't the only person who didn't know anyone. Strangers like you were plentiful. Also like you, some of them belonged to parties not out of belief in the dogma spouted by their leaders, but to find food, shelter, and protection.

The only place I felt safe was the morgue. The dead bodies gave me an aura that only those bold enough to look at the dead could see. People were afraid of me when they knew that I wasn't only the guard of the dead but also stuffed and washed the corpses. In the morgue, I became another person. When I crossed its threshold, the fear and suspicion that accompanied me outside fell away. The dead protected me.

25

I HAD COUNTLESS DREAMS WHERE I saw myself washing and stuffing Mum's corpse, or Dad's corpse, or the corpse of a relative. I would wake up from the dream afraid, and spend the day depressed as though there was a boulder hung around my neck. But the most vivid dream was where I saw my dead self strewn among other corpses in the morgue.

First, I thought I was asleep. I went and shook my body gently, then harder and harder. I checked the neck for a pulse. Nothing. Now I was sure I was dead.

I was afraid my body would decompose if it stayed where it was for too long. I moved a corpse off the refrigerated slab, picked up my corpse, and put it in its place. I was shocked when I saw a patch of blood between my shoulders. To discover the source of the blood I tried to raise the upper part of my corpse. I didn't complete the task. I was afraid that the living, dreaming me would faint in the morgue. The nun might get mad if she saw two corpses of the same person in one place. One on the cold slab and one on the floor.

I saw myself, her, and Robert standing around my corpse. In the dream I wished that she would take on the job of stuffing and washing it. I would help her and Robert when needed. I imagined her holding my penis to bind it, then it slipping out and she grasping it again. After it kept slipping out of her hand, she would ask me to hold its head, so she was able to knot the thread around it.

Unfortunately, she called Robert to come with her, and charged me with stuffing and washing my own corpse. Before he left, Robert helped me remove the corpse's clothes. Shirt, trousers, and vest we cut open. We put the pieces in a plastic bag. The underpants were next. I took the scissors from him—I felt ashamed at him seeing me completely naked.

Washing only took a few minutes, although I meant to do it slowly. Wasn't I someone saying goodbye to his corpse?

I watched myself stuff it as though it wasn't my own corpse. I don't know where I got the courage from. I shut the two wide-open eyes and stuck down the eyelids with clear tape. I kept to the usual routine, closing one orifice after another.

When it was my penis's turn, my hands failed me. This was my penis, the one my mother had treated playfully when I was small. In summer she often left me naked from the waist down, so she could flaunt her baby boy, at a time when most births happened to be girls. It was my penis that in my early teens lengthened and thickened if I played with it. What a revelation. I remember the first pleasure that shook through me, proving to me that another life existed far above. I often soared away when I conjured up specific anatomical parts of the girls at school. Many times, I watched our neighbor sweeping her house. Imagining her beautiful breasts splayed under her baggy robe sent me off to the heights. My penis that attained manhood from a forty-year-old Bedouin woman the day I took her in my grandfather's orchard. My penis that I touched the moment I woke up and ran to the bathroom so that my mother did not spy my morning erection. It was my penis that demanded I conceal it under my gown so that the nun did not discover its disobedience. My penis that I imagined between Nahla's breasts—she was my colleague in the emergency room. There it stood. Still in its prime. How could I choke it with a fine thread? I hesitated, but in the end, procedures had to be followed. I knotted the thread tightly around it.

I saw myself looking confused when it was time to dress the corpse to hand over to the next of kin. My next of kin. I had nothing in the wardrobe that suited a corpse. The custom was for bodies to look smart on the way to their last resting place. Bou Moussa had a black suit that he only wore to funerals. I saw him approaching with the suit on a coat hanger, and a white shirt and black tie in a bag. I didn't believe it. He looked like he'd just brought it from the dry cleaners.

I saw my corpse on the point of going stiff. Touching the fingers made me realize. They wouldn't stay evenly spaced like a hand stretched out for a handshake. I wanted my corpse to make it to the coffin and then the cemetery undamaged, without fractures, just as it had come into the world. Putting on the shirt and suit had to be done at top speed. But that required some flexibility in the limbs. I headed to emergency and explained the situation to the nun. At once, she told Robert to stop what he was doing and help me.

Robert lifted the body from the shoulders and I inserted the left hand in the left-hand sleeve of the shirt, then the right hand in the other sleeve. While I put the buttons through the buttonholes, he did up the tie then folded the collar down over it. We put the jacket on the corpse in the same way. Putting the two legs into the openings in the trousers was not hard. Once we had done with that, I took a couple of steps backward to take in the whole image. I looked like a bridegroom. That's what my Mum would say when she saw me.

I saw myself and my Dad in the front row inside a church full of people. Not the church in our village. A strange church, but beautiful. I saw the coffin, my coffin, before the altar on a table covered with a white sheet. My full name and the year of my birth and my death were on its front:

Abir Habib Litani
(1958–1979)

Condolences were exchanged at the entrance to the cemetery, and I overheard a lot of what was being said about me. The nicest thing they said was that the whole village had turned out for the funeral.

I saw myself leave the graveyard alone. On the way back, I met a boy carrying a large picture of me. It might have been the same picture held aloft in the funeral procession. The boy walked like someone lost. When he saw me, he stopped and gazed between the large picture and me. Then he gave a smile that mixed sarcasm and cunning. He wanted to make me know that he knew that the dead person wasn't me, and that the person alive wasn't me either. That boy wasn't a stranger. Eleven years before he had been me.

Whenever I recalled the dream, I recalled his face, and I doubted that I was myself. The me now working at the morgue, stuffing and washing corpses, pining for the nun, could not be that boy who served at Mass on Sundays, trapped birds, and was scared of his own shadow at night.

26

I CONTEMPLATED THE CORPSES THAT nobody had claimed and were starting to turn blue. I was used to the way they looked. Their faces and clothing. The pose their stiffening bodies assume. A vague bond grew between us.

I memorized the features of every corpse, despite the hourly changes they underwent. Features brimming with health and toned with life faded into a blue-stained yellow, a mixture that stood for death. I hated the color blue, the first sign that the body had started to decay and decompose. On clear days, I often avoided looking at the sky to stop the blueness reminding me of the blueness of death.

I was sad about the corpses when I knew the story of their death. Their memory roiled through me. The smell of bread, ink, or chalk, or of sweat from toiling in a factory or restaurant, clung to their souls and bodies. The cake seller, the oven hand, the lad on the school bus, the tramp, the wretched scavenger in the garbage dump. The corpses of those, and those like them, pained my heart and shook my faith in God.

Wasn't the daily grind to find something to eat enough? What had they done to deserve to die like that? They were chance victims. We, who still enjoyed the breeze, the sunshine, and a few pleasures, were alive by chance.

Corpses that showed signs of an easy life did not evoke the same sympathy as the corpses of the poor and ordinary. It was something involuntary. I often demeaned a corpse whose body was dressed in a jacket and tie and still reeked of perfume. An elegantly dressed corpse seemed to put the others down, or at least I thought so. Other corpses I thought humble in comparison. I would lift the leg of the chewing-gum seller and place it on the chest of an elegant corpse or do something else to redress the balance of justice.

I could not be impartial, even though it was against hospital rules. I was biased toward the corpses of the wretched, those whom fate had oppressed and turned into humiliated beings living on the breadline. I was biased toward them because I was one of them. I felt we had many things in common, and I tried to make their corpses comfortable in this place where I was in charge.

Sometimes, I would delay the turn of a corpse whose time had come to be shrouded on the refrigerator slab, jumping the queue with a corpse that had come in later, because the second corpse was someone poor and oppressed while the first was someone well off. No guilt complexes for me. I did it with an easy conscience.

A lot of corpses I didn't handle the way the living should treat the dead, in the way someone with my job was supposed to behave. I often spoke to the dead and revealed my innermost thoughts.

It's not true that people die when their heart stops beating and the brain stops functioning.

Often in the morgue, when there wasn't anyone there, I felt I wasn't alone. Especially when it was quiet, I felt the place was chockfull, its cramped confines almost bursting. The silence freed the souls from their bodies and they hovered around them. I listened to breathing fraught with strangled words in voices that wanted to say something but did not speak.

I wasn't imagining it. To begin with, I convinced myself that what I heard was a total illusion, or just voices in my head. I didn't dare say anything about it. I was afraid people would say I was a tad crazy, or that I conjured up spirits and communicated with demons. Now, I am certain that what I heard, and still hear, was not a figment of my imagination or a result of the films I had seen. I rarely watched television at the hospital, and I hadn't watched horror films at home. I only went to the cinema to see porn films: a double bill on continuous play.

I often deliberately went down to the morgue at the end of the evening. Patients' family and visitors would have left the hospital, emergencies would have calmed down, and the calm had a mysterious effect. I visited the morgue to listen to the buzz of the quiet. Often, when I saw the bodies discharging water and disgusting fluids, I wondered whether the mind like the body discharged its fears, its secrets, and its memories. It discharged them as whisperings embraced and circulated by the silence. I was certain about it. I was hearing the discharging of souls and minds, not something carried on the wind, as some people liked to say commenting on such a situation. Minds and souls emptied themselves so they could ascend to Heaven free of earthly cares.

When I reflected on the state of the corpses, I went beyond the bounds of logic, and imagined minds and souls at the moment of death ejecting their contents and secrets, in the way that a typewriter ejects the sheet of paper once the words have been typed. The contents and the secrets were written on sequential sheets coming out of the earholes, or the mouth, being a larger orifice. Papers to be cherished by those dearest to the departed, even though they, or anyone else, would never read them unless the deceased left instructions in a will to go through them and sort them out because of their general benefit.

It was an injustice against humanity for the contents of the mind and the secrets of the soul to die with the death of the body. Assuming this plan could be put into practice, who knows what riches would fill human history and the numerous achievements that the distant future would see.

All the scientists who died, taking their theories with them. All the poets who passed away with dozens of poems they had no chance to write down. All the lovers who met their Maker with so many words to their beloved left in their hearts unsaid. All the mothers taken by illness, whose maternal love was still fertile and who could fill the world with tenderness. These and other thoughts assailed me in the morgue and kept me company.

I had not previously been enamored of philosophical speculation. All my life I disliked the dryness of philosophy and had no sympathy for its proponents. Our philosophy teacher at school, who in our final year drummed into us the theories of Socrates, Plato, Aristotle, Ibn Sina, al-Farabi, and others, was fun. He often made jokes about philosophers, ancient and modern, to attract our adolescent minds, but we listened to the jokes, not the lesson. For us, the sum of philosophy lay in a smile from the girl next door, and in the shiver that went through us at a glance from a student at the high school for girls.

In the morgue I found myself philosophizing. The daily confrontation with death spurred me to think. I did not say a word to anyone about my musings. They were reflections that appeared and disappeared of their own accord. In the gap between their appearance and their disappearance, my soul would soar above its web of cares into the riddles of existence.

When he heard me talking about the murmurings of souls and stifled voices, Bou Moussa said he was worried about me, and advised me not to stay too long in the morgue after my shift. Andretti did not comment. Minnow, who never smiled even when tickled, laughed a lot. Since then, I've kept my thoughts to myself, which has deepened my love for solitude. The morgue became the only place I felt warm and safe. The dead became the companions of my solitude. They listened to my ideas in their profound silence. I did not speak to them or express my fears out loud, but they heard me. I felt that my words settled in their souls that had yet to separate from their bodies or had separated but were still hovering close to them. These feelings made my isolation open to the world, as though those corpses were just windows for me to look through and see Heaven.

27

AT EXACTLY QUARTER TO NINE a massive blast shook the hospital. The explosion was so powerful I suspected it was in the neighborhood. My heart started racing and my body sagged as though I was about to faint. Total chaos ensued.

I was in the morgue, getting ready to start a fresh day after spending half the night in surgery. I was too weak to stand, so I sat on the edge of the refrigerated slab. Once I recovered, I stood up. I rushed to the bathroom and washed my face that looked yellow in the mirror and only needed a touch of blue to look like the face of a dead man. That was down to lack of sleep, and the worry that went with every explosion in our area and the adjacent suburbs.

Ambulance sirens drew closer, and as they did the hospital went on the alert. Patients and visitors looked out of the windows to watch the scene that had often been repeated since the beginning of the war.

The radio announced that a car packed with explosives had detonated in a crowded residential street near the bakery. There were dozens of fatalities and many wounded. Enormous panic surged through the people. A man was asking about his mother who had gone to the market and not come back yet. A woman was looking for her brother who had left the house a few minutes before the blast. A child in the road was crying, with snot over her mouth and dribble down her front, and nobody paid her any attention. Perhaps her mother, whom she had been with, had met a sudden death. A woman looking out from a third-floor balcony was wailing. Her son worked as a baker at the bread oven, and her heart was telling her that something terrible had happened to him.

Armed men from several militia kept the crowds back by shooting into the air, fearful that another car was primed to explode. The people dispersed, not out of fear of a second explosion, but afraid that the armed men would disagree over the pecking order. Then, those who survived the explosion might die from the bullets of local people.

Ambulances arrived full and left to fill up with corpses and human remains once again.

An old man asked why the people were so agitated as he cursed a lad who almost pushed him over without meaning to. His deafness saved him from hearing the terrible news.

That was some of what I heard.

I wanted to go to the site of the incident, but that was impossible in such circumstances. Alone in the morgue (it was Robert's day off), I helped first responders empty the stretchers they were carrying in. Various size body parts, half corpses, and corpses. There was no room left in the morgue.

The nun pointed out to the first responders how small the morgue was and how they needed to take the next batch of victims to another hospital. She scolded them, and she knew some of them well, saying that they were acting as if this was the only hospital in the area. She hoped she would not see their faces again.

Separating the new corpses from the old, and laying them out in a separate spot, tired me out. The ambulance men might come back and take some of them to hospitals with morgues with space for them. I made room for the body parts in a corner where I had spread out a couple of charity blankets that I often put under a bleeding corpse to soak up the blood. Once its job was done, I would roll up the blanket, put it in a plastic bag, and throw it in a waste bin. I sprayed the room with disinfectant when the smell got too strong.

Once I was sure that the ambulance men had respected the nun's request, I counted the bodies. Twenty-one complete corpses, of which fifteen had been brought in that day; two half corpses, one severed horizontally, of which only the head, chest, and stomach remained. One hand was missing below the wrist; the other was fine. The shirt on the corpse was splattered with mud and water. Perhaps the force of the blast had thrown it some distance. The other half corpse was severed vertically and lacked a leg and the right arm from the shoulder.

I didn't count the body parts. The way they looked all stacked up was enough to make me look away. I fetched a third blanket and covered them. I had never seen so many severed limbs before, some of which were still dressed in tatters of clothing. For the first time since getting used to the work in the morgue, I wished I did something else so that I didn't have to see that horrific scene. The sight of the body parts and lacerated flesh reminded me of the offal that the village's only butcher would fling into a corner outside his shop, next to the edge of a water conduit running beneath an iron grille. All the flies in the world met over those scraps.

I will never forget that sight, the sight of the body parts, or what happened after, when the next of kin started doing the rounds of the hospitals in search of limbs missing from corpses. They implored me by all I held dearest to help them rummage through the pile of human remains in search of a hand for example—they told me the shape and brand of the watch that might still be around the wrist—or for a leg or any other part of the deceased's corpse.

I wasn't up to sorting through the remains in search of the missing limb. I asked the next of kin to send someone in to search through the pile. Some of them offered me money to spare them and do the search myself. I didn't take it, and

181

would never take it even if the person asking paid me his own weight in gold.

I spent the day on my feet without food or a break. Even my pack of cigarettes remained untouched. I just smoked two cigarettes, which I puffed down with a cup of coffee. My ears were glued to the radio that we often resorted to during the hours of bombardment and when major incidents like that explosion took place. It was broadcasting news flashes about the tragic event, and the familiar intro music made us nervous until we'd heard the latest. Between each update, martial patriotic songs played at low volume making them hard to hear. Anyone standing next to the radio would turn the sound up when the intro music for the update began and turn it down again after the news. That person might be a visitor, a patient, a nurse, or Sister Christine herself.

Everything that happened during the day fitted in one scale of the balance, and the events of that night in the other. Two young men showed up. One had a pistol visible under his shirt. He said their cousin had died in the explosion and they hadn't found his body at any of the morgues. They had found one of his shoes among the stuff gathered up by first responders and deposited at the Red Cross HQ nearby. I let them look through the pile of remains, keeping my eye on them. They checked all the body parts, then did it again and a third time, but did not find a single limb connected to their relative. Then Mr. Concealed Weapon said that they would have to take some body parts from the pile and make the deceased's relatives believe that they were from the corpse of their beloved boy. He said there had to be some piece of the corpse in the coffin, apart from the shoe. Holding a funeral for a shoe was not on.

I remembered the story of a Greek philosopher that our philosophy teacher told us. This philosopher threw himself into the mouth of a volcano to end his life. The fire grabbed him, and the lava spat out his shoe. The philosopher died and the shoe survived.

I refrained from answering the angry guy with the gun. Then in the tone of someone harboring evil, he said, "We'll take this hand and this leg." He picked a hand up off the floor and pointed at a leg. I said, "You're cheating the family of the dead man, and stealing the limbs of corpses whose next of kin might not find anything else. Is it reasonable that they should carry empty coffins?" He immediately put the pistol to my head and with his other hand pulled me toward him by the collar of my coat and threatened me. He implied that if I knew who he was, I'd shut up. I didn't ask him who he was. I wasn't interested in who he was, or whose son he was. I pleaded with him to put the gun away so that we could look for a solution together. He got angry and said that the only solution was to give him what he wanted and that he would kill me if I refused.

I complied. I wasn't willing to be a needless victim for the sake of body parts. He wasn't joking. Evil glinted in his eyes. There was nothing to stop him killing me. The area was out of control, the bastards hiding under party names were in charge, and woe to anyone who dared to say no. Someone who had a pistol under his shirt and used it to threaten people was one of them.

I started ingratiating myself with the man holding the pistol and his cousin with emotional stuff about the sanctity of death and the need to respect the dead. Perhaps something would happen and extricate me from the awkward situation. Like the nun turning up, she sometimes made her nightly rounds about this time. Or a patient in critical condition turning up with some of his family, or one of the nurses passing by perhaps. . . .

But none of those possibilities happened. The guy with the pistol said, "Gimme a bag to put the arm and leg in, or something to wrap 'em in." I gave him a bag and tried again to address his conscience and dissuade him from what he was doing. I asked him whether the deceased's father would accept the burial of the remains of strangers once he found out they weren't his son's. I kept going, although he wasn't looking at me. "That hand you're putting in the bag now," I said, "isn't the hand that the father kissed when his son was little, and not the hand that shook his hand and which he shook when the deceased became a lad. Just as this leg . . ."

He did not let me finish. He let go of the bag, picked up the pistol off the floor next to him, and attacked me. I ran out of the morgue and down the corridor. I thought he would follow me, but he stayed where he was.

I thought about telling the nun but changed my mind. She was resting at the nuns' house, and getting there in the middle of the night was risky enough. Even if I went to tell her, there was no guarantee that I would find the pair of them still there when I got back. So I went straight back. I was worried they would take other parts besides the hand and leg.

When I arrived at the morgue, I was surprised that they had gone. I heard the roar of a car engine and raced to the entrance to emergency. The car had taken off. The driver's fist stuck out of the window, giving me the finger.

28

SOMETHING HAPPENED THAT HAD NEVER happened to me before: sexual desire for a dead girl.

They said she had been killed during an exchange of fire between ill-disciplined party fighters. A bullet lodged in the back of her skull and killed her instantly. The poor girl was taking her dog for a walk near home when bullets rang out in the street. She drowned in her own blood on the pavement. The dog went home.

From the foot of the slab, I lifted up the sheet. I contemplated her in the nude like someone who wants to memorize the details. Then I put the sheet back. I was awestruck by the sight of her naked body. The girl looked asleep, not dead. Her whiteness wasn't overly bright, hinting at coldness, but tinged pale red. She had not gone pallid, even though the time of death was about three hours before.

Her face was well-proportioned and without makeup. Her shut eyelids shrouded the color of her eyes. Her auburn hair was clumped together, as though the wind, not a hairdryer, had dried it after her shower. Her breasts, slightly bigger than average, were firm with a slight droop that gave them an attractive shape. Their skin tone was paler than the surrounding area, which, like the top of the shoulders and the waist, kept a faint tan from summer sunbathing.

The down on her thighs indicated they were strangers to hot wax and the razor blade; blond fuzz, whose lightness was intensified by the blackness of her beautifully geometrical pubic bush (an inverted triangle). The pubes were quite long—she might not have taken care of them since days at the beach. From their curl, I concluded she wasn't cruel. Perhaps their softness was like the softness of my mustache in puberty.

As I gazed at her small vulva and her clitoris nestled between two frilly lips, I wondered if she was a virgin or not. Satan whispered to me to find out, but I let him down, and did not heed his repeated calls.

I stared at her feet and was blown away by her beautiful toes, their nails painted aubergine. A trained beautician had done an excellent job. Her feet looked as if they walked on air, not the ground. I imagined myself touching them leisurely, like a visitor to a museum handling a rare artifact. I imagined myself unable to control myself and kissing them, toe by toe.

In a moment of abandon, I had a strong urge to spread her legs apart and drag her body until her ass was at the edge of the slab, then raise her legs up onto my shoulders to make penetration easier. I sketched the scene in my head and found it arousing and easy to put into practice. For a moment I thought I had devised it myself, but I remembered the same thing from a porn movie.

That such a body should wither away hurt. A body that many men must have wished to touch, embrace, or possess, and which they lodged in their imaginations, weaving dreams and fantasies around it. I was unable to treat it like a corpse. It still aroused emotions and the imagination. I felt that life was rippling through it despite its silence, the prelude to decomposition and decay.

I looked at it as though I was about to be sucked in. I snapped out of it when I became aware of the squeak of a wheelchair in the corridor. I covered up the girl, leaped over to the door, and stuck my head out. Nobody.

I left her covered for a little while then raised the cover and stood there holding it as though about to place it back over her body. Caution was essential in such circumstances. If the nun caught me leering hungrily, she would punish me by not allowing me near the corpses of women, leaving all the procedures for their corpses to herself and Robert.

My mind came up with a good idea. I dirtied the sheet with a little of the blood oozing from one of the corpses, so that if Sister Christine saw the body uncovered, I could claim I was changing it.

I was nervous. I checked the corridor from time to time. I walked up and down it, to make anyone who saw me think I was pacing to kill time. When I was reassured, I went back to the morgue and lifted the cover once again. I studied the body of the young woman as if seeing it for the first time, even though during my short absence, it had not left me. Wherever I looked, there it was.

On the nun's request, as relayed by one of the nurses, I didn't start readying the body for collection. That could happen for various reasons, and I didn't find it strange. I hoped I would be excused from stuffing and washing the corpse. If I was assigned the task, I was afraid I might not respect the sanctity of death. Sometimes, desire does not follow rules and brooks no objections, oblivious to the voice of conscience.

If I was assigned the task, there was nothing to stop me putting into practice what had occurred to me shortly before, particularly if I remained on my own in the morgue. I would never forgive myself if I carried out such a sin. I prayed to be saved from the experience I had played out in my mind, but which I did not intend to play out in practice. I prayed and was compelled to remember the body of the girl. The prayer invoked it rather than banishing it.

I didn't know why I was attracted to it in particular. I had seen corpses of girls and women, some beautiful, and not been aroused. Here in the morgue and also in surgery I gained a true knowledge of women's bodies. At the training camp, I had had the chance to screw the woman in the Honda, but I didn't venture to. At the village, I was fourteen when a Bedouin woman twenty years older than me taught me how. I often had sex with her under the fig tree and in the shack my grandfather had put up in the orchard.

I learned about sex as a teenager from the porn magazines I borrowed from Bou Zahran. He was an old man who behaved like a child and ostensibly sold lupine seeds, cotton candy, halva, and plums from his three-wheeled cart. I would conceal a magazine under my clothes and race off to be alone with myself.

The bodies of pinup girls were no different to the body of the girl prone on the cold slab. The difference was that those bodies were spread about, and those who made them emerge from the glossy colored paper, and slept with them in solitude, were limitless in number. The body of the girl stretched out now within reach of my hands, would not be shared with anyone. I had the power to do whatever I desired with it.

For an unknown reason, I longed to be able to leave the morgue and only return once the girl had gone. Running away would not make me forget the sight of her body sprawled on the slab but would stop me doing what I might regret for the rest of my life. I could not guarantee that I would be able to keep my cool, whether it was me preparing the corpse or the nun, who might ask me to help her in Robert's absence. If I helped her, I would be embarrassed. It would be excruciating if I had the chance to make a direct comparison between the girl and the nun. I would not judge fairly, because I was already biased toward the girl, even if I did not deny how much I liked the nun. My bias had nothing to do with the age difference between them, nor that I had seen the girl's naked body but had only seen the nun's hands, face, and neck. The reason for my partiality was the taste of farewell, since every time I saw the girl, I imagined I was seeing her for the last time.

In my imagination I went back to childhood with her. There she was, clutching her doll and falling asleep after her mother had told her an enjoyable story or sung her one of her favorite songs. Then she was nine, and I watched her at the mirror putting on lipstick and wearing her mother's high heels and carrying her purse. On to fourteen, and I saw her by the window waiting for the boy next door to pass by, and the letter he would throw her, which she would hide under her pillow or inside a book.

I imagined her as a young woman walking. Was there a seductive swagger to her walk or a gravity tinged with flirtation, I wondered? I imagined her talking. Was her voice high, medium, or low? Did she speak quickly or slowly, or in between? I imagined her smile and her frown, her wince when she hurt herself, and her moans when she climaxed, her composure, and her anger.

I was lost in a whirl of thoughts when I heard fragments of conversation coming from a room in emergency. I covered up the girl and stood by the door like someone bored of waiting. Sister Christine came in with Isabel, the Jester of Emergency, as we called her. When I saw Isabel, I was sure that I would be relieved of the job. I said bye to them and left and did not return to the morgue until the next morning, but the body of the girl did not leave me. Her body, not her corpse.

29

BEFORE GOING TO BED I would stroll on the hospital roof. That little break took me back to the village. Whenever I looked at the stars, I remembered Mum, when she saw me looking at the night sky, telling me not to count the stars so that my hands didn't end up covered with warts. I don't know where that superstition landed from. I had often wracked my brain and the brains of my friends, who had also heard the same warning from their mothers, but no one knew its source.

When I was a little older, I took to sitting on the mud-and-straw roof of our house in the evenings and watched the stars and the motion of the clouds passing beneath the moon. Mum's theory was disproved when I did count the stars. I waited for a month, but no warts—small and round like a chickpea or smaller—appeared on my skin.

The roof of our house often came to mind here at the hospital, where I spent the day between its four walls and corridors. When I walked around the courtyard, I only saw buildings hemmed in by buildings. As a son of the open country, I felt suffocated.

I took the radio and went up. I walked slowly, mostly looking into space, with the small device pressed against my ear. I studied the moon before it went behind the buildings. In the city, it isn't possible to enjoy its journey. Do lovers in Beirut have an intimacy with the moon like that of lovers in the village? Someone who doesn't love the moon cannot be in love, and in order to love it, you have to see it in its various phases: waning and waxing, as it rises and at the end of its traversal, shining bright when lonesome, and obscure when shrouded in clouds.

I changed my opinion of the village moon once I started to spy on the neighbor's daughter. A pleasant complicity developed between us. The moon alone observed my emotional adventures. I often relied on its light when going up and down to the roof. I confided my secrets to it and turned my back on it without fear. I had never heard of the moon stabbing someone in the back. That only happened in the world of man.

On the hospital roof, I only saw it briefly and, to compensate, I would keep watching. When it went out of sight, I searched for a station not playing martial songs and not pumping venom into its news broadcasts and commentary. I left it tuned into the station broadcasting one of Fairuz's plays. One of those plays which my father never tired of hearing, and which he convinced me to like because he praised Fairuz so extravagantly. He would say that her voice was a gift to the Rahbani brothers, since without it their poetry would never have reached the people.

During my nightly walk, I avoided the area that overlooked the nuns' house. As soon as I spotted a corner of the house, I turned back. I was afraid one of them would see me and get suspicious, then I would be under a fatal cloud.

I don't know why I broke that rule one night. Perhaps out of curiosity to learn something private about Sister Christine. Concealed by the darkness and by caution, I started walking in the area off-limits. I crossed it listening to the radio with my head down. My eyes, however, were aimed at the windows with identical curtains.

There were ten rooms, one for each nun. The house contained other rooms for guests, as well as a spacious lounge, a storeroom for provisions, a large dining room, and a kitchen managed by a cook, who was assisted by two young women under the supervision of Sister Clemence.

I hadn't visited the nun's house. Visits were only permitted to those with work to do, or a relative of the nuns. Nahla described it to me. She had been able to go inside quite a few times. She had had lunch with the nuns.

The lights were off in the ten rooms, even though the time was before ten thirty. The nuns slept early because they were used to getting up at dawn for morning Mass. I thought I was dreaming when one of the rooms was effused with a pale light. The light of a lamp in a corner of the room. Perhaps the occupant had woken up to go to the bathroom or for some other reason.

I walked slowly until I was directly opposite the room. I didn't see a shadow. That indicated that its resident hadn't come back from the bathroom yet or hadn't gotten out of bed. Perhaps she was having trouble sleeping and turned on the lamp to read something, the Gospels perhaps, to overcome her insomnia. There's nothing like reading to send you to sleep. Sister Christine said that she never went to sleep without reading, and that she read any book except the Gospels. Surprised by her admission, I asked her why. "Because I know every word by heart," she said.

Perhaps the nun in the room with the light on was Sister Christine. I wondered what book she kept at hand near her bed. Was it in Arabic or French? Did she read for pleasure or edification? What kind of books was she interested in?

I didn't seek answers, even though I was itching to know them. I was drawn to know intimate things about people I admired. Their daily habits, their bedrooms, the contents of their drawers, wardrobes, and desks. Anything connected with them that I didn't know. When I thought about Sister Christine, as I was looking at the light coming out of the window, I imagined the bed she was sleeping on; the colors of the bedspread and sheets and of the pillowcase; the color of her pajamas or her nightdress. I went further than that. I imagined her underwear. Did it differ from the underwear of laywomen? Did nuns have special nightclothes?

I interrupted the questions as soon as a shadow appeared. The pale light doubled its size, and it was impossible to make out the features that might lead to the identity of its owner. I saw the shadow bend over and disappear. The nun turned off the lamp and went back to bed.

30

I LOVED WORKING UNDER SISTER Christine, unlike most of my male and female colleagues. They'd rather have worked with the Devil than her, but they did admit that she was the only nun who'd been able to rescue the emergency department.

The nuns before her had failed, and the department almost fell apart into chaos. She came along and got it back on its feet, and it became the most productive and organized department at the hospital. With her strong personality she imposed herself. She didn't do anything extraordinary. She allotted roles, put the right person in the right place, and adopted a system of accountability. That specifically had been missing and caused the department to fall apart at the seams.

Sister Christine's marked success bolstered her position and she was listened to by the mother superior, who was in charge of the hospital and the nuns working there. She was showered with praise, and even the metropolitan himself congratulated her personally at a celebration held to mark the hospital's thirtieth anniversary.

Maintaining the success and fear of failure made her run the department strictly and treat the nurses firmly. This made those who disliked her outnumber those who liked her.

She never rested. The morning cup of coffee we had in the department, she drank standing up. I never once saw her sitting down, even when she came back from her village in the south with a limp and supported by a cane. They said she had slipped over and broken her leg. Some said she had fallen off a motorbike, and had it not been for the intervention of divine providence, she would have fallen into a gulley.

She was fastidious and always complaining. She chastised everyone in front of the patients and their relatives. She could not bear mistakes or those who shirked their duties and did not follow the rules.

A hell of a nun. Me, a convent-school boy until graduation, didn't know another nun like her. I knew cruel nuns, like Sister Phenomène, who taught geography. She hit us with an oak rod for trivial reasons: if we yawned in class; if we failed to pronounce the name of a country or city using her Beiruti way of saying it; if a student did not stand up when she entered the classroom. She often punished me by making me kneel in the corner by the door because I was looking at the birds outside and not the map that was the subject of the lesson.

Sister Phenomène was unjust because she picked on young pupils for reasons that did not warrant punishment. Sister Christine, however, was just because she ran the department inspired by the rules of the hospital. She didn't treat the nurses badly. She was fiercely protective if another nun tried to interfere in her department's business, and kept her off her territory.

She was made of different stuff. Few women were like her. Her favorites were lucky. None of the senior staff would dare say a harsh word to them whatever their mistakes, while their colleagues put on an outward show of affection but harbored envy.

I was one of the lucky ones. In the first few weeks, I did not feel the significance of the prestige I enjoyed with her; a prestige whose cause was unknown to me. Was the recommendation of the doctor for whom my cousin worked behind it, or some other reason?

I was the only one who used to make her laugh. None of the staff in the department had seen her teeth before I came along. That's what they said. They didn't know that I told her dirty jokes. I'd give odds of a thousand to one that she told them to her sister nuns at their evening gatherings. She wasn't shy to ask me for a new joke after a day or more had gone by without me telling her one. She seemed indifferent if the joke fell flat, but if it was a good one, she cracked up. She put her hand over her mouth and kept up a stifled laugh. I cadged jokes to guarantee her favor, and made them up if needed, but Sister Christine could tell the genuine article from the fake.

I liked her the first time I saw her. Then I started thinking about her. It wasn't just the way she looked that attracted me, but her mystique. Her voice stayed with me. In secret, all on my own, I would invoke its rare sweetness and also invoke her fingers and take flight. My fantasies did not exclude her mouth with its full lips, the lower lip especially, which protruded compared to the upper one. It always seemed to me that the words rested momentarily on it before reaching the person she was speaking to. It was enough to hear her voice for me to be filled with feelings that lightened my mood and made working in the morgue bearable.

When she stood next to me washing a corpse, I would perspire and my heart pound. It was so strong, I was afraid she would hear it. I couldn't conceal the shaking of my hands. Moving around and hard work warmed me up, but I felt cold. The gloves masked the coldness of my hands, but not the trembling. Fortunately, for the first two weeks Sister Christine put my trembling down to fear and lack of experience. I went along with her deduction to stop myself revealing the feelings I had toward her. My clothes absorbed the sweat coming out of my pores and hid my erection, which I had no control over in such circumstances.

What made me agree to continue working in the morgue was love. Without it I would not have endured so long. I was the only one of all those who'd come before who didn't turn around and leave after a month or two. It was the first time I experienced such feelings, wonderful and tortuous at the same time.

Many times, fantasy took me where I would not have dared go when fully conscious. For example, I wrote her a letter where I told her I loved her, and if it hadn't been for her I wouldn't have stayed in the morgue five minutes. I kept the letter for days. Then with the end of a lit cigarette I burned holes in it and tore it up. With every hole I smelled the words. My heart was burning, not the letter.

Once, I decided to confess to her face to face how much I liked her while we were preparing a corpse or whenever I could find an appropriate moment for such a confession. We worked on many corpses together, and I had many opportunities, but I didn't say it, and the decision remained pending.

I thought my confession would pave the way for her confession too. She wasn't an ordinary woman to take the initiative and open up her heart. She was a nun who had taken vows of chastity, obedience, and poverty. Breaking her vows was a sin that could only be absolved by His Holiness the Pope himself. Yet, at the same time, she was a flesh-and-blood woman. Her body had rights. She might curtail them with prayer and mortification some of the time, but not all the time. If she could bridle the hunger of the flesh, it was not a simple matter to bridle the raging heart's inclination to love. Perhaps she loved me and was waiting for me to reveal it first. She wasn't the first nun to fall in love and give up the cloth to follow the call of her heart and she wouldn't be the last.

My mother had been a nun. She fell in love with my father and left the convent, even though in becoming a nun she had gone against the will of her three brothers. She had told them, "It's my vocation, and none of your business." They didn't leave her be. They said, "You're our only sister, and we want to share your joy and see you with sons and daughters." She made them believe that she would not disappoint them, so they eased her confinement, but deep inside she was set on the matter. One day at dawn, she escaped with only the clothes she was wearing, helped by a taxi driver from the village. He took her to the convent and promised her that if he was asked, he would say he hadn't seen her and knew nothing about her.

My father, who taught Arabic at the convent school, took a fancy to the pious nun who was my Mum. He convinced her he loved her a lot and that having a successful Christian family was no less worthy than vowing herself as a bride of Christ. She was convinced, and they got married nineteen years ago. I was the fruit of their love. They had me after a year of marriage, and were content with me an only child, as they planned, not for any other reason.

I didn't intend to marry Sister Christine. She was older than me by at least seven years. For sure she would not accept me as a husband. That's if I assumed she decided to throw off her nun's robes and return to ordinary life.

Perhaps in Sister Christine I loved the nun who had been my mother. My far away mother who I now imagined going through photographs of me in the hope that it would make her miss me less. My Mum, whose tenderness or contented smile I never found the likes of, nor any bread better than the bread she made in thin sheets on a hot metal plate. I imagined her listening, her hand over her heart, to the names being read out on the radio after every round of shelling, and taking a deep breath when her son's name wasn't among the victims.

No, I didn't see my mother in Sister Christine. From first sight, I saw the woman, not the nun. Ambiguous reality sometimes made it seem that she reciprocated love for love, and the world would become garbed in wonderful bright colors. Sometimes I felt I was living a one-sided love, my side, and the days dressed in black. Every now and then, hope would spark again following some action of hers that I translated to fit with my fancies and I rebuilt the dreams that I soon realized were nothing but fantasy.

While I was in love with the nun and had eyes for no one else, Nahla, my colleague in the department, had a secret passion for me. Robert pointed it out. "She devours you with her eyes," he said, proud to be an expert about women, and their eyes. I became sure of her fondness for me when I went back over some incidents.

She was often friendly to me in the cafeteria, and for weeks she sat at the same table as me and we shared our food. I had the dish of the day prepared by the hospital kitchen, while she brought food from home. More than once at lunch she whispered that she wished the place was empty so that she could put her feet up on my knees to give them a rest from standing up for so long. I didn't take that desire of hers as having any inappropriate intent. I believed she was tired out and wanted to relax. All of us in the department spent our eight-hour shifts on our feet.

A few times, she asked me to rub her shoulders. They hurt her, since they suffered from what she called cramps. She claimed she turned to me because my hands were strong and were used to getting rid of the cramp and easing her shoulders. When I gave her a massage, she would be wearing her pinafore with a blouse or T-shirt beneath, and I deliberately worked my fingers under them so that they touched her shoulders and I could feel their softness. I would massage them gently at times and quite roughly at others, which was how she always insisted for certain spots on her back. Whenever my fingers went over her shoulders and the upper part of her back, she relaxed and stifled the groans that revealed I was making her happy. That happiness was not the result of the absence of pain, but from the sensation produced by my hands running soothingly over part of her body.

During the massage, she rotated her head right and left, and I would hear the sound of her neck vertebrae cracking. I discovered afterward that massaging the back of her neck in a way that combined hardness and softness turned her on. I concentrated on that tender spot and she squirmed in silence, worried that someone might notice how aroused she was. I also got aroused and hid it by having superficial conversations with Nahla herself, or one of our colleagues, to give the impression that there was nothing more to it than an innocent massage, and that nothing was happening to us physically.

I remember that she often volunteered to massage the shoulders of any female colleague who asked me to do it. She wanted me as her exclusive masseur. I didn't care about such behavior. I was somewhere else entirely. There was only one woman on my mind: Sister Christine.

I can't remember the number of times I didn't fulfill Nahla's request for a shoulder rub, always giving a different excuse: my hands hurt; a corpse needed urgent attention. . . . I refused because I thought that Sister Christine would get angry if she saw me touching another woman, and she would take her revenge, whose intricacies and timing God alone knew, against me or Nahla or against the pair of us. I got jealous when I saw her and Robert whispering together or when she joked with him and laughed at a comment he made. If ordinary situations like that inflamed my jealousy, then how would *she* react to my hands touching a woman's body for ten minutes, and sometimes for longer? I avoided hurting her feelings, not just by refusing to give a massage to Nahla or any other of the nurses in the department in her presence, but by refusing to joke with them too.

When she caught me massaging Nahla, she would pass quickly by without looking at us, as if we weren't there. I would feel embarrassed and wished I was able to shrink so it would be easy to hide.

At other times, it was the opposite. I deliberately appeared happy when massaging Nahla and raised my voice if she passed by during the massage and didn't notice us—for real, not pretend. I wanted to know how she would react. If she loved me, she would avoid looking once, twice, three times, but in the end though she would show her hand. If I was just another member of staff to her, she wouldn't care.

However, her darting glances at us, me in particular, held both indifference and interest at the same time. At least, that's how I read those looks. Perhaps I read indifference by mistake, because deep inside I wanted her to declare her jealousy. More than that, I wanted her to order me to stop such actions, the massaging, during my shift. If that had happened, I would have been the happiest person in the world. But it didn't happen. I remained swinging on a pendulum of doubts. The situation continued until I adjusted. Confusion strangles love if the bright star of certainty does not shine through the doubts.

Nahla might have been the only person who suspected I was attracted to the nun, but she pretended not to know, confident that the attraction did not cross any lines, and certain that the nun would never stoop to an experience that might, if it became known, destroy the promising future awaiting her as a nun. Also, events proved to her that in the eyes of the nun I was just a member of staff whom she had taken under her wing when he started work so that he didn't feel a stranger. That was nothing new, because Sister Christine had treated those who worked before me in the same way. Nahla had her finger on the pulse of the department: she knew all and sundry and what was being cooked up in corners. With feminine intuition, she could have discovered that the nun held special feelings for me. She wasn't blind. She didn't lack alertness and sharp powers of observation, or the experience derived from much daily contact with all kinds of people.

After Nahla told me how much she liked me, she was unable to conceal her jealousy and expressed it in various ways: she concentrated on work and only spoke when necessary; she ate alone and did not sit with me as usual in the cafeteria (that was if her jealousy caught fire before noon); she avoided looking at me if we met in the corridor or elsewhere, and if she did look it was with fierce reproach; she would leave at the end of her shift without saying goodbye and without having talked to me for a few minutes at the morgue door when I had work, or at the entrance to the department as was usual.

But her sulk did not last long. The morning meeting of the emergency staff around the coffeepot dissipated the dregs of the day before. She often brought me a cup of coffee, as a sign that she intended to start her day by turning over a new leaf.

Mostly I drank my coffee with my head down to avoid looking at the nun and not hurt Nahla's feelings. I also avoided looking at Nahla in the belief that doing so might annoy the nun. Being absent from the meeting was not an option, although that would have spared me the awkwardness. I liked the conversations and the comments that punctuated them, and enjoyed the aroma of the coffee that filled the room more than drinking it.

The first time I felt the heat of Nahla's femininity, and wished we were alone together away from everyone, was the afternoon of September 10, 1979. She always reminded me of that date, because, in her words, it reminded her she was still alive. (The newspapers called it the 'War of the Hospitals' after hospitals in East and West Beirut were shelled.) We were immersed at work when shells started to fall around the hospital. We all— male and female nurses, patients, and visitors—gathered in one of the safest rooms in the department. By chance, I found myself in the same corner as her.

The bombing shook the hospital and prayers accompanied the quaking of hearts, the knocking of knees, and the groans of those in pain. Things continued like that until a shell landed on the top floor. Nahla, shaking with fright, turned around and grabbed me. I grabbed her, and my face lodged between her neck and shoulder. I inhaled her perfume which was infused with her sweat. I had inhaled it many times when she passed close to me in the morning before its intensity faded. It's impossible for me to describe the softness of her skin and the warmth brushing me and spreading through my being. I also felt strands of her hair tickling me. Her black hair was confined by her white cap, but when free it flowed halfway down her back. I drew my lips lightly from the top of her shoulder up to behind her ear, following the curve of her beautiful neck. Despite the fear and the critical situation, the path of my lips caused her body to tremble, and goose bumps appeared that my lips sensed immediately.

In my heart I prayed that more bombs would rain down on the hospital so that our embrace did not end. God answered my prayer. A shell landed on the nuns' house, and voices rose in supplication again. Nahla and I carried on hugging. She had her arms tight around me, and I didn't know if that was down to panic or the desire our brief clasp had sparked in her body, or both those reasons combined. Her proximity to me made my body shudder right through and I closed my eyes as if in ecstasy. I did not want to open them before I was full of her. I felt her breasts brush my chest, and her thighs brush mine. I squeezed her waist closer toward me in the hope she would feel how aroused I was. For a few moments I imagined she had bent down and buried her head under my coat and was bringing me relief.

When her mouth rippled over my neck, I filled with pure joy. Her breaths were saturated with the desire that might have been kindled by fear of possible, or imminent, death. I don't know where I read that desire flares up with the approach of death. Her hands roamed over me as if she wanted to depart this life hugging someone she loved.

The shelling quieted down, and everyone remained where they were in expectation of its starting again. Nahla and I remained in the corner. She was standing in front of me observing the terrified faces yellow with fear and listening to comments from here and there. Our bodies were no longer stuck together, so that we didn't draw anyone's attention. I brought my knee toward her legs and placed it between them, and she squeezed her legs around it. That position was not discernible because other people were standing in front of us. From time to time, I placed my left hand on the left side of her waist. She raised her hand when she was certain we were safely out of sight and took my hand. Her fingers entwined with mine, then she unclasped them and with her palm started stroking the back of my hand. I moved slightly away from her and gave people looks to camouflage what was going on between us.

Once we were sure the bombing had stopped, since we no longer heard the echoes of the blasts or the whistle of the shells as they passed, everyone left the room, and we returned to work.

In the department, I and Nahla spent the rest of the day exchanging looks brimming with an unfulfilled desire that we could not satisfy. Those moments, less than an hour, had been enough to take us from one side of the river to the other. We took to meeting alone. One of us would kiss the other as though we would never meet again. Our stolen kisses recurred: in the department when the atmosphere permitted a few snatched seconds; in the lift, which, provided we were alone, we went up and down in again and again; and on the stairs to the cafeteria. Whenever I kissed her and returned to the morgue, I avoided looking in Sister Christine's eyes, so she didn't see something in my eyes I didn't want her to know.

Nahla didn't invite me home. During our conversations over lunch, she dropped many hints to make me understand that no man had entered her house since her husband's disappearance, not even his brothers. She often mentioned that her neighbors had tongues worse than vipers, and that her son was alert and would not be happy to see a strange man with his mum at home.

I did not mention going to her house, although I wanted her to invite me for a cup of coffee, an innocent invitation that concealed behind it what it concealed. Our quick meetings at the hospital were torture for both of us. There was nowhere for us to put out the burning desires.

If the room where I slept had been safe, I would have invited her in, even though I was sure she wouldn't agree. I would have tried to persuade her to come after making a surefire plan. The room was empty for most of the day. The problem was getting to it, since it meant going past a number of rooms some of whose doors were often left open. The rooms were allocated to trainee doctors for them to rest between shifts and between operations. They were not permanent residents, but stayed for six months then left, then another group took their place. For that reason, as soon as I got along well with most of them, their training period came to an end and they left. It was possible, under the cover of friendship, to ask those who happened to be in the rooms to close their doors when the situation demanded. Unfortunately, the reality wasn't like that. I couldn't ask a person to whom I only said good evening and good morning to close the door of his room.

I wasn't sure she would come, even assuming that getting to the room was easy. She was cautious. She worried about her reputation, especially as everyone knew and respected her. Her caution went as far as paranoia. She often broke off from our furtive kisses and hurried off, leaving me standing in amazement at her illogical reaction, particularly when the opportunity was a good one. I got used to that behavior and was surprised when she acted differently. I would ask myself what had induced her to change. I put it down to the longing that she could only translate into kisses.

We carried on like that, a few furtive kisses here and there, until Bou Moussa took pity on me and lent me his VW car for a night. I promised him that I would ask the woman I was going out with to bring a friend along next time for him to meet. I didn't tell him that I was in a relationship with Nahla, that she was the woman I was borrowing his car for. He knew her well, and I wasn't sure he wouldn't divulge the secret if I told him. Besides, I'm not the type who brags about his adventures with women, which are mostly figments of the imagination anyway.

Nahla was delighted when she knew about the car. We agreed a time and place and met three hours after the shift ended. I drove her in the car. It was raining that night. She said that she hated the winter but liked going out in the rain and exchanging kisses under an umbrella. She wished the car had had a tape player, so we could listen to a tape of Fairuz songs together. She opened her purse and gave me the tape for me to listen to later and think of her.

When we reached the place that Bou Moussa had suggested, which was next to a well-known resort, I parked the car on a dune close to the sea. The sound of the waves was audible, and the foam spreading over the beach glistened in the dark. If a distant streetlight had not cast a faint glow over us, neither of us would have seen the other's face. I loved that place, because the road leading to it came to an end, and only those heading for the resort used it.

I was happy when I saw that she was relaxed. She repeated what she'd said before and committed to memory. She said that I was the first man she had been involved with since her husband, and it was the first time she had been in love with a man three years her junior. She swore on her son's life that if she didn't love me and trust me completely she would never have agreed to go out with me at night. She said that she didn't consider what had happened and was happening between us as cheating, because it was born out of love, not physical hunger. She told me that in her heart she felt her husband wasn't missing. He wasn't coming back. She said that she didn't know of anyone who had been missing for two years during the war and come back. She cried. She put her head in her hands in an effort to stop her crying and bent forward until her face was on her knees. I left her to cry. Perhaps she needed to let it all out in order to relax.

Then she sat up, took her jacket off, and threw it on the back seat. She came closer and I took her in my arms. When she calmed down, I started softly kissing her neck. She melted and pulled me toward her. Then she drew her head away and kissed me like she never had before. She thrust her tongue into my mouth. I took it in, then thrust my tongue into her mouth, and she took it. I found this delicious and I sent the ball back into her court and she responded. While I was kissing her, my hand slipped under her thin sweater and groped around her shoulders and upper back. Then it found the clasp of the bra and, with some difficulty, undid the two hooks. She did not react. I thought that perhaps she hadn't felt me unclip her bra. I was worried she would refuse and think that I had brought her to this place for that end alone.

My suspicion was out of place. She seemed responsive, so much so that she only released my lips from her mouth to take them back again. Once they were free, I immediately bent down to her breasts which looked beautiful under her blouse. Her bra was still cupping them, so I removed it, sniffing at it with eyes closed and inhaling the heavenly perfume lingering in the cups where her breasts had rested. I contemplated her breasts once they were at hand. They were taut and firm despite their size. I rubbed my face on them. I kissed them, taking pleasure in them. I sucked the nipples, chewing them with my lips. Her breasts were as I imagined them before seeing them. I don't deny that I had caught sight of them without her knowing and without her intending to reveal them to seduce me. She often had to bend over at work to lift a patient or pick something off the floor, and part of her chest would become visible. Whenever I needed company during my secret flights, I remembered the image of her breasts in the department.

I helped her pull her jeans off. Then I got out of the car and went over to the other side. I opened the door and reclined her seat. She leaned back into it and I lay on top of her, after also removing my jeans. The small car started rocking with us. It seemed to me, momentarily, in the midst of our vigorous motion, that the parking brake released as a result of the vibration and the car rolled down the beach with us and into the sea.

As we rocked to the rhythm of our bodies, the rain pattered on the roof and windshield of the car in a melody I had long wished to hear with a woman in such a situation. Now, however, I paid no attention to the melody until we were about to get dressed.

Our panting had steamed up the windows and stopped us seeing around us. It was like we were inside a cloud. Two prisoners uninterested in freedom but only in remaining inside the cage of mist they had built with their breaths, words, and moans of pleasure. With a finger she wrote on the residue of our panting, 'I love you' and drew a heart with an arrow through it. Then beneath the words and the drawing she signed her name, threw herself into my arms, and hugged me.

The whole way back, she rested her head on my shoulder. Her hand stayed in mine until we were near where she lived. She got out in the street parallel to her street to avoid one of the neighbors seeing her get out of a strange car in the middle of the night. Also out of caution she did not want to kiss me as she was getting out. She was just content to kiss the tip of the finger she had used to write 'I love you' in the condensation and put it to my lips. I kissed it.

I waited till she disappeared into the darkness of the alleyway and returned to the hospital.

31

THE HOSPITAL WAS A WORLD of its own.

I discovered that from living there. My view from outside was totally different to the view from inside.

When I heard Sister Christine describe the hospital as a cabaret, I was amazed that a nun should compare a hygienic, humanitarian place like a hospital to a commercial, brazen place like a cabaret. I wondered how she could make such a comparison, given that she had never even been in a cabaret, and did not know what went on behind the scenes at night. I answered the question myself: Robert, who had worked at a nightclub, might have told her about behind the scenes. Maybe her information came from films and novels.

At the time, I didn't understand why she used that description, which left an impression that came to mind on various occasions. She said that the hospital like a cabaret was visited by rich and poor, cruel and kind, atheist and believer, the thief and those who earned their bread by the sweat of their brow, the chaste and the whoring. She said that you had to get along with everyone and put up with their annoying dispositions, their body odor, their stupidity in some cases, and with all of that you had to smile and be patient.

I didn't know anything about nightclubs, except the one time I went with Guevara, Conger, and Charno to Weeds. That was when we met Domino, who got down on all fours on stage and the girls took turns riding him. An unforgettable night. Still, I couldn't claim that I was a regular at bars and an expert on clubs. Robert told me about his work at the club Etoile de l'Aube, and I gained an impression.

Just as nothing remained hidden in a club, the same applied at the hospital. It was as though the walls had eyes and ears twenty-four hours a day. Reports and stories were always doing the rounds. When you heard them, you couldn't work out whether they had really happened or had been made up by an imagination fed only by gossip and the trashing of reputations. New reports circulated every morning. Should a morning lack fresh news, the stale was given another airing.

For example: Nurse so-and-so slipped into the cardiologist's clinic whenever she found the chance, and come out a quarter of an hour later, her face aglow with happiness, while the doctor went back to work as if nothing had happened.

The nurse responsible for the radiology department took a risk with a handsome patient when she was getting him set for an X-ray. The man submitted to her caresses. Her colleagues were in earshot in the next room.

The apparently saintly anesthetist was caught in the bathroom with a cleaner. They said the cleaner was the active partner and the doctor the passive. I was dubious about that report until the doctor started coming on to me. I made him understand that I was straight. So that he didn't try it on again, I said I would agree to a relationship with him provided I could also sleep with his wife.

The night switchboard operator listened in on calls and blackmailed married women patients having affairs, some of whom paid up. One day he fell into the hands of a woman who knew how to take her revenge. He spent a week bedbound after her husband or her lover sent someone to teach him a lesson with a big stick in the hospital parking lot.

Many times at the end of the night a male nurse would be caught in a female patient's bed, or a female nurse between the thighs of a male patient, not for medical reasons, but because the night was long and she wished to make him and herself happy.

Even the nuns were not safe from venomous tongues. Sister Fontaine was witnessed putting her hand on the ass of trainee doctor Alphonse. Before Alphonse, Wadie's ass had been the resting place for the nun's hand as he went back and forth. They called her the nun with a taste for a nice ass.

Sister Fabiola, who was over fifty, had a penchant for young guys. Whenever she came across one, she pinched his cheek and stroked his face with her palm. Straightaway, her chubby cheeks blushed red and her eyes gleamed strangely. They called her the patron saint of the young.

Sister Christine, though, was the nun who was most often the subject of gossip because she was the best looking of them. Not only that, she was better looking than all the nurses and the rest of the staff. They said the metropolitan was crazy about her. He never said no to her. They said she liked dirty jokes. (That was true, and I have proof.) They said she had a complex about men, since it was incomprehensible that a young woman as beautiful as her would have become a nun if a failed love affair wasn't involved. They said that her aversion to men had messed with her desires until she inclined toward women. (That's baseless, and I also have proof.)

They talked about her extreme thrift, and said she never threw anything away that might be of use. In an empty biscuit tin she put her sewing kit. She kept empty cans of olive oil and sent them to her mother who filled them with rose water, orange blossom water, or vinegar, or any of the drinks they made in her village. She kept empty tubs of halva to put left-overs in. They said that when she was young she always licked the lid of the ice-cream tub, as though "Please lick the lid" was a direction for use.

No one was spared vicious and sarcastic gossip, not even those who made it up. I didn't know what they said about me when I was out of earshot. Had the walls observed me looking hungrily at the nun, watching her walk until she went out of sight? Fortunately, such eyes could not perceive the desires and secrets of the heart.

Nahla and I often wondered whether anyone knew about us. Did they know and only discuss it in our absence? Did the nun know but keep it secret because she liked and respected Nahla and was fond of me?

We often wished that someone from the department would tell me or tell Nahla the gossip about us. We were burning to know whether our furtive kisses had remained unseen and unremarked upon. True, we ate lunch together most days, but we rarely sat just the two of us at a table in the cafeteria. There were always other people with us. The tables were few, the staff many, and the break short. The cup of coffee she poured out and brought to me at the morning meeting was not proof of a relationship between us. She sometimes poured the coffee for other people, and also brought it to them.

I confess that the gossip fascinated me, especially when there was more to come. Just like the TV serials, we waited for the next episode to keep up with the plot. That was virtually our only diversion in the midst of people's pain and the drudge of work. There were endless stories. Some were boring and lacked excitement. Some forced you to ask how it would all turn out.

There were horrible stories of doctors who hid their black hearts with their white coats. I wished I had never heard them so that the halo that I ascribed to doctors did not slip off. I considered a doctor a demi-god who saved you from death when you were seriously ill, eased your pain, and cared for you until you were cured.

I did not believe that a doctor could operate on a patient unnecessarily, just for the money, which benefited him and the hospital. However, there were many examples of such doctors who made patients believe that their condition required an operation and sent them to hospital. Among them were people who had gone into debt or sold a piece of land or pawned their wife's or mother's jewelry to meet the costs of the operation. Doctors who trafficked in the pain of the poor, exploiting their ignorance about medical matters and their absolute confidence in medics, so that they could drive the most expensive cars, live in the most beautiful houses, and educate their children at the most prestigious schools. When their crimes come to light, they should be hung up by their feet at hospital entrances and their corpses thrown to the dogs.

I thought that taking a commission only applied to some fields of business and real estate. That it was also widespread among doctors came as a shock. If a doctor referred a patient whose condition was outside his specialization to a colleague, he would ask for a cut. Imagine, a doctor selling the drugs he got as promotional freebies to his patients at half price. A doctor bribing the admissions clerk and the nurses to send patients to him and not a rival doctor. In contrast, there were doctors who did good. For them medicine was a vocation, not a profession. Sadly, they were few in number.

During my work in surgery, I got to know most of the doctors at the hospital. Over time, I became able to distinguish a skilled doctor from one who quaked in fear at the prospect of anything unexpected happening during an operation, like a mistake or something that went beyond his scientific knowledge. When a doctor made an error, he became disconcerted and disconcerted the team assisting. I, the new member of staff, discovered that a mistake had been made when the anesthetist standing by the head of the patient started exchanging looks with the intern assisting and the supporting nurse, looks that mixed anxiety and discomfort. Those looks worried me, and I inferred from them that the patient was inevitably heading for the morgue, unless there was divine intervention and a miracle saved him. I often saw patients go into surgery alive and leave as corpses. In the morgue I gave those corpses special treatment because

I had seen and spoken to their owners when they were getting ready for the operation. In a place like surgery, death became one of its rituals. It left behind a transient sadness that passed as soon as the corpse left the department.

A cruel world—the world of hospitals.

32

Two exhausting weeks went by. Nonstop work in the operating theater at night and in the morgue by day. I was collapsing from tiredness and felt almost unable to support my body. If I got a moment to sit down, it was an effort to stand up again. What made it worse was that you heard only orders and were told you weren't any good. Words of encouragement that might give a worker a boost were out of circulation. Complaining or raising your voice wasn't allowed, even if you had to work overtime.

I was about to go up to the cafeteria for lunch before it shut for cleaning at four o'clock sharp, when the nun called me. I knew immediately what awaited. The way she called me, and others, during a shift was different to the way she did it once the shift was over. In the former there was an imperious tone, while in the latter there was a hint of kindness and affection.

I didn't ask her what she wanted after I saw a number of workers and nurses heading for the storeroom. There was a truck full of medicine and medical supplies. A donation from a charity in West Germany, they said. This wasn't the first truckload. Trucks from other charities had come before, whose cargo we took to the same place.

Unloading the truck took three hours. Twenty of us formed a line from the truck to the storeroom, with about one meter between each of us, and passed the boxes from the first person to the second and so on to the twentieth, quickly to begin with, then slowly when tiredness set in and arms flagged.

The storeroom filled up. Boxes piled on boxes that had become lairs for rats and mice. Some of them were definitely not fit for use. It wasn't just the smell that told us that, but the fact that boxes piled up in the corners were virtually unreachable. These were left over from donations that had flowed to community groups and hospitals. Unfortunate victims and displaced people, the intended recipients, had never benefited from them.

I don't know why the hospital kept all those medicines, which was more than needed. I didn't ask so that the question didn't reach the ears of management and annoy them and brand me a troublemaker. Here at the hospital, just like at the barracks, it was sensible not to ask questions unless it was directly relevant to your work.

One question, however, I could not shake off, and it changed my view of many things: why did the hospital charge patients for donated medicine? Even those wounded by shelling or fighting and the poor weren't exempt from payment.

I saw injured people who did not belong to any party bleed for hours at the entrance to emergency unable to find a doctor to treat them because the hospital had refused them admission on the pretext that there were no empty beds. Some of them died during the hunt for a room at another hospital. I can't bring myself to recall the hard cases I witnessed. They were many and heartrending.

A mother in her forties with a shrapnel wound to her chest dying with the cries of her three children ringing in her ears because she didn't have the money for treatment. An Egyptian worker hopping about with his hand half cut off, pleading from the outside courtyard of the hospital for a doctor to ease his pain. An old homeless man who stayed at the entrance to emergency for a whole day until he passed away. Poignant scenes did not rouse mercy in people's hearts.

Party members, however, and their relatives to the umpteenth degree, found the doors wide open, and enjoyed generous service and care. No one uttered a cry of protest when their visitors came and went in their muddy boots, with their weapons and their argy-bargy. The administration, from top to bottom, mollified them with smiles and greetings.

Frequently, we took medicines out of boxes that were stamped as donated. On the orders of the administration, and under the oversight of a nun, we removed the stamp. Sister Christine would say that the hospital was heavily in debt to the state, and that the money made from selling donations plugged the gap and paid part of the wage bill.

Only hospitals benefited from the war. Their owners got rich, and even so they still complained endlessly and stuck out their hands to beg. Their motto was "Complain and prosper." The emergency department used up part of those donations, and it took the cost of treatment in cash from the patient. Treatment (setting an arm or a leg in a cast, third and lesser degree burns, an injection after a dog bite, and so on) mostly only took a few minutes, and the patient paid and left.

Sister Christine was personally in charge of receiving the money. She put it in the drawer of the small table that she bent over writing out receipts. What the nun was doing was out-and-out theft. There was no other explanation for the sale of charitable donations given by Europeans and Arabs for handing out free of charge to the poor of this unfortunate country.

The staff knew all about it and participated knowingly or otherwise, but they could not object. If they did, it might cost them their jobs. Nobody was happy about their salary. I was shocked when I found out that some staff made only just above the minimum even though they'd been in the job for more than ten years.

I also felt exploited. The money I made, even though I was new, did not equate with the effort I made. No one else at the hospital worked in two places: the morgue and surgery. No one else was on shift day and night like me.

The sense of unfairness drove me to the verge of heresy whenever I saw the nun playing with the money as she calculated the day's takings, while us hard-working staff deprived ourselves of clothes and food. Deprivation did not make us immune from borrowing off each other or for asking for an advance against your wages.

There's no justice in this life.

33

WHENEVER I FELT AGGRIEVED, I looked for excuses to lessen the effect on me, but sometimes I despised myself after making an effort and only hearing words of blame rather than praise. At a moment of clarity, I devised a plan to still my aggravation and restore my self-esteem.

This plan, just like all plans, was waiting for the right moment to begin. That moment arrived when the nun forgot her bunch of keys on the table when she had hurried out after hearing a shout in the next room. I had my eyes peeled and grabbed the opportunity I had long awaited.

I picked up the keys and followed after her to give them back. In a movement only perfected by professional conjurors, I pressed the key for the drawer onto a piece of putty I kept for that purpose in a matchbox. Then I put the bunch back on the table and did not hand them to the nun. Luckily, no one had noticed me, or so I assumed.

The shout had secured the right moment, and I exploited it. Chances didn't come twice. The putty had been in my pocket for about two weeks, during which time I had been unable to copy the key. I was careful to keep the box in good condition. I hid it under a corpse and would collect it when it was time to go up to the room.

At the end of my shift, I changed my clothes and left for a key-cutting shop in a neighborhood far from the hospital, even though there was a similar shop close by. In cases like this, caution was essential. No one knows what the future holds in store. Perhaps the nun would notice that the money in the drawer was short and suspect that a strange hand had opened it using a key, not by force. Then she might send the original key with a nurse she trusted to the shop nearby to ask its owner whether he had made a key like that for someone. If the man said yes, he would be pumped with questions: Can you describe the person you cut the key for? When did he come? Would you recognize him if you saw him?

Before adopting the idea of copying the key, I often saw the drawer full of banknotes of every denomination, some of whose edges peeked out of the drawer. Many times I managed to get a hold on the edge of a note, making good use of my long fingernails. As soon as I extracted it, I folded it up and palmed it or put it in the pocket of my apron. Often, when no nurses were in the room with the table, I tried to pull the drawer open. Perhaps the nun had forgotten to lock it.

At the shop, a solitary man sat behind an antique table. I couldn't tell whether he was the owner or an employee. I gave him the putty and asked him to cut two copies of the key. When he looked at the matchbox, I was worried he would ask an awkward question, because thieves often used this technique. But he looked at me and was content to state the price. I didn't haggle, contrary to my habit. I paid up, and claimed I had work to do. Before I left, I asked him when I should come back for the keys. "No more than an hour," he said as he compared the putty with the rack of keys behind him so as to choose the right key to cut grooves like the imprint in the putty.

I wanted two keys cut for two reasons. If I lost one, I had a spare. It was possible the opportunity would not arise again, since the nun would have to forget the bunch of keys and I would have to re-imprint the key in putty. The second reason was the possibility that the grooves on the key didn't fit the grooves of the padlock, and I would have to file them a little or a lot. I couldn't exclude the possibility that I might file badly and so damage the grooves and make the key useless. Then I would file the second key, taking advantage of my experience with the first.

I avoided waiting at the shop so that the man didn't memorize my features and clock my accent. Remaining silent wasn't feasible, for if I didn't start a conversation, he would. Politeness required that I join in and exchange a few words. Returning in an hour was a good solution. If he only saw me for a few minutes, he might forget my face, but if I hung around for an hour, it would be imprinted in his mind. This too was out of caution. He also might face questioning if a case was opened against persons unknown after the mechanics of the theft came to light.

I went back ten minutes after the agreed time, took the keys, and walked back. I liked walking in the evening after a day spent standing up. As I walked, I imagined myself keeping tabs on the room where the drawer was and at the right moment, hurrying over with the key and trying to open it. I felt a shudder of fear go through my whole body even though I was still imagining it. What would happen in the real world? Different scenarios occurred to me.

First, the drawer opens easily. The key turns in the padlock like the original key. I pull out some banknotes. (No need to be greedy, so it isn't obvious and the nun realizes the money is short. Like that, the plan and the proceeds keep going.) I slip out of the room as if on air, and head straight to the morgue. I hide the money under the ass of a corpse, or in the pocket of an unwashed corpse. Then I pick it up at the end of my shift and take it up to the room. I put it in the bag for my dirty socks. I'm sure no one would dare go near it because of the smell.

Second, the drawer doesn't open. I insert the key and turn it left and right, but it doesn't turn fully. I leave the room, giving an impression of nonchalance as I hum a tune so as to seem surrounded by a host of angels. I go away and think about which groove has stopped the drawer opening so I can file it down a little. Then I try again.

Third, as I'm about to open the drawer, I hear the jangling of keys or the sound of footsteps or a slight cough, and I disappear.

The fourth scenario almost made me give up trying, but I didn't give it much weight. I excluded its happening provided I was careful and planned every step.

When I arrived back at the hospital, a frightening feeling possessed me. I felt that all the workers in emergency could see the two keys in my pocket and knew my scheme and what I intended to do. I walked past them like a condemned man on his way to the gallows.

34

"A MORGUE IS A GOLDMINE." A line whispered to me by a guy who claimed to have worked a few years in a morgue at some hospital. I didn't get what he meant until later. In time I was convinced. He came to mind when I caught Robert red-handed. I saw him pocket a banknote he took from the father of a dead guy whose body he had just finished preparing.

The man wasn't one of Robert's relatives or neighbors. I knew most of them and often helped them out at the hospital when he wasn't there. As soon as he saw me he looked shifty. That raised questions for me. The questions prompted suspicions about similar incidents I recalled. I had often seen him talking with someone's next of kin. I thought he might be consoling him, or knew him, or was introducing himself. He was the type who liked to strike up relationships and interfere in visitors' business.

My suspicions were soon confirmed. Whenever Robert took a step to get close to me, doubt took a step closer to certainty. I found out why he disliked me and made up stories to cast doubt on my competence and honesty at work. With those stories he intended to sow a bad idea about me in the mind of the administration, in the hope that it would take root and I would get fired. At that point, the field would be open to him and he would get all the tips to himself.

He thought himself the victor when we agreed to split the tips. "Fifty-fifty," he said as he split the air in two with his hand.

The expression was current in my village, especially among the gamblers, but I didn't recall ever having used it. I needed the money. Those suffering like me in a city that had no mercy for strangers had to save up for the days to come. The agreement did not last long, though.

Robert was very suspicious. He had doubts about how much money I was getting and made up his mind that I was a liar and double-crossing him. He often accused me of being greedy, but I wasn't a liar. I was pleased with what the families of the dead gave, and, when we were away from prying eyes, I gave him half the tip.

His constant suspicion of me made me suspicious of him. I started keeping an eye on him. More than once, I was certain he was cheating me. He put the money in his pocket, but, when he came over to me, he took a banknote out of his other pocket, pretending it was the one he had just received. When he kept doing it, I felt he was taking me for a fool. It wasn't like me to keep quiet about such behavior, and I confronted him at the critical moment. He swore he wasn't cheating me. I didn't believe him. He insisted, and I insisted that he show me what was in his other pocket. He confessed and asked me to forgive him, claiming he hadn't done it before.

Our mutual suspicions led us to come to a new arrangement. The new arrangement worked out, and things went perfectly. It had one provision: each of us would take the whole tip, however large, for washing a corpse, provided we took turns. Neither of us had the right to wash two corpses one after another and take the tip unless the other was unable to take his turn for work reasons. To keep things equal, they had the right afterward to wash two corpses and keep the tips.

We also agreed that our personal relationship should be limited, so as not to rouse suspicions among the staff who enjoyed chitchat. Everyone knew that we were as good as enemies. If he was present, I withdrew. If I was present, he withdrew, and if the pair of us stayed in the same place, we avoided looking at each other except askance.

We kept up the image. Outwardly, our relationship continued to appear prickly. He told me what was said about me behind my back, and I did the same for him. Later on, it turned out that the plan served both of us and saved me from a sticky situation that almost caused me to get fired, not to mention the possibility of going to jail.

We often swapped information in a whisper as we washed a corpse. Bent over, to someone passing, especially the nun, we looked hard at work. I worried that Sister Christine would pick up a signal that revealed our complicity and ruin my image with her. She would regret having treated me well if I let her down. She might, if she knew, withdraw her protection, and I would become easy prey for those out to harm me. Working without protection at the hospital exposed the staff to plots that could strike out of the blue.

I think Sister Christine knew about the tips and turned a blind eye. It wasn't just Robert and me who got tips, most of the nurses did. Previously, the administration had banned it for the hospital's reputation, but backtracked on the ban when it proved impossible to enforce. Salaries were meager and prices went up day by day, and they were going to deprive you of tips? It was as though they were fighting against the virtue of generosity enjoined by all religions. Jesus himself, symbolized by the crosses hanging on the chests of the nuns, said to the rich man, "Sell what you possess and give to the poor . . . and come, follow me." How then could the mother superior issue an order banning giving?

From just the tips, I made a quarter of my salary. To prevent any suspicions being roused, I carried on borrowing against my wages. When concealing my little wealth became a hassle, I decided to open an account at a bank in a neighborhood far away from the hospital. I'd heard that the banks had started to pay high interest rates. Depositing the amount

I had and making some money, even if not much, was better than nothing. I was not desperate for interest as much as I was desperate for my savings to be in a safe place, and is there anywhere safer than a bank?

Hiding the deposit book was easier than hiding a bundle of banknotes. I stuck it to the underside of a plank at the bottom of the cupboard, toward the floor, after covering it with cardboard cut to size. It would have been hard to find other than by chance. Agatha Christie taught me that a good hiding place is one that no one would think of as a good hiding place. The cleaner who swept and mopped the room twice a week was content to run the broom and the mop under the cupboard. I watched her and noticed that she did her work to the same routine.

Caution was vital. If someone knew about the deposit book, and the balance written within, awkward questions would be asked. From my salary alone, I wouldn't be able to save such a sum, even though I wasn't extravagant. I spent on essentials, and essentials meant food. I ate a meal every day at the hospital cafeteria for three lira. The woman serving gave me double helpings in exchange for me singing the praises of her beautiful dark eyes, which I likened to the eyes of Samira Tawfik, the famous singer. A snack was manousheh with zaatar or cheese. Dinner was a labneh sandwich I made in the room. To economize, I tried to stop smoking, but failed. I smoked two packs of Winston Supers a day, which cost two and a half lira. If I stayed up late, I might get through half a third pack.

But after another source of income opened up, not the tips, I started treating myself in secret. I'd have a bowl of beans twice a week at a small restaurant behind the hospital, and I'd have lunch there when I didn't like the look of a dish like Samira Tawfik.

The key to this new source of income was Robert.

35

ROBERT WAS FORCED TO UNLOCK the new source of income.

His mother fell ill, and he had to take unpaid time off to look after her. She had no one else to care for her following the death of her husband, Robert's father, at fifty-five.

I was startled when he whispered to me that he wanted to let me in on something important. He asked me to meet him at a spot two blocks from the hospital. I went along and arrived at the agreed time. He was waiting for me in his car. As soon as I sat next to him, he put his right hand on my shoulder and said that he wanted to tell me a secret that he hoped to add to our other shared secrets. Time had proved I was trustworthy, he said, but he still made me swear on my mother's life to keep his revelation to myself.

I urged him to leave off the introductions and get straight to the heart of the matter. We could build on what we had as long as we were in it together. There was no need to repeat platitudes about trust, secrecy, and the like, when all that was behind us. Otherwise our meeting was pointless.

He was silent, then asked me if I knew Bou Radwan. I answered yes—he drove the pickup that delivered canisters of gas and oxygen to the hospital two or three times a week. He came to emergency for the nun to sign the dockets. Whenever I met him, he greeted me in the way that only people from villages do. Just two words that I considered the most beautiful greeting since it contained an invocation of blessing: "Good health!" I seldom heard someone from the city use such a greeting.

Robert said that Bou Radwan would be the third partner, or more accurately, I would be their third partner. I didn't get what he meant. What business did Bou Radwan have to be our partner? What did he have to do with our work in the morgue to partner with us? Besides, what was I going to be their third partner in?

Before I asked those questions, Robert flashed a smile to show how cunning he was and said that he and Bou Radwan shared the proceeds they made from the canisters. He stopped talking to observe the impact of his words. He asked for a cigarette, even though he didn't usually smoke. I gave him one and lit it for him.

He asked me whether I wanted the story from the beginning or the end. He seemed to be playing with my nerves. I made to open the door and leave, but he grabbed my arm and started talking. He told me it was Bou Radwan's brainchild.

Bou Radwan had discovered the possibility of unloading three full oxygen tanks used in the operating theater, taking away three empty ones, and making the nun believe he had unloaded four full ones. That couldn't happen without the complicity of the person overseeing delivery and collection, which was Robert, whom the nun had assigned to help Bou Radwan with loading and unloading. They made an agreement and split the price of the cylinder, which was eighty lira. Nobody had discovered their secret even though the agreement had been in place for nine months.

Robert said that Bou Radwan had agreed to my being the third partner after long negotiations, not because he didn't trust me but because he refused to split the money three ways. In Bou Radwan's opinion, a three-way split made the gains too small to justify the risk. When Robert failed to make him change his mind, he backed down and agreed that Bou Radwan's share would remain unchanged while I and Robert would split the rest.

Listening to him, I discovered an explanation for why he came in on his day off when it coincided with the day Bou Radwan came to the hospital. As usual he helped him, and of course collected his share, then passed by emergency, said hello, and left. He always accounted for his unexpected appearances in a way that everyone, including the nun, believed. He claimed that he had forgotten something and had come in to get it, or that he had nothing useful to do at home and had come in to have fun and help out if needed, or that he'd come for lunch because he loved the daily special cooked in the hospital cafeteria. Every day a different dish and all of us looked forward to our favorite dish of the day. Only Robert never expressed a preference. The dish of the day Bou Radwan showed up was his favorite dish.

Why did Robert concede half his share to me when he could have kept it all? What motivated him to suggest a partnership when it wasn't needed? He was worried that during his absence, which might be lengthy, the nun would appoint me, or someone else, to help Bou Radwan. At that point, both of them, Robert and Bou Radwan, would be losers. So he pre-empted what might deprive him and his partner of a not insignificant sum of money. By choosing me as a partner, he guaranteed getting half his share even if he was away from work for a long time. The share was fixed, and there was no room for games.

I accepted the offer. He did not forget to mention that in his absence, I would be getting all the tips from the morgue. He said that he would look in at the hospital from time to time to see me. He reassured me that the agreement would continue even if he came back to work.

He let me in on the plan devised by him and Bou Radwan to make the nun choose me, and not anyone else, to help unload the canisters. It wasn't a complicated plan, what mattered was that it succeeded from the outset. It required Bou Radwan to come to emergency between ten and twelve when work was at its peak. If he saw that the two nurses, one of whom Sister Christine was liable to chose, were both busy, and I was sitting idle (the nun would have to see me in the department at that moment), he would ask Sister Christine for someone to help him. Then, logically, she would choose me. Should that happen, it would mean I would be the permanent helper.

Two days after the agreement with Robert and it was time for action. The first time Bou Radwan came into the department, he didn't see me. He went by the morgue and saw me busy with a corpse. I spotted him and nodded my head as a sign of acknowledgment. When I finished, I wondered around in the hope that the nun would see me. She did. I saw that both the nurses were occupied, and motioned to Bou Radwan to come in. He came in and spoke to the nun, who was playing with a little girl clinging on to her mother's dress. She immediately called me and asked me to help out.

The plan worked, and we implemented the agreement. However, like everything in life, it didn't last. Another driver took over from Bou Radwan for some reason to do with the business. The new driver refused to keep the venture going even though we enticed him with an increased share. He was religious, God-fearing, and refused to take tainted money. The new situation reduced my income, and I decided by way of compensation to visit the nun's drawer more often.

36

IT WAS ATTEMPT NUMBER SEVEN.

Half the staff from emergency were at lunch, the rest were taking care of patients. At that time of day, the earnings in the drawer were good, and taking a little would not arouse suspicion. It was also the time that the nuns met around the dining table. After surveillance, I noted that Sister Christine rarely missed the event, but she soon came back to the department, as if the work there only went well in her presence. She was absent for twenty minutes at most.

Once I was certain the opportunity was ripe, I determined to have a go. I made for the drawer, but before getting there, a voice screamed out of the darkness in my head, "Turn back!" So I turned back.

As I was leaving the room, the nun rushed in. I don't know what made her come back so unusually soon. When my eyes met hers by the door, I was hit by conflicting feelings. First, I was afraid that in my looks she had seen what I was hiding. Second, I was happy that the voice of fate had saved me at the last moment.

I stood chatting with a colleague in a room next door. Perhaps I would find out why she had come back suddenly. After about a minute she left the room, putting one of her hands into a glove in preparation to start work.

If she had seen me opening the drawer, she would have fired me. Or at a minimum, given me a stern talking to then forgiven me, since she had taken me on and would refuse to have it said that she had employed a thief. That would damage her reputation as a manager and diminish her sway with the mother superior. She would keep it between herself and me in the hope that I wouldn't do it again.

I choose midday for my attempts because, apart from the nun going for lunch, it was a better time than the morning or afternoon. In the morning, the drawer only contained a pile of coins and some small notes. Taking anything was dangerous and not worth the risk. In the afternoon, another batch of nurses came for the night shift. Anyone who turned up early would sit in the room with the drawer. In the evening, I often saw the nun bent over the drawer sorting the notes by value. At intervals she raised two fingers to her mouth and moistened them with her tongue to make counting easier. Then she recorded the day's takings in an account book. After putting the account book back, she folded the money into two bundles, put them in her pocket, and left.

Nobody knew whether she kept part of the money for herself and gave the rest to the administration, or kept the whole lot for herself. Perhaps the mother superior was her silent partner. She might have been compelled to do it to help her family on the sly. There was a war on, and many people had lost their jobs, been fired, or forced out of their villages.

The money that came into the department was under her sole control. There was no written record of the amount. True, there was a receipt book, but she only wrote out a receipt when a patient, obliged to give one to his boss or for some special reason, requested one. She could write whatever amount she wished on the receipt. She issued the orders and the prohibitions and had no overseer other than her conscience. Now I understood the meaning of a phrase I had often heard in the village: So-and-so doesn't need a job as long as his sister is a nun or his brother a priest.

Once I treated a patient in my time off. I got a small sum out of him and kept the money. The patient left then came back to ask me for a receipt. He put me in an awkward situation, and I was scared the nun would find out. I gave the money back to him, claiming that the receipt book was unavailable that day.

Not using receipts was to my advantage. I had put my hand into the takings three times, and nobody suspected they were short. Opportunities to open the drawer were few. The room it was in was rarely empty. It was more like a passageway between two rooms, one for triage, and one for receiving serious cases before their admission to the hospital.

Attempts would have been easier if someone had been watching one of the entrances and, using a prearranged signal, warned me at critical moments. I thought about involving Robert. That would have been returning the favor. He had made the tips and the gas and oxygen bottles available to me. I should thank him with the drawer. He trusted me, so why didn't I trust him?

I held off all the same. Then I dropped the idea. I was worried that a partnership would involve taking more money than I was used to taking. Then the whole thing would come tumbling down on both our heads. I had no objection to splitting what I made with him, provided I remained at the helm.

I was worried that he would insist that once we were partners I cut him a key too. Why should I have a key and not him? I knew it would happen sooner or later if we were in partnership. If I had a key cut for him, he could open the drawer by himself whenever the opportunity arose, and without telling me. When two hands, his and mine, visited the drawer on the same day, as was likely, it would mess up the nun's accounts and raise a question. When she got suspicious, her vigilance would grow and eyes would be watching. At that point, taking a chance would be stupid, and my income would be stopped.

Alone, I could manage it better and keep it under my control. I would never leave my fate in Robert's hands. He might get greedy, and greed would induce him to be reckless. Then he'd get caught out and have me caught out. All my attempts had succeeded so far. Once or twice a week was enough. True, I didn't make much money. But on top of the tips it was equivalent to a third of my salary.

Before every attempt, I was seized by fears beyond description. They started the moment I made up my mind and magnified with every step toward the target. The peak came when I opened the drawer and took what was at hand. At those moments, I not only felt that the pounding of my heart was reverberating throughout the hospital, but that I was sweating as if I'd just come out of the sauna. Even my hands were sweating, and I was scared the key might slip out of my fingers at the crucial moment and fall on the floor with a clang that, in the situation, sounded like a bomb exploding at night.

The fear persisted until after I left the room and did not fade away until after I had hidden the money. The fear often crept into my dreams, and I would see myself between two policemen who dragged me off to a military jeep and threw me into a filthy prison full of thieves, druggies, and pedophiles.

In a dream, I often saw Sister Christine catching me in the act of opening the drawer and firing me in front of everyone. I also dreamed of Robert threatening to reveal the secret if I insisted on keeping him out of it. I sometimes imagined myself being caught red-handed, and it being impossible to fabricate any innocent explanation. Innocent until proven guilty would not apply then. That image almost persuaded me not to try again, but greed spurred the opposite.

37

SISTER CHRISTINE WAS SURPRISED TO see me shaving a dead man. The reason for her surprise: I had refused to do it when she suggested it before. It was extra work in exchange for a tip from the next of kin. I told her I was willing to do anything apart from shaving. "Please don't make me do something I'm not up to," I said. When she realized that I was sticking to my guns, she didn't insist, but she did find it strange that I agreed to stuff and wash but refused a comparatively easy job like shaving.

I refused to do it because it put me, even if only for a short time, in close proximity with the face of the dead man, since it wouldn't be okay to shave without looking at the spot where I placed the razor. If I was inattentive, a razor cut wouldn't go down well because it would scar the face of the deceased. It might provoke his family to berate me or complain to the nun. In contrast to a slip when shaving, other errors passed without problem, provided they were not immediately apparent, such as a broken arm or leg.

Many relatives of the dead asked me to shave off the beard of their loved one, but I brushed off the request on the excuse that it was not in my job remit. When demand increased I convinced myself that this was a new way of making money and it would be stupid to leave it unexploited.

Just as there were rules for plugging body orifices and washing and stuffing corpses, the same applied to shaving. The nun showed me the easiest way, a lesson that only lasted a few minutes. She said, "Hold the head with the left hand and shave with the right." Straightaway, she put the explanation into practice, hoping it would be useful and make my work easier. She wet the beard of the corpse, a man in his forties, fitted a new blade in the razor, and set about shaving. She explained as she shaved, "Take care to keep your hand straight, because any deviation might cause a cut, and it's impossible to conceal a cut. Then the family will get angry and some of them might have the nerve to ask the hospital for compensation." She didn't say this sarcastically or to be funny. It had really happened, and some nurses still brought it up when conversation turned to comical stories of hospital life.

She reinforced her explanation with a series of recommendations: use the razorblade once only; wet the spot with water a few seconds before shaving; avoid shaving without water; concentrate; don't put your face close to the deceased's face if you're not wearing a mask; don't work without gloves.

I was struck by the way she gripped the razor and the elegance and speed with which she carried out the task. I stood opposite her, impressed by her skill and imagining myself doing the same.

Whenever I heard the noise made by the blade scrapping over the beard, I compared it to the sound I heard when I shaved in the morning. The sound was more or less the same, even though I used shaving cream that I lathered for a while to make cutting the stubborn hairs easier.

When the nun finished, she handed me the razor and the packet of blades. "Show me what you've learned," she said, and pointed at the corpse on which I was going to apply what I had learned. The corpse was of a man in his fifties, and his beard was slightly longer than that of the example from the lesson. My hands trembled as I inserted the razorblade, flipped down the cover, and screwed in the handle.

She noticed my unease and must have put it down to her standing there watching me, so she left. A few minutes later she came back, and I had completed the shave. She went near the dead man's chin and inspected it closely. She made no comment, good or bad. No comment meant she was satisfied, and that I had done the job as well as could be.

Now I had become the expert. The nun said so. I was faster than her. A shave only took a couple of minutes. Sometimes less. I swapped the old-style razor of the kind I had seen my grandfather and father use for a disposable one. I had got used to using them to shave myself because they were cheap and better than the old-style ones. With that new razor I set about shaving off beards.

Once, as I was about to shave off a corpse's beard, I looked at the pack of razors and saw that it was empty. I didn't have time to let the nun know about it. I was worried that she would tell me off for being remiss, since I was supposed to let her know as soon as the razors ran out. I went up to the room, picked up the razor I'd used in the morning, and shaved the dead man's beard with it.

The feeling I had at those moments was indescribable. The blade that had passed over my chin a few hours before was now passing over the chin of a corpse. Hairs from my beard that were stuck in the gap between the blade and the plastic casing mixed with hairs from the dead man's beard. I was troubled when I reversed the situation: I was shaving my beard with a razor that I had used before to shave a dead man's beard.

The act of shaving, which demanded attention and patience, brought me closer to the dead man, and I would memorize his facial features. Looking in the mirror as I shaved, I would often see someone else's face. Faces and ghosts of faces overlaying it. I shaved and conjured up beards I had wetted and shaved, or they appeared spontaneously. I took to shaving my beard in the same way that I did the dead. I would pull my skin down with my left hand and shave with the right. That wasn't the way I did it before the morgue, or specifically before I shaved the beards of the dead. I used to shave using one hand and used two fingers from the other every so often, and not all the time, as I took to doing.

I hated mornings because I had to shave. I also hated shaving because it reminded me of what ruined my day, but I had to do it. The hospital required all the staff to. Violators were given a warning for the first offense, and if they didn't heed the warning, the mother superior summoned them for a lecture on shaving and masculine hygiene, and how people shouldn't have to see a man letting himself go when he was quite capable of looking smart. A repeat offence meant dismissal.

I hated shaving my beard but didn't hate shaving the beards of the dead. It became quite the vocation, bringing in a good amount of money. I didn't fix a price list. When I was asked, "How much do we owe you?" I would answer, "Whatever you think appropriate." Some paid unexpected sums. I was startled, for example, by a man whose clothing did not suggest that he might pay ten lira, an amount equivalent to a day's wages. I often made a quarter of that from men with cigars in their mouths who didn't remove their sunglasses even in the shade. Some just turned around and left, thinking that giving a shave was part of my job. My insults followed them all the way home. When that recurred, I did not volunteer to shave, but waited to be asked.

By chance, I discovered a sideline that could be included with the shave: trimming the nose and ear hair. For that purpose, I bought a small pair of scissors that I kept in my apron pocket and used to trim the hair poking out of nostrils and earholes after the shave. I discovered that job when someone who had come to collect a relative's body pointed out the tufts of hair coming out of the late man's ears. He implored me to trim it, and I did not disappoint him. I asked him to wait while I fetched a pair of scissors from emergency and then trimmed the hair. In return, he did not disappoint either, giving me two lira on top of the five for the shave.

After shaving the beard, I often told the family of the deceased that I had cut the nose and ear hair for free, in the hope that they would be embarrassed and increase the tip. Many times I asked them before starting the shave whether I should cut the deceased's nose and ear hair so as to avoid telling them directly that the job was separate from the shave, and that if I did it, they would take it into account when paying my fee.

So often did I clean noses and ears of excess hair, I started unconsciously looking at the nostrils of the person I was talking to and slyly inspecting his earholes. Even hospital visitors and passersby in the street did not escape my curiosity.

38

ELEVEN AT NIGHT AND THE room phone rang. I woke up to Sister Christine's voice asking me to come to the morgue. I put my clothes on and went. She asked me to wait for the next of kin to come and collect a body that had been ready since the early evening.

To take advantage of the wasted time, I entertained myself with an Agatha Christie novel. The long wait and the reading tired me out. I wheeled a trolley for patients up against the wall next to the morgue door. Then I lay down on it fully dressed. Desperate for a rest after an exhausting day, I dozed off on my back with my hands crossed on top my stomach.

I did not anticipate that the sudden sleep would be followed by massive panic. Panic whose likes I had never felt before when I woke up to the insults of a stranger who was trying to grab hold of me and, at the same time, evade two guys who were trying to stop him hitting me.

I was thunderstruck when I realized I was laid out inside a coffin. Then the questions pounded in my head. How had I ended up inside this coffin? Who had played the trick on me? Was it a joke or a trap to get me in trouble with the nun or the hospital administration? What was the objective? What connected me with these three men, especially the one who would not have hesitated to kill me given the chance? The bastard was treating me like an enemy or as if I had killed his father or screwed his mother or sister.

I had no suspects. I excluded Robert because he wouldn't have come at night for a prank like that. I wouldn't, however, have exonerated him if it had happened during the day.

I couldn't properly understand the situation. I had been in another world, dreaming a most beautiful dream. I was in the village, walking in the open country, the shotgun ready to fire, a dog by my side, as I tracked the flutterings of a woodcock. Then the bird flew off. As I aimed the gun, a hand lifted me out of the open country, and an angry face spraying me with spittle and curses loomed over me. For some moments I didn't know what to do. Should I defend myself, or, at least, make some show of resistance that might stop the man going too far?

The last thing I remembered was wheeling the trolley from the department and parking it up against the wall by the morgue door. I placed the stretcher for carrying corpses from morgue to coffin on top and lay down on the stretcher. What followed I knew: I was in a coffin and around me were the nun, three men, and a corpse waiting for me to get out to take my place. But what happened in-between I had absolutely no idea.

I came back to reality when the man bawled at me to get out of the coffin. I was about to get out when he raised his stick (I subsequently found out that he supported himself with it because he was lame) suggesting he was going to give me a beating. I ducked unconsciously and tried to avoid it. Sister Christine intervened, begging him to calm down so the situation could be sorted out.

I found her long silence strange. She thought I was acting, and stood there holding in her anger, waiting for me to stand up and end the bad joke, but she knew that when it came to work, especially dead bodies, I behaved most responsibly. Perhaps she was waiting for the man, who appeared to have lost his mind, to calm down.

In her looks I read the question that she did not want to ask me in front of them: what's going on? She also read the answer in my puzzled looks: I don't know. Really, I didn't know. My account was clear. I had lain down on the trolley, then woken up in the coffin with four people and a corpse on top of me. More than that I didn't know. I was extremely curious to learn who had carried me from the trolley to the coffin, and why.

Sister Christine didn't believe me. I swore to her by my exile, and my mother and father, that I was telling the truth. She maintained her position but, at the same time, did not call me a liar. She said there was a missing link that had to be found to reveal the truth. We agreed to keep the details of what happened a secret between the two of us. Finding the missing link did not take long. It happened by chance.

One afternoon, I was in the morgue preparing a corpse for collection when two guys appeared in the doorway and said hello. I remembered them instantly. Their faces were still etched before me as if I had seen them yesterday and not two months ago. They were the two guys who had witnessed my emergence from the coffin that unforgettable night. Could anyone forget falling asleep on a trolley and waking up in a coffin? An occurrence only believable to those with faith in strange ironies that don't happen on screen let alone real life.

The two of them were there to carry a corpse I had just prepared to a car parked at the entrance. While they waited for the man who had gone to complete the administrative formalities for collecting a corpse, they introduced themselves: Moustafa and Ahmad. They were Egyptian and worked in a carpentry shop. The driver of the hearse asked them for help to carry the coffin from the morgue to the car and on to the house of the dead man's family. Once they were confident I was in a good mood, they reminded me of that ill-fated night, taking turns to speak.

Moustafa revealed the secret that led to the missing link. He said that he and Ahmad thought I was the dead person and hurried to move me from the trolley to the coffin.

Everyone—they, the dead man's brother, and the driver of the hearse—was in a hurry. It was a long way to the village and they needed to beat a snowstorm that might close the road.

He divulged that he was surprised when the nun opened the morgue door and pointed to the corpse ready to be moved to the car. At that instant he deduced that he and his companion had made a mistake. His deduction proved correct when the dead man's brother was unruffled when he saw the body.

Ahmad said that he and Moustafa were startled when they saw a living person in the coffin. They found it weird that they had not sensed that the person they were carrying was not dead but alive. They felt guilty and stupid, so they opted for silence and neutrality. They admitted that whenever they remembered the sight of me waking up in a panic inside the coffin they fell about laughing.

Before they left, I asked them to wait a minute. I went to the nun and told her I had found the missing link and asked her to listen to the truth herself. She came and listened. As she was leaving she commented that I had broken our agreement to forget all about it.

39

"Watch out. The nun suspects you." A short remark Robert uttered in passing. I did not understand the intent of that oblique reference. Why did he say, "suspects you" and not "us," seeing as we were still partners dividing up the spoils from the oxygen canisters and the tips. If I had been caught out, then the game was unquestionably up for him too, and vice versa. He uttered his words of warning and vanished. I couldn't go after him to explore the reasons behind them because I was preparing a corpse that had to be delivered as fast as possible.

Once I'd finished the job, I avoided leaving the morgue. I was scared of meeting the nun face to face. What did she suspect, I wondered? The key to the drawer? That was possible, even though I was vigilant and careful. I often stopped visiting the drawer for a fortnight, longer sometimes, to dispel any doubts she might have should she think the money was short. When she found nothing missing for two weeks, she would discount her suspicion and put the shortfall from the days before, if noticed, down to a mistake in counting or some other reason.

Could her suspicion be the result of the suspicions of others? Could someone have seen me without my noticing and told her?

I decided to act as normal, as if I hadn't heard the warning. I left the morgue and headed for the bathroom. I washed my face and went back. I intended to pass by Sister Christine and make small talk with a nurse in earshot of the nun.

Assuming she only suspected me, that meant she had no proof and I was therefore innocent. The novels of Agatha Christie taught me that the accused is innocent until proven otherwise. They also taught me that the fingerprints left by the killer at the scene of the crime might bring him to justice. I wore gloves out of caution. If anyone saw me leaving the room with the drawer after I had completed my mission, they would not ask why I was wearing gloves. I seldom took them off during my shift. They were part of the job. I often roamed the department with them on. To be extra cautious, after visiting the drawer, I would flush them down the toilet, not taking my eyes off them until I was sure they had gone down.

If Robert had suspicions about the drawer, he would have confronted me and demanded that we share the proceeds, just as we did with the oxygen cylinders. He would use fairness as an excuse, and give his famous motto, 'Eat and feed.' It wouldn't have been wise to turn him down.

He had found a way to let me know that something dubious loomed on the horizon and that caution was needed. We still pretended that we weren't on good terms to protect each other's backs. He uttered his words that darkened my day and disappeared. It wasn't like him to disappear like that unless his sick mother needed him. I didn't dare ask after him. If I did, everyone would find it strange, become curious, and start inquiring about the reason for his sudden absence.

I stayed in the emergency room although my shift was over. I walked around the hospital courtyard watching the visitors and passersby in the hope of spotting Robert. His height made me exclude short people. He would have made a good basketball player. He didn't need to jump to throw the ball into the net. It was enough to stretch out his arm for him to score.

In the evening, I hid the two keys to the drawer in a place that even a bluebottle fly couldn't find. I stayed up with Bou

Moussa who was on duty that night. We had a drink and listened to part of the biggest poetry slam of 1972 held at Sports City in Beirut and featuring sixteen poets. I went to bed and he stayed up listening to the incendiary dialogue between Zein Shuaib and Jriss al-Bustani.

When I got up in the morning, I had a feeling that it was going to be a long day. I shaved, showered, and sprayed on cologne. I wanted to give the impression that I was in a good way.

I was alone in the morgue when Robert came in. He said I should know that the nun suspected that a hand other than hers was opening the drawer, and that I was at the top of the list of suspects. He surprised me by not placing me in the frame, but accused the woman who managed the nurses in the department. He wondered how she had got hold of the money to buy a smart car like the one she had bought a while before. I did not comment. I deliberately appeared astonished. A great weight was lifted from my shoulders, and I felt as happy as if I had won the lottery.

There was a vast difference between my being the only suspect, meaning I was the culprit, and my being one of a number of suspects. I resolved to forget all about the drawer. Grasp all, lose all. I had made a tidy sum from the drawer, even if I didn't know the exact amount. I didn't count what I took. I thought counting unlucky. Luck runs out if you count your money, so said my grandmother, my mother's mother. I often thought that the money I saved ought never leave its hiding place, for when the lira sniffs the air, away it flies.

Lost in these thoughts, I heard a colleague calling me. She was standing at a distance because, since the death of her only brother, she avoided coming too close to the morgue and seeing the bodies. She said that Sister Christine wanted to speak to me, and that I should drop everything and go.

I was startled and confused. A host of paranoid thoughts hit me. She didn't normally summon me like that. Only a very few times that could be counted on the fingers of one hand. I had gotten used to her coming herself and talking to me here in the morgue, or inviting me to come with her to the room where the drawer was to speak to me. Sending a nurse to tell me that she wanted me to come to her did not inspire confidence, but there was no escaping the confrontation. I dropped everything and went.

She was sitting on the chair for visitors with the receipt book on her knees and a blue pen moving continually between her fingers. With her was Sylvie, the longest-serving nurse in the department, who was resting a side of her large ass against the table with the drawer, and the jester Isabel. The three of them were expecting me. I went in and said hello. The nun pulled ten lira out of the receipt book, stretched out her hand with the money toward me, and asked me to go the nearby market and buy a new padlock for the drawer, the same size as the old one. She gave me the lock. I stared at it intently with the eyes of someone who had never seen it before.

I took the ten lira and went.

It was a smart message and an indirect accusation. Or suspicion not cloaked in accusation. The nun wanted to make me understand that I was under suspicion, and that perhaps I was the only one she suspected. So she chose me especially to buy the lock. If after fitting it, she noticed that money was missing, or felt anything suspicious, she could be sure I was the culprit. Who else other than the person who'd brought the lock would be able to have a key made and then rob the drawer?

40

I DIDN'T SEEK OUT A new way of making money after they changed the lock on the drawer and I lost the income from the gas and oxygen cylinders, but once again luck compensated me, taking away with one hand and giving with the other.

I was shaving the chin of the corpse of a man in his sixties. Two of his relatives were waiting for me to finish to collect the body. I don't know why, but I opened his mouth, which hadn't stiffened shut yet, and saw three gold teeth inside. I had the idea of pulling them out, keeping them, and then selling them. I tried and failed to pull out the first tooth. There wasn't enough time to fetch something metal to use to pry it out—the two men outside the room were insisting I hurry up, and my absence, even for a few minutes, was not on.

I took my watch off my wrist and with the clasp on the strap I worked away at the tooth until it came out. Using the same method, I took out the other two teeth. Then I hid them all in the pocket of my apron. To ensure nobody discovered what I had done, I bound the corpse's head vertically and horizontally with a length of gauze so that the mouth could only be opened if absolutely necessary. We often used that trick when the jaws could not be shut with the usual adhesive tape.

At the end of my shift, I went up to the room and took the gold crowns off the teeth. I wrapped them in the corner of a blanket and gave them a few light stamps of my heel to change their shape.

I went to an Armenian goldsmith. When he saw the three pieces of gold, he said the gold was high quality and used to make dental crowns. I was taken aback, and nearly picked up the pieces and left. Perhaps he knew where I had brought them from and wanted to scare me into selling them cheap. I avoided asking him the questions his assessment had prompted.

He inspected them, turning them over in his fingers, and said he would pay thirty liras, that was ten lira a tooth. I told him I just wanted to value them, not sell them. It wasn't because of the price that I didn't sell them, but so I could show them to other jewelers, one of whom might pay more.

I wrapped the crowns up in a piece of paper and hid the paper in my sock bag. I decided to sell them once I had amassed ten. Over the following days, I opened the mouth of each corpse while I was preparing it. I learned that people over forty tended to have their teeth capped in gold. I did not come across a gold-capped tooth in the mouth of anyone younger than that, so my interest focused on the elderly. From time to time, however, I would inspect the mouth of a young person's corpse to silence any doubts I had that I might find what I was looking for. More than once I got lucky. That persuaded me not to exclude any corpse, as long as the effort cost me nothing. As I washed a corpse, I would open the mouth and inspect the upper and lower jaw. If I spotted a crown, I took a sharp implement, something like a knife blade without a point, and prized it out.

The extraction only took a few seconds. With the fingers of my left hand I stopped the jaws from closing, and with my right hand I worked at the crown with the instrument. Very often, when the crown was well implanted, the extraction took longer, and I had to stick the blade right into the gum to lever out the crown. There was no worry about bleeding, however deep the gash. The dead do not bleed when cut, just a little water comes out. The blood coagulates in the veins once the heart stops pumping.

Gently and slowly, I would apply myself to a difficult case, so as not to repeat an earlier mistake. One day, an upper wisdom tooth fell right out as a result of decay to the jaw from neglect and age. As soon as I applied pressure on the crown with the blade, the tooth fell out. I hid it straightaway in my trouser pocket and then went to the bathroom where I removed the crown and threw the tooth down the toilet.

I did it as quickly as possible. I was afraid Robert would see me and set his sights on a moneymaker that I still could not believe he hadn't worked out.

Barely a day went by without my bagging a crown, sometimes more. Whenever I had enough to justify the risk, I would go to a goldsmith I had befriended and become used to dealing with. To avoid him becoming too suspicious, I amended my story and did not deny that the pieces of gold came out of people's mouths. Not, of course, the mouths of the dead, but the living.

I told him my uncle was a dentist, who kept the gold crowns he extracted in a box for the purpose. When there were enough of them, he would call me, and I would sell them. He donated the proceeds to poor families, or to help fund the building of a church. He was embarrassed to sell them himself, lest it be said he was selling the gold out of the mouths of his patients, and his reputation get ruined. To confuse things and disguise my tracks, I explained to the goldsmith that there was a material, called 'composite' in English, which replaced the crown and preserved the patient's tooth for longer. During my explanation, I hinted that my uncle was not stealing the crowns as long as the people concerned did not ask what happened to them once they were removed. Perhaps they didn't ask because they thought they had gotten a few years use and now the time had come to bear the loss, even if the fitting had been expensive. They preferred to gain a tooth and lose the crown, not the other way around. The goldsmith believed the story and commended my uncle's behavior. He expected me to show up once a month.

He said he gave the pieces he bought from me to the workshop, and after a few days he got them back as earrings, bracelets, chains, rings, or icons of saints. I imagined the emotions of a lady or young woman if they knew that the chain adorning their neck, or the saint's image on their chest, had come from the mouths of the dead. An experience I had been through in my own way with every crown I pulled out.

Whenever I touched or remembered a crown in my pocket before adding it to its counterparts, the face of its owner would appear to me. I even recalled what the inside of their mouth looked like. Those feelings faded when I counted the crowns, which, after crumpling their edges, all looked alike. Then, it was hard to tell whose crown was whose, and out of which jaw I had extracted it.

The stranger who once whispered to me, "A morgue is a goldmine," was right.

41

THE SONS OF BITCHES KIDNAPPED me.

When I came round, I knew the long-feared event had happened.

I remembered that I had been preparing a corpse when I was struck hard on the head. I did not lose consciousness instantly. As I was falling, I saw the cross flanked by its two lamps as many overlapping crosses and a great number of lamps.

It hurt where I was hit. I felt an urge to scratch but couldn't. My hands were tied behind my back with rope, as were my legs. A strip of plastic sticky tape covered my mouth, and my eyes were blindfolded with a piece of cloth that might have been torn off a shirt that someone had just taken off. It still retained the body odor.

Azizi's killer had finally found me. I had believed he had forgotten me amid all the worries of the war. But who had led him to me? A strange question seeing as I was working at a hospital visited by hundreds of people a day.

I had long expected one of my old comrades to see me and inform on me. Most of them knew my deep connection with Azizi, and perhaps they also knew, even if they didn't admit it, the reasons why he was killed, the mastermind behind his death, and the perpetrator.

Nothing remains hidden, but secrets, especially those to do with murders, remain covered up, even if they are found out. Discovery makes them twice as secret. The knowledge might lead to the grave.

My close relationship with Azizi would not have reassured his killer, and he would have tried to get rid of me. He waited a while so that my killing not be linked with Azizi's. The killing of two known friends in mysterious circumstances would raise questions.

True, there was a war on, and in wartime everything is permissible. There were matters that might not give pause to the derelict lawful authorities, but the party would not keep quiet about them.

Azizi wasn't the only person to take his secrets with him to the grave. Many others had disappeared in mysterious circumstances, their bodies found under bridges, by garbage dumps, or on the beach. No one would dare inquire about the reasons for their death.

Many times, we knew the reason, and held the confession in. Fear that we would meet the same fate made us deaf and dumb. We buried the secrets at the very bottom of memory and cruelly suppressed ourselves so that a fatal word didn't slip out of our mouths. Forgetting equaled life.

Smart people didn't ask too many questions. A question might lead to death, because it stood for doubt, and doubt doesn't go away until the truth comes out. Truth costs.

I haven't been one for asking questions since school, but after what happened, masses of questions gnawed at my mind. Who kidnapped me? Why? How was I kidnapped from the hospital, from inside the morgue in fact? Was Sister Christine there when I was struck and kidnapped? What was her reaction?

How many of them were there? What did they look like? Why had they dumped me in this place and left? When were they coming back? And when they did, what were they going to do to me? Was I being held in an inhabited or an abandoned room, and in what area?

Was someone sitting in the room watching me in silence?

I decided to keep quite still but heard nothing to prove that anyone else was there. They knew what they were doing leaving me without an observer. Tied up, how could I escape or ask for help? No sound reached me from outside, as if I was suspended in outer space or under the ground.

I lay on my back to explore the floor with my hands. It was covered in a layer of dust, suggesting that the place wasn't inhabited, or that its inhabitants didn't care about cleanliness. After crawling around the room, it seemed there was no furniture.

With difficulty, I was able to stand up. With my head and shoulders, I rubbed along the walls in exploration. A windowless room, just like the morgue. Houses with only a few windows were horrific. They were like tombs.

A year ago, I had been homeless and slept in the doorways of buildings and in cars without the owners' knowledge. I spent the day on the streets, delighted by the surprises a stranger discovers when visiting a city for the first time. Whenever I remembered that period, I wished I had never given it up and gone to the barracks. Despite hunger, thirst, poverty, and loneliness, I was happy. At least I wasn't always looking over my shoulder fearful of people's glances, as I took to doing after Azizi's murder and my leaving the military. Regret was no use. What happened had happened.

Time passed slowly. I felt out of space and time. I began to feel hungry. Hunger was my way of telling the time. It showed that it was now past two in the afternoon. At the hospital I usually had lunch around twelve. Most likely, I had been kidnapped two hours before lunchtime.

The boredom of waiting made me doze off fitfully, despite the buzzing of a fly around my head, and its adopting my wound as a stage from which to invite its sisters to the feast. I dreamed I was in the morgue. A corpse stood upright in front of me. It chased me. I ran. When I was within arm's reach, I sped up. I turned around and saw the corpse falling into pieces. The skull rolled behind me letting out a frightful laugh. I woke up. I took it as a good sign that the corpse did not grab me. If it had, it would have been a bad sign. I had often heard that if a living person obeyed the call of a dead person in a dream, then something bad was going to happen. Did anything worse than this await me?

I would be a liar if I said I wasn't scared. I submitted myself to God, since nothing happens without His knowledge. If He wanted His deposit back, let it be. Perhaps there was a lesson beyond my ken in it. The imminent prospect of time being up, my time, was a harsh punishment. Waiting for the moment of death was a difficult exercise in the acceptance of the idea of death.

If they intended to kill me, why had they kidnapped me? They could have finished me off with a bullet outside the hospital, when I was taking my usual stroll in the streets to breathe air untainted with the smell of corpse and germicide. They could have ambushed me in an alleyway, finished me off, and fled.

They might kill me after interrogation. Perhaps they would delay killing me if they thought I had revealed secrets to others. Like that I would have protected myself if the identity of my killer became known to them. The secrets were the evidence that would lead to him. This supposition made him hesitant. Perhaps he blamed himself for leaving me at liberty all this time.

The problem was I didn't have any secrets. If I told them that I didn't know anything, and that Azizi had not let me in on any of his secrets, they wouldn't believe me. A lack of belief might push them to torture me so that I got scared and blabbed everything I knew, including the names of those I'd let in on the secrets.

If I held my ground, they might try various torture techniques to loosen my tongue. Such techniques were well known.

I had often heard talk of them from comrades who had used them themselves on prisoners or hostages, or which had been used on them or a relative in enemy detention.

It would be dumb to fabricate secrets to avoid being beaten and abused. They might work out I was lying. Then they would think I was making things up to mislead them. That wouldn't be in my interest.

Saying that I knew nothing (or, from their perspective, not confessing) was preferable to lying. It was better to be honest and convince them that I was telling the whole truth, even if they hit me, insulted me, and abused me.

Fate had dropped me in it, and only fate would save me.

I expected them to arrive, dreading the unknown destiny that awaited me.

I didn't anticipate that Azizi's killer would interrogate me himself. He would allocate the task to one of his subordinates. This subordinate would not be someone I knew or who knew me, so that memories of the past and having been comrades in arms would not affect the interrogation. He would choose him from the new recruits—there were always new recruits— and furnish him with the questions to ask me and the method to adopt if I confessed or if I refused to open up.

This subordinate would not come alone. As least two people would accompany him. It was probable that those three carried out my kidnapping. It was to the best advantage of missions like that that they involved only two or three participants. A small number guarded the secret, and quickly led to anyone who blurted it out. This was a technique favored by the police and spooks.

There seemed to be movement outside. It went on for some moments. It wasn't the sound of footsteps. It might have been caused by the wind or by a passing animal. I stuck my head against the door in the hope of picking out the source, but all I heard was the deep hum of silence. The movement might have arisen inside my head, which was overwhelmed with imaginings. I stayed by the door, holding my breath, so that I didn't miss any movement should it recur.

While like that, it occurred to me that Azizi's murder might not have been the reason why I had been kidnapped. Perhaps Napoleon wanted to get rid of me so there were no witnesses to the theft of the gold dealer's briefcase. He had killed Ninny, the third accomplice in the job, and today was my turn. Napoleon was ready to eliminate anyone who tarnished his image. He was scared I might not keep the secret, and my giving it up lead to his death. Secrets were sold. It was a legitimate trade and he knew that.

But why had Napoleon waited all this time before deciding to snuff me out? I didn't remember when exactly the robbery took place. Perhaps ten months ago, although it seemed like it was happening now.

The briefcase might not have been a reason for my kidnap. If I had wanted to reveal the theft, I would have done so. I promised Napoleon when I joined his unit that everything I saw and heard would remain secret. I kept the promise. I saw many outrageous things and heard about outrageous things that made the robbery look minor by comparison. Everything I knew about, witnessed, or took part in, I left behind at the barracks as soon as I walked out the door.

Excluding the robbery led me on to a new possibility. The gold dealer had been injured. I had seen him clutch his stomach and fall onto the hood of his car after Ninny shot him. If he didn't die instantly, he would have definitely been taken to hospital. He might have been treated for months then died. So that he did not leave a single witness to his crime alive, Napoleon had kidnapped me in preparation for killing me.

True, it was Ninny who shot the gold dealer, but Napoleon organized the job and was its sole beneficiary. His own interest demanded he kill Ninny and kill me. Since we'd made nothing out of it, he was scared one or both of us would spill the beans. Killing us shielded him from blame or made finding him difficult. There were no other witnesses to the robbery. The license number of the car we'd used for the job (which might have been noted down by a passerby and handed to the authorities) would be of no use to the investigators if the car had been stolen.

It was also possible that the gold dealer had died as a result of his injuries, and his family wanted to take revenge themselves, given that recourse to justice in wartime was not going to prove of benefit. After a long hunt, they had learned the names and addresses of the criminals and wanted to dispose of them. They asked mercenaries to carry out the mission, since they themselves weren't qualified, or didn't want to get blood on their hands. Those mercenaries succeeded in finishing off Napoleon and Ninny because it was easy to locate them and monitor their movements. I remained at large because my place of residence was unknown. But in the end, they found me. Who sent them my way, I didn't know, or how they knew I was working at the hospital, the morgue specifically, from where they snatched me away. The local area was small, and informants and snitches were having a ball. You could keep out of sight some of the time, but not all the time.

If their orders were to kill me, they would have killed me. They were postponing it to interrogate me. They would want to know the names of my accomplices, once they realized that by my capture they had found the clue leading to them.

If they had already killed my accomplices, they might still be looking for information they had not gotten out of them, like where the briefcase was. It might have contained secret documents and incriminating papers that only Napoleon knew about. I thought the briefcase contained jewels since it was in the possession of a jeweler. They would take the information they needed, then kill me and dump my body. A number of people would likely be sent to interrogate me, all of them close to the victim. Some would put the questions, and some might come to see the face of the criminal, which was me.

The biggest surprise would be if my interrogator were the jeweler himself. He might have survived and wanted to get back the briefcase and get retribution from those who had harmed and nearly killed him.

I couldn't imagine myself in a scene like that. The man whom we tried to kill interrogating me. What would I reply when he asked why I wanted to kill him? He wouldn't believe me if I told the truth and nothing but the truth.

The truth being that I found myself in the back seat of a car watching him come out of a shop and sit behind the wheel of his car. Then the car tailed him. Its driver got out, threatened him, hit him on the head with the butt of a pistol, and came back with a black briefcase and wounded in his forearm.

I wouldn't blame him if he didn't believe me. I probably wouldn't in the same position. I would relate what happened candidly, and he would have to take the view dictated by his conscience.

These suppositions took me back in time, to events that I had witnessed, participated in, or heard about. One of them was the reason I was here in this room, tied up, hungry, and frightened.

I recalled Domino's eyes, flashing with unstated menace when Guevara, Conger, and I said goodbye to him at the cabaret the night he had gotten down on all fours and the girls had ridden on his back. He might have wanted to rehabilitate his injured manhood by killing the witnesses. Someone like him had no compunction about hurting people for a reason like that. It was rumored he had shot a woman because water from the clothes hanging out on her balcony had dripped onto his shirt. It was said that he had detained his niece's French teacher in an unknown place because she did not give her high marks. It was said he threw a grenade into his neighbor's bedroom because the man had the radio on loud during his siesta. Someone who acted like that would not be deterred from anything.

Of the witnesses to that evening, he did not care about the waiters or the owner of the club, the girls who had ridden him, or their colleagues who might have watched the spectacle. None of them knew who he was or what he did. They knew he was a vicious thug who carried out his threats and could close down the club on a whim.

It was the three of us that concerned him, because we were in touch with his men. If we spread the scandal among them, it might be the end for him, and his glory turn into a joke passed on with a great deal of gloating by those who hated him. His friends would find it amusing, unable to believe that the cabaret girls had mounted him, and that one of them had slapped his neck in imitation of a cowboy striking the neck of his horse with a whip to make it go faster. When he lost his aura, he would lose the respect of his followers. No subordinate would respect his boss once he imagined him on stage on all fours with a girl riding on his back. Domino wouldn't allow that to happen; he was used to people being afraid of him, lowering their heads as he passed, and kissing his hand to gain his approval.

It was likely that had happened. The tale had leaked out somehow and spread. A story like that of the cabaret did not die, even after a long time. I had forgotten the date of our evening at the club, although it was a date impossible to forget because it was the day one of the most important areas in the control of our enemies fell to us.

I imagined Domino at the moment he heard the news banging his hand on the table and swearing on his honor to kill all those who had helped tarnish his reputation. Right away, he mobilized his men to respond to the campaign against him, which he would pretend was mounted by those damaged by his presence in the party and who started rumors that tarnished his reputation, like the rumor about the club. The first people he would have suspected were Guevara, Conger, and me. He might have kidnapped them individually and interrogated them. Questioning me was left. He must have put in some effort to find out where I worked. Guevara and Conger had not left the party, and it would have been easy to find them—at the barracks or the pinball place opposite, or at a barricade. If he didn't find them in those places, he would find them in the club where he had been turned into a horse to be ridden by four horsewomen. Perhaps one of the two was the culprit but had denied it and accused me and our other comrade of revealing the secret. That made Domino capture me to hear what I had to say. Then he would decide whether to release me or I know not what. Perhaps Guevara and Conger agreed to put the blame on me, not to sacrifice me maybe, but because they thought I had gone back to the village, and it would be extremely difficult to get hold of me. Perhaps Domino in a moment of madness decided to get rid of us, but in a singular and well-planned way. Like that, the scandal would be buried with us. He had finished off Guevara and Conger, and only I was left.

The sudden blast of mortars brought me back to reality. I didn't hear the sound of a mortar being launched but the sound of the explosion. I wished that a shell would land near my place of detention and blow open the door. If that happened, I would crawl away and escape. I would bump into a passerby who would help me free just my hands. I would deal with freeing my legs and pulling off the tape over my mouth and the blindfold.

Then I would disappear. I would avoid going back to the hospital except to pick up the deposit book hidden underneath the cupboard. I would go back once and then hide in a mountain village under an assumed name, rent a little house, and keep hidden until things calmed down. My life was destined to be uneasy since the incident with the teacher. I decided to face up to it. I had no other option.

The explosions from the mortars were still reverberating when I heard an out-of-the-ordinary movement. A movement unlike what I had heard a while before. I heard footsteps and intermittent voices. They had come. It was definitely them.

My heartbeat changed the moment the key started to turn in the lock of the door. Cold sweat broke out on my body.

The door opened. People came in, how many I could not tell. One of them picked me up off the floor until I was on my knees. Then he pulled the tape off my mouth so that I could speak. I felt a need to scratch where the tape had been and asked him to untie my hands. He didn't respond.

None of them uttered a word. Even their steps were few in number and almost soundless. It was so quiet, I could hear their breathing. What were they doing? Why were they silent? Why didn't they interrogate me? What were they waiting for?

I pictured them looking at me, holding clubs or iron chains in their hands, ready to hit me before beginning the interrogation. Beating was the best way to make a suspect confess to his crimes, and sometimes to confess to crimes he had not committed to make the torture stop.

I longed for them to insult me so I could hear their voices. If they did, the insult would have landed like a sweet melody. But they remained quiet, as if they had swallowed their tongues.

I asked them why they had kidnapped me and what they wanted with me. I might as well have been asking myself. They remained silent.

I didn't know what made them pull the tape off my mouth. I decided to take advantage of the opportunity and talk about my relationship with Azizi, about robbing the jeweler, about the night at the club.

However, I thought it better to go slow. Perhaps they were setting a trap for me. They had removed the tape so I could talk, and they gambled that I would speak as long as they remained silent. In that way something they were waiting to hear might slip out and the jaws of the trap snap shut around me.

I also kept quiet. If only they would put the tape back over my mouth.

I don't know why during those moments I thought about the woman in the white Honda and what happened the last night at the training camp. Perhaps the organizer of my kidnap was her companion who begged us that night to take what we wanted, even the car, and let him and his girlfriend leave unharmed.

If it wasn't him behind the operation, then only her brother or her father would have been willing to get revenge from those who had besmirched the family honor. Or perhaps her husband if she was married.

It was possible that the woman herself wanted revenge. Perhaps she had befriended someone influential in the party, or a warlord, and told him about being raped. He took on the revenge mission to win her favor and prove that he loved her. He found out our names and started looking for us. He found Starling and Shakespeare and killed them. Today was my turn. Perhaps she had planned the whole thing, seeking help from hired killers to get her revenge.

I was going to tell all the details of that ill-fated night but didn't. I held back because they would never believe me if I disclosed that I had nothing to do with it, that I was there but had not harmed the man or touched the woman. They would think that someone who didn't screw a beautiful woman when she was open to him wasn't a man but a fag. They would think me a charlatan if I said that I had tried to stop Starling and Shakespeare from what they intended to do, but that they didn't listen to me.

Lying would prove the charge against me. There was no evidence corroborating my story. If an oath was sufficient proof, I would have sworn on the Bible that I was telling the truth, the whole truth, and nothing but the truth.

The continuing silence forced me to curb the rush of such thoughts. If it hadn't been for the sound of their breathing, the clicking of lighters when they lit cigarettes, and the smell of the weapons they were carrying, I would have thought they were ghosts.

After some thought, I decided to speak in the hope of loosening their tongues. I began with an account of the night of the rape. I don't know why I chose that incident in particular. I related what happened from the moment we left the camp to the moment we got back. I went over the scenes and described them in detail. If they were smart, they would ask me to repeat the account to find out whether I was telling the truth or not. That way, if I was lying, it would be easy to tell. It was virtually impossible for a liar to give the same story twice without some addition or omission or getting things out of order.

I would have loved them to interrupt me so I could know how much my words had affected them. Many times, I intended to break off the narration to arouse the curiosity of one of them, who would order me to resume the account, but my ploy didn't work.

I asked for water. I asked for food. I asked for a cigarette. Yet I was unable to drink, eat, or smoke. They did not respond.

I went on speaking about various personal things. I kept talking to fight off the fear that the silence instilled in me. My voice kept me company, and I enjoyed the tales I told. They seemed to work that out, and shut me up, leaving me a prisoner of my isolation, for without warning, two hands closed in on me and sealed my mouth again with plastic tape. The smell of the tape was mixed with the smell of tobacco that burning cigarettes left on the fingers.

I was made as happy by being deprived of the company of my voice as I was annoyed. I felt that my guards had been listening to me and weren't indifferent.

Then followed something I had been expecting to happen sooner or later. I was even looking forward to it since I would learn my fate.

Four knocks at the door shattered the calm: two in quick succession, then a short pause followed by two more raps. It might have been a prearranged signal.

The raps were not followed by the sound of footsteps or any movement to suggest that someone was outside. Perhaps the visitor was wearing sneakers that did not make any noise when he walked, unlike shoes with a hard sole. Alternatively, perhaps he had deliberately approached the door slowly to give himself the chance to listen in on us in the room for some reason of his own.

A guard got up and opened the door. The others made faint noises as they readied themselves to meet the visitor, whom they must have been expecting. Perhaps he was the one who had the power to free and confine and decide my fate. The door closed.

I didn't know whether he stayed with them or left. Perhaps he spoke to the guards using his hands and left as silently as he had come.

I wished that he was the companion of the raped woman, because he knew I was innocent and would pardon me. Even more than that, he would apologize to me. If he wanted to eliminate all the witnesses to bury the scandal, then he would surely order for me to be killed. This assumption also supposed that the fate of my guards would be no better than mine, since they knew about the scandal, but if the person were someone else, my chances of escape were slim.

I might be spared if the visitor, who had given no indication as to their gender, was a woman. This woman would be none other than the woman in the Honda, and she knew who had hit her and taken her by force.

But what if she hadn't seen our faces clearly in the dark? Then she wouldn't recognize me and wouldn't know that it was me who had been sitting on the bundle of dry branches watching what was happening.

She had come to see me. She had come to see the third person, who might be one of her rapists, or a witness to her rape. After having seen me, she would order my death and leave, or stay behind in silence to see the kind of death I was going to have.

I imagined that the visitor was Azizi's killer.

I imagined he was the jeweler.

I imagined he was Napoleon.

I imagined he was Domino.

I tried to speak, but the words bumped into the tape and turned into splutters and stifled half-sounds.

Silence reigned when a shot sounded. I thought it had been fired by mistake, but the burning in my guts disproved that idea. The bullet lodged in my innards. I reckoned I was just being softened up for a severe interrogation. If they had wanted to kill me, they would have shot me in the head, not in the stomach. Then the second shot rang out. And the third.

I came round on a riverbank in an industrial zone. My lower body was in the water, and my head on the pebbles. Drizzle was washing my face, and two sparrows next to me flew off as soon as I moved. My hands and legs were still tied up and the tape over my mouth. My eyes though were not blindfolded. I didn't know whether one of the guards had removed it before I was taken out of the room or it had slipped off by itself.

They had dumped me under a bridge. A favorite location for dumping the bodies of victims of robbery, drug smuggling, and the settling of personal scores.

Between life and death, with flickering eyes I implored the shadows of those walking over the bridge to help me.

SELECTED HOOPOE TITLES

The Watermelon Boys
by Ruqaya Izzidien

Sarab
by Raja Alem, translated by Leri Price

Fractured Destinies
by Rabai al-Madhoun, translated by Paul Starkey

*

hoopoe is an imprint for engaged, open-minded readers hungry for outstanding fiction that challenges headlines, re-imagines histories, and celebrates original storytelling. Through elegant paperback and digital editions, **hoopoe** champions bold, contemporary writers from across the Middle East alongside some of the finest, groundbreaking authors of earlier generations.

At hoopoefiction.com, curious and adventurous readers from around the world will find new writing, interviews, and criticism from our authors, translators, and editors.